To: Paul Burek

Minn's best
golfer.

[signature]

T H E
CHAIRMAN

Kevin J. Dunne

authorHOUSE®

AuthorHouse™
1663 Liberty Drive
Bloomington, IN 47403
www.authorhouse.com
Phone: 1-800-839-8640

Published by AuthorHouse 08/25/2014

ISBN: 978-1-4969-3289-1 (sc)
ISBN: 978-1-4969-3288-4 (hc)
ISBN: 978-1-4969-3287-7 (e)

Library of Congress Control Number: 2014914067

DEDICATION

My wife, Heather, and I have much to be happy about, but our greatest joy is our family. We thus dedicate this joint venture to:

Erin and Chris Caldwell, and their children,
Brandon, Tyler and Riley;

Kevin and Stacy Dunne, and their children, Sydney and Sophie;

Patrick and Marci Dunne, and their children,
Libby, Ashley, Kinsey and Gardner;

Sean and Catherine Dunne, and their children, John and Patrick.

THANK YOU

To the Sedgwick law firm which has given me so
much support throughout my legal career.

CONTENTS ⅠⅠⅠⅠ ⅠⅠⅠⅠ ⅠⅠⅠⅠ ⅠⅠⅠⅠ

CAST ▐▐▐▐ ▐▐▐▐ ▐▐▐▐ ▐▐▐▐ ▐▐▐▐ ▐▐▐▐ ▐▐▐▐ ▐▐▐▐

Atlas Insurance Company
> Jackie Jones - CEO
> Fortune Jones- VP Claims
> Francis O'Neil - Outside Counsel
> Woody Wilson - West Virginia Private Eye
> JJ Strauss- Outside Coverage Counsel
> Drew Richmond - Outside Malpractice Counsel
> Bay Area Insurance - subsidiary

Jonas Pharmaceutical Company
> Patrick Jonas - CEO
> Jayne Jonas - wife of CEO
> Al Purcell - Medical Director
> Kenny Clark - General Counsel
> Nobo Extract - Brand name for pancreatic cancer cure

Thompson Firm
> Tommy Thompson - Senior Partner
> Bill Dawes - Partner
> Sam Hawthorne - Partner
> Mary Smith - Associate
> Karen Klein - Paralegal

Malloy Firm
> Bryan Malloy - Senior Partner
> Miller Johnson - Partner
> Boxer Tate - Associate

Laura Flood - Secretary
Audi Johns - Headhunter

Cases
Lumpy Griffin - 1906 Bouncer Case
Todd - Nevada Brain Damage Case
Dr. Vegas- Plaintiff Expert
Mamie McDermott - Cook County Pancreatic Case
Danny McDermott - Brother
Florence Duffy - Bridge Friend
Oso Lynch, MD - Treater and Co- defendant
Dodge Lee - Plaintiff Attorney

Plaintiff Lawyers
Jim Scholer - San Francisco
Dodge Lee - San Francisco
Jim Rocky - West Virginia

Plaintiffs:
Lumpy Griffin - San Francisco
Rex Annex - West Virginia
Craft Smith - Fictitious West Virginia Case
Mamie McDermott - Pancreatic Cancer Case

Judges
Earl Max - Federal Court San Francisco
Bruce Friendly - Feeder Judge
Jethro Pugh - Presiding Judge Cook County
Charlotte Higgins - State Court Cook County
Homer Frank - State Court Cook County
Bobby Waco - State Court West Virginia

Boxer Tate

"I thought he was going to choke me to death. Now he's suing me," said the young man, who called himself "Boxer" Tate. His real name was Baxter.

Tate was Miller Johnson's last interview of the day. Johnson conducted these interviews in one of the firm's conference rooms rather than his private office, which was filled with legal files and telephones and a laptop computer.

The interviewees were defendants insured by Atlas Insurance Company, which had referred them to the Malloy law firm. Miller Johnson was a senior associate in the six-person firm. He replied to Tate, "The complaint alleges that you beat him up at the 1906 Club."

Miller looked over the police report and hospital forms detailing Lumpy Griffin's injuries and his version of events. Miller shook his head, sizing up the kid sitting opposite him at the table.

Miller finished refreshing his memory of the events of the night in question. According to the statement by one Lumpy Griffin, the plaintiff, Tate had assaulted him in the 1906 Club, resulting in broken bones, missing teeth, and many stitches. Miller knew the 1906 Club, but he never went there. It was a trendy place capitalizing on the 1906 earthquake way back when, exactly the kind of club Miller avoided. Evidently, the kid in front of him worked there as a bouncer. The thought made Miller laugh. Boxer was maybe five feet, ten inches tall—in a good-size pair of boots—and skinny as a broom handle. Maybe his friends had given him the nickname ironically.

Regardless, the kid had great posture. He wore his suit well, even if it was an old one. He was clearly trying to impress. He had a focused look, like he could get mean if he needed to. Maybe the nickname wasn't ironic. But with that frame, who did he think he was kidding? He must have had something to prove.

"You go to school, Tate?"

"Yes, sir."

Miller couldn't be sure, but he thought the kid was keeping himself from saying more. "Where?"

"Douglas, sir."

"Douglas Law?"

The kid nodded. So that was what he had to prove. Miller had to stifle a chuckle. Graduates from Douglas had less than a 10 percent job placement rate, and that was of the graduates who could even pass the bar. He might as well have said he was just out of high school.

Still, you couldn't fake that confidence or the look in those eyes. And when he nodded, confirming he went to Douglas, there was no shame there. Tate might have made something of himself if he'd gone to any other law school in the city.

Miller asked, "How'd you become a bouncer? That doesn't look like your expertise."

Tate said, "You're right. Two of my buddies are boxing champs and tough as nails. The money is great, and they said that the owner gave them authority to add a third member to the crew. Since I was in law school, I was to be the negotiator of the three."

Miller asked, "How did that work out for you, son?"

"Good and bad. I could charm the ones with dates, and it was relatively quiet during the week but it was mayhem on the weekends."

"Why?"

Tate seemed anxious to tell his story. "Not only were the local college students on the loose but teenagers with false IDs invaded from Marin and Contra Costa and San Mateo counties, where IDs are more closely inspected for birthdays than in San Francisco's drinking joints.

"It was so crowded on the weekends that the college kids had to wait in line to get in. The line ran up the stairs and halfway down the block. Most of the kids had started their serious drinking Friday afternoon, and some even carried a pint with them through the line. Not only was crowd control a problem, I also had to chase down the occasional undergraduate who bolted on the bill. Some of the bolters would stop and pay up; others had to be tackled before they would cough up the money. Frankly, most of the time I lived in fear.

"This particular Saturday night, my buddies did not show up for work, and I was on duty alone. I felt that the inmates were taking over the asylum. Out-of-town teenagers were bucking the line, and local grad students were rebuffing them. I was guarding the door, admitting the next in line after examining government IDs and photos to make sure customers were over the legal age limit."

"Okay … the fight?"

"One of the local grad students, Lumpy Griffin, decided he should not have to wait for the teenagers and pushed to the front of the line. I raised my hand to stop him, but Lumpy continued walking into me and grabbed me around the head with both arms. I panicked. All I could see was Lumpy's head, and I started beating it with my fists as fast and hard as I could. Lumpy fell to the floor bleeding. I later learned he lost five teeth.

"I never hit anyone with my fists before in my life. The police and ambulance arrived. Lumpy was taken to the hospital, and I was taken to jail, where I was booked for assault and battery, kept in a holding cell overnight, and released on my own recognizance in the morning. I can't believe this is happening. I was defending myself. I've lost my job at the 1906, and I spent the night in jail and now I'm a defendant in this lawsuit."

Baxter did not know it, but this was not going to be the last time in his career that he would spend the night in jail.

Miller added, "Lumpy has not only sued you, but he also sued the owner of the 1906 Club. Fortunately, as an employee of the 1906, you are covered under the 1906 insurance policy even though you have been fired. The insurance is with Atlas Insurance Company."

After the meeting with Miller, Tate adjourned to a downtown bar to meet his buddies for a drink before they had to go to work at the club. This night the buddies treated Tate because he had just been fired. They also enjoyed reliving Tate's fight. Tate described each punch. His buddies applauded anew with each boxer blow, and they started saying that he too could now be known as a boxer. Indeed, the regulars at the 1906 were already calling him Boxer. Tate was proud of his new moniker, but deep down he knew he had no pugilistic skills. His real strength was his mouth.

The buddies reported that the 1906's owner was claiming that he had no knowledge of the fights or bouncers chasing down customers bolting on their bills. In fact, he described the bouncers as "managers." Everyone but Tate found this very humorous. He knew he was not going back to the bouncing business.

His buddies asked how the meeting with Miller Johnson had gone. Instead of responding, Tate just said, "I'm going to get them to give me a job." Everybody laughed into their beers, and Tate slowly sipped his Maker's Mark whiskey.

Depositions

Lumpy was represented by Jim Scholer, an experienced plaintiffs' personal-injury attorney. In an effort to intimidate, Scholer had a process server personally serve Tate with the file-marked copy of not just the summons and complaint but also the notice of Tate's deposition. The prayer on the complaint was for ten million dollars.

Tate telephoned Miller with news of the service. Tate tried to act nonchalant, but Miller still wanted to ease any tension. Miller explained that most plaintiffs' attorneys, as a courtesy, ask the defense attorney to accept service rather than having a sheriff's deputy formally serve the documents personally on the defendant.

Boxer said, "I figured he was trying to jam me since I'm in the middle of studying for the bar. Well, he's got the wrong guy."

Miller said, "I know you're busy, but if you can make the time, I think we can show our confidence by scheduling Lumpy's deposition for the same day as yours. I will need your help to get ready. Can you come in?"

"Yes."

Boxer and Miller Johnson met at Malloy's offices a week before the deposition. Douglas School of Law did not teach trial practice or depositions. Boxer was later to become an expert in these areas. But for now Johnson explained the basic mechanics. "Lumpy and his attorneys will be with us in a conference room at the office of Lumpy's attorney. You will be put under oath and will be asked questions by Scholer. If the question is inappropriate, I will object and say why and instruct you either to answer it or not to answer it. Listen to what I say and carefully follow my remarks. Sometimes my comments will give you hints at problems in the question. In other words, I may say, 'Object. Vague and ambiguous.' Thus, your response could be 'I don't understand the question.'

"Everything that is said in the room will be transcribed by a court reporter. It will be typed in a booklet, and you will be given the opportunity to read the transcript, make any corrections, and sign it under oath. If you make corrections, counsel for Lumpy can comment on these changes at trial. Thus, we will talk before you sign the deposition.

"Scholer and I may get into arguments about some of the finer points. I don't want that to worry you. It's what we do for a living. Indeed, you will probably like the experience."

Miller explained further that the deposition would be videotaped and the video, or parts of it, could be played at trial. Thus, Boxer should wear a tie and jacket. He should listen carefully to the questions and answer them honestly and directly but give no more information than called for. "The more information you volunteer, the more follow-up questions will be asked. The longer the deposition, the greater the risk of giving inaccurate responses."

The day of the Boxer deposition, Lumpy arrived with Jim Scholer and one of Scholer's associates. Scholer expertly started the deposition with admonitions to Boxer about the penalties for perjury and the importance of giving full, accurate answers. Scholer then asked Boxer background questions about prior DUIs (none), arrests (none), and his height and weight (five feet, ten inches and 145 pounds). He also asked about his education and employment history. Scholer then asked Boxer if he had been drinking on the night of the assault. Almost immediately, he accused Boxer of looking at his attorney, Miller Johnson, for help with the answer. When Boxer denied drinking, Scholer followed by saying, "Isn't it true that you told one of your fellow bouncers that you had a drink?"

Boxer then remembered. "Oh, yes, but all I had was a beer between the time of the incident and the time police arrived because I was so shaken."

Boxer remembered what Miller had taught him. A simple no was the cleanest and most impressive negative response you could give, and Boxer had just answered yes.

Scholer thought, *I can make this cocky young man my witness.* "Isn't it true you and your fellow bouncers revel in beating up customers at the 1906?"

"No."

"Isn't it true you received no training for the job?"

Miller quietly interjected, "Object. Vague. Ambiguous."

Boxer paused and said, "I received on-the-job training from my two buddies, who are experts at keeping the place under control."

Miller wanted to applaud.

Scholer looked at Miller and in a raised voice said, "You're coaching the witness."

"Not true," said Miller. "You're trying to mislead the witness."

Boxer, whose face was on video, remained impassive. Scholer continued being argumentative, and at one point he became so frustrated he stuttered. On the surface, Boxer was placid. Beneath, he seethed.

The deposition of Boxer took three hours, during which time Boxer suffered dry mouth, sweats, and anxiety, but he kept his composure and coolly and carefully recited how Lumpy was the instigator and aggressor in the confrontation at the 1906.

Boxer's deposition was finished right before lunch.

At the lunch break, Boxer went to the restroom and nearly collapsed. He was furious. He was shaken. He wanted to punch the mirror. But as he looked at the mirror, he promised he would never be in this position again. He was at risk of not becoming a lawyer, of losing what money he had, of being found guilty of a crime, and he knew that Scholer would try to prove he had committed perjury. He vowed to be successful no matter the obstacle. He wanted to be in control. To do this, he would have to devote himself to his career. It might hurt his golf. He might have to give up cocktails with his buddies from the Club. He had to start by getting a job.

Boxer was thrilled at lunch when Miller told him he had done great. The two of them then had the videographers roll back the video to the questions about drinking, and the video showed that Boxer did not look at Miller for help to answer the question.

In the afternoon, Miller started his examination of Griffin. Lumpy's look played well for the camera. His face was swollen and bandaged. He looked like he had been beaten up. Miller recited his admonitions, such as "If you answer a question, I will presume you understood it."

He then proceeded with the usual background questions:

"Occupation?"

"Student."

"Prior personal-injury lawsuits?

"None."

"Height?"

"Five feet, seven inches."

"Weight?"

"One hundred forty pounds."

"Prior fights?"

"None."

"Prior arrests?"

"None."

Then Miller asked about the details of the fight. Lumpy denied it was a fight. He said, "I was cold cocked." He testified that the 1906 Club was his first stop and would have been his first drink of the night. He said he was coming to the front of the line to find out how long the wait was. He tripped and fell into Boxer, and Boxer commenced to beat him in the face. He was hospitalized, lost five teeth, had sixteen stitches, had disfiguring scars, missed his final exams, and spent $3,600 in dental and doctor bills and would have to spend another semester in school, incurring another $12,000 in tuition, and would thus lose six months of work at $35,000. These numbers were called *specials* and totaled about $50,000. Many plaintiff lawyers argued that cases should settle at six times specials.

Settlement

At the end of the deposition, Scholer made a settlement demand of $450,000. He explained that $200,000 was for punitive damages for assault and battery. He also said the demand would only remain open for ten days.

Privately, Boxer and Miller discussed the possible settlement further. Miller explained that the Atlas Insurance policy did not cover punitive damages. Further, if Boxer was found guilty of felony assault and battery, it would put his bar admission at risk.

Miller said, "I think I can get Atlas to contribute two hundred thousand, and if you put up fifty thousand, I can settle the whole case including punitive damages for a total of two hundred fifty thousand dollars, saving Atlas two hundred thousand." Boxer could see the practical benefits of such a settlement, but he was appalled that a lying plaintiff could so easily abuse the justice system. Boxer asked Miller Johnson why Scholer would be seeking punitive damages knowing they were not covered by insurance and further knowing that he probably didn't have that kind of money. Miller said, "He probably knows that this will cause you to lean heavily on Atlas to pay everything even though Atlas might not think they owe for everything. You should want this case settled, because you don't want to be at risk for uninsured punitive damages."

Boxer said to Miller, "First of all, I don't have fifty thousand dollars. Further, I refuse to borrow it, and I don't want to pay Lumpy a dime.

He's the one who started the fight and tried to rip my head off. I don't care if Atlas settles as long as it includes me, as I would just as soon see this case go away."

Both of them knew that Lumpy's father was a policeman who was well known by the San Francisco assistant district attorneys. They were aware that Lumpy's father was pushing to have a criminal suit brought against Boxer to put his bar admission at risk. Boxer was appalled that such a gold digger could create such hell in the life of a good citizen. Boxer vacillated between fury and depression. He knew that defense costs might cause Atlas to settle, but with increasing fury he said, "I won't pay Lumpy any money, and I'm not sure I will authorize Atlas to pay or to settle with Lumpy." Miller pointed out that such a position might cause Atlas to deny coverage. Miller suggested a meeting with Atlas, and Boxer readily agreed.

The meeting took place at Atlas the next day. Miller said that the head of Claims, Fortune Jones, would be at the meeting. Boxer and Miller were ushered into Jones's office, which was modest in size but on a corner and very tastefully appointed. Jones was on the phone but murmured, "My two o'clock is here. I have to call you back." She quietly rose and came around her spotless desk and firmly shook hands with Boxer and then Miller. She was drop-dead gorgeous and looked way too young for her job, but she immediately took control.

Jones said to Boxer, "Well, I guess your job at our insured is the cause of your new name?"

Boxer, who intended to be all business, smiled and said, "My real name is Baxter, but I wear Boxer like a badge ... nevertheless, this lawsuit is a pain, and no, I won't put up fifty thousand dollars of my own money to settle it."

Fortune said, "I have been reading the file, and I can't say I blame you. It looks like you will be a good witness on your own behalf and on behalf of your employer, the 1906 Club."

Boxer, realizing that Miller really was in a conflict situation, said, "I have been thinking about this case, and I have an idea. Would you be willing to invest some time and money into conducting a background investigation of Lumpy and to see if there are any favorable eye witnesses to the fight?"

Miller intruded by saying, "The more money Atlas spends on defense, the less they have for settlement."

Boxer snapped, "Whose side are you on, anyway?"

Fortune wanted to keep her best witness happy and immediately volunteered to spend five thousand dollars for a private investigator who would report to Boxer.

After several days, the private investigator reported that Lumpy had several prior arrests for being drunk and disorderly in public and that Lumpy had been drinking for several hours at another bar before he came to the 1906 Club on the day of the fight. Finally, a witness stated that Lumpy had grabbed Boxer around the head and started twisting his head before Boxer started punching in self-defense.

Boxer felt justified in his opposition to contributing to any settlement, but the 1906 Club registered concern that if there was no settlement, Scholer would start discovery against the Club and try to learn the number of fights and injuries that had occurred there. The 1906 Club wanted out immediately. And they also thought their best defense was attaching themselves to the attractive Boxer Tate. Fortune and Miller wanted Boxer to agree to settlement. They realized that they had a conflict of interest. Their one client, the 1906, was desperate to settle; their codefendant client, Boxer, was not. At least he acted as if he did not want to settle. He said to Atlas and Miller, "What you want is for me to give up time I should be spending studying for the bar and interviewing for a job. I think Scholer will realize that his case gets better if I'm not in it."

The solution hit Boxer like a bolt of lightning. He stood up in front of Fortune's desk with a huge smile and announced with a flourish, "I have an answer." Fortune, who had stopped looking at Boxer, looked up.

"What's that?"

Boxer said, "If you will let me negotiate the settlement, I will pay out of my own pocket any settlement above seventy-five thousand dollars. In turn, you will give me any money saved below seventy-five thousand dollars. Thus, if we settle the whole case for fifty thousand, you will pay me twenty-five thousand."

Fortune saw what was really going on. Boxer figured he'd start practicing law before he had been admitted to the bar. He intended to get Atlas and the 1906 Club out of a big pickle and would be making money for himself at the same time. Fortune was enthralled and pleased when all nodded favorably to the proposal. They all agreed to the unusual proposition and gave Boxer $75,000 settlement authority.

Boxer then arranged a meeting with Scholer, Lumpy, Lumpy's father, Fortune, Miller, and the owner of the 1906. The meeting was set for 3:00 p.m. Friday. With the authority of the team, Boxer ran the settlement meeting. He passed out pages from the Lumpy deposition transcript. He then produced all of the private investigator's materials. He pointed out the inconsistencies, outright lies, and indeed perjury. He said if this case went to trial, all of this information would become public. Looking at Lumpy's father, he said he should not want his son's reputation to be harmed. Boxer said he was opposed to settlement but with the consent of the defense team he had a one-time, last and best offer. The defense would pay the fifty thousand dollars in specials and, in addition, the 1906 Club would exempt Lumpy and his father from the line. They would be allowed in the back entrance of the 1906 Club ahead of their compatriots. They would be given a written pass, and the manager (no longer called a bouncer) would be instructed to honor the pass.

The plaintiff team asked for time to discuss the offer privately. The defense team yielded the room. Miller could not help but wander close to the door. He "tried not to listen" but reported that Scholer could be heard fighting to accept the offer. Scholer sounded worried. If the case was tried, he could lose, and it would cost him time and money. Lumpy's father was unhappy with his son and worried about a possible loss of reputation. The only one who wanted to take a flyer was Lumpy, but the rest of the team opposed him. After about an hour, Scholer emerged and said they would not settle for fifty thousand dollars but would settle the case for seventy-five thousand. Without any discussion with the defense team, Boxer said, "Absolutely not. We will try the case. All offers are withdrawn."

Scholer said, "Give me ten minutes," and Boxer did not say no. Within ten minutes, Scholer reemerged and said they would accept the offer if Boxer would apologize to Lumpy, which he immediately did.

In the meeting afterward with the defense team, Fortune said she was surprised that Boxer had apologized, and he said, "I have no job, I have no money, and I have the cost of the bar examination all coming up. For my twenty-five thousand-dollar fee, I would have kissed his ass."

Boxer loved getting twenty-five thousand dollars in cash. He had no idea that he would be handling much larger sums in the not-too-distant future.

The Bar Exam

Boxer could hardly remember taking torts, or real property, or the rule against perpetuities, or civil procedure as taught at Douglas Law School.

If he wanted to practice law, and he now knew that he did, he could not miss any of the law review lectures or tests. He was able to make the steep payments for the lectures out of the settlement fund. For the first time, he came to enjoy the majesty and discipline of the law. The articulate, sophisticated Boalt and Stanford professors brought the law to life. His scores on the practice tests continued to improve, but he did not pass all of them. In fact, he barely passed just a few of them. He was trying to learn a three-year curriculum in three months. He worked at the law twelve hours a day, seven days a week.

The *Lumpy* case had been an eye opener. Tate did not like being at the mercy of others. He now wanted control of his life, and he knew that the practice of law could give it to him. He liked the idea that he had beaten the system. He had gotten paid twenty-five thousand dollars for winning a fistfight and charming a pretty insurance executive.

He missed his golf and his buddies. Ironically, he even missed the 1906. One night when he had just started the bar review course, he joined his buddies for a drink and they laughed about the Club and the cute nursing students coming for drinks. The bouncers were pleased to be making a hundred dollars a night. A woman like Fortune Jones was an abstraction. They didn't know anyone like her and could never have gotten a date with someone like her. Boxer wasn't sure he could either. He thought about calling her. He thought there was something there. He thought his chances would improve if he had a job. A license to practice law might help also. He remembered how close to ruin he had been. Boxer had spent several years after college playing golf on the secondary tour. He had never made a dime and, after two years, had realized he had to do something else—thus his three years at Stephen A. Douglas Law School.

In retrospect, to apologize to Lumpy had not been as easy as he made it out. He now reaffirmed to himself that he would be successful at all costs. He loved his buddies, but their interests were diverging. There was just no time for the drinking life, and he decided to go home early.

Several weeks later, his favorite buddy stopped by his apartment. Tate showed him the mountain of course outlines he had to review and had to decline his invitation to go out on the town.

His friend tried several more times but ultimately stopped.

The one person Boxer had time for was Miller Johnson. After he got his $25,000, Boxer called Miller and said, "Let's celebrate. My treat."

Miller said, "My treat."

Boxer said, "Okay, fifty. Agreed."

Boxer picked ex-Mayor Willie Brown's favorite luncheon place, La Central. Boxer called for reservations. He said, "If Willie isn't coming, could I have his table for lunch? I have a very important client who would love it." Boxer got the table. It was surrounded by pictures of Willie, and Miller was impressed. They both had sand dabs and talked leisurely.

Boxer said, "Tell me about Fortune. I was a little surprised that the head of claims would get involved in such a small case."

Miller said, "I should have told you. Her father owns Atlas."

Boxer's head snapped up. "So that's the reason such a young person has such a powerful position."

Miller said, "Not exactly. Fortune Jones could get a job anywhere she wants. She has an MBA from Stanford and became wealthy in the insurance bond market back in New York. She did not like New York City and decided she wanted to come to San Francisco. At the time, Atlas was having financial problems with its latent asbestos claims.

It stood to lose billions of dollars in late claims. Her father, Jackie Jones, persuaded her to return to San Francisco to resolve these claims. Fortune agreed but not for a salary. She wanted a percentage of the savings, which turned out to be a lot of money."

Miller continued, "Indeed, the *Lumpy* case was small in the context of all her responsibilities. Not stated in all our meetings was the fact that the owner of the 1906 Club is a personal friend of Jackie Jones. The club was scared to death of the case and wanted the very best claims handling. As a favor to the owner, Jackie asked Fortune to get involved. As it turned out, both the owner and Fortune were mesmerized by your clever take-charge approach. Both were thrilled with the settlement and were thrilled that you made money off the deal. That's how they operate."

Boxer said, "To be honest, she looks too hot to be head of claims. Is she seeing anyone?"

Miller said, "She is older than she looks, but she has several boyfriends. They are PhD-in-economics types. She doesn't flaunt it, but she is an intellectual."

It was not cool, but Boxer had to ask, "Do you think I could get her to come out with me?"

Miller said, "She generates a lot of interest wherever she goes. I have no idea if she would go out with you, but she did spend more time on the *Lumpy* case than I ever expected."

Boxer switched gears. "How's the practice going?"

"Great."

"What's hot?"

"Suits against pharmaceutical companies. Some courts have ruled that mere compliance with FDA regulations does not immunize a drug company from a personal-injury suit."

Boxer decided not to mention his premedical studies, since he had been rejected by every med school he applied to. Unfortunately, his law degree from the little-known Douglas told the story.

Boxer knew Malloy was not a top-tier law firm, but he still very much wanted to get his foot in the door. He did not have many options.

The lunch ended with Boxer thanking Miller for taking on the *Lumpy* case. He said, "When I pass the bar, can I send you a résumé?"

Miller was impressed that a kid with such a pedestrian academic record could be so confident of passing the bar. But Miller thought, *With his tenacity, I'll bet he does.* Miller said, "Yes, send me a copy of your résumé. We are not hiring right now, but things could change quickly in a small firm."

In California, the official results of the bar examination are mailed to the applicants in mid-November. Several days later, the names of the individuals who passed are published in the statewide newspapers. Mid-November came and went. Boxer received nothing from the state bar. He was devastated. He realized how desperate he was to become a lawyer. It was his only chance at real success. He hid in his apartment and wouldn't leave.

When the newspapers came out, Boxer looked to see which of the compatriots he had met during bar study groups had passed. To his shock and awe, there was his name, Baxter Tate. Boxer called the bar examiners and was told that they had him listed under his real name, Baxter, and hadn't mailed the results to Boxer. They then came to realize that he was now also known as Boxer, and they congratulated him on passing.

Now Boxer was going to practice law no matter what. Even if he could not get a job at a going law firm, he would practice solo—doing what, he did not know.

Atlas Insurance Company

Atlas was a large, nationwide insurance carrier. Among other things, it wrote liability insurance coverage for individuals and companies. Thus, if its insured was sued, Atlas would defend and settle or try the matter. If the case couldn't be resolved in-house, Atlas referred it to an outside attorney. Atlas received hundreds of thousands of claims every year. It had a staff of almost a thousand claim handlers and claim managers to handle these suits. Atlas paid out billions of dollars a year in claims. Fortune Jones was in charge of the claims side of the business. She rarely got involved in individual cases unless they were huge. Most of her managers were in charge of retaining outside counsel to defend Atlas Insurance's individual cases.

The claims managers reported to Fortune, and Fortune reported to her father occasionally. She had more power than most head claim managers.

Fortune had set up a system for selecting outside counsel. She called it the panel counsel system. Claim managers could only refer cases to lawyers Fortune had personally approved to be on the panel.

Atlas had many claims in Cook County—Chicago—considered by many to be one of four or five judicial hellholes in the country.

Fortune had one of her Midwest claim managers in town for a meeting with a Chicago attorney she was considering for the panel.

Fortune had a conference room attached to her private office, which she used for these meetings when her private office was not pristine.

The Chicago lawyer was Frances O'Neil. O'Neil watched how Fortune ran the meeting. She started with some introductory remarks about Atlas. She understood that most lawyers did homage to the majesty of the law, but she was not a lawyer and Atlas was not a law firm. She ran a business. She had to offer her insureds the best defense for the lowest premiums. For the most part, she would not take on a vendetta. The Atlas business model was to investigate claims thoroughly and quickly, evaluate them, and make reasonable offers. Atlas would even pay on a questionable claim if it made sense economically.

As far as its attorneys, Atlas wanted courtroom trial lawyers who were skilled litigators. Fortune explained that while the attorney would have input in evaluating each lawsuit, it was Atlas who would put the final dollar value on a case. Finally, Atlas expected its attorneys to give it a discount on its bills in return for volume.

Fortune paused, but O'Neil was savvy enough not to try to fill the void. Fortune concluded, "What's your reaction to this?"

O'Neil had heard this or similar speeches from other insurance people, but there was more electricity in Fortune's presentation and O'Neil suspected she usually got what she wanted. O'Neil asked, "Ms. Jones, what's your role in this?"

Fortune said, "Call me Fortune. I am hands-on. I know all of our lead panel counsel. I keep statistics on how quickly and inexpensively they turn over cases. In our experience, lead lawyers can get more done—they're better and quicker than a young associate even if the lead lawyer's hourly rates are higher. I keep track of how much you are paying on varying types of cases. At the end of each case, my claim people report on your strengths and weaknesses."

Atlas had already done a background check on O'Neil and a search of the results of all of his trials. He had a good win-loss record but for one big defeat for $1.5 million on a single trial. Fortune asked about the case. O'Neil said, "Oh, that was before Judge Charlotte Higgins. She was a former plaintiffs' attorney who used to sue insurance companies.

She ruled against me on all legal issues, but I got the case reversed on appeal."

Fortune liked O'Neil and, after the meeting, told the claim manager to put him on the panel counsel list.

After the meeting, Fortune retired to her office, where her secretary had sorted her mail. One envelope was marked personal and confidential. The return address was Boxer Tate. Fortune was curious. After the *Lumpy* case, she had thought they might get together but realized their difference in status could be a turnoff. She opened the envelope and saw a résumé with a handwritten note stating, "I passed. Boxer."

Instead of going through the San Francisco claim manager, Fortune forwarded the Boxer résumé directly to Miller Johnson along with a new case against an Atlas insured. The note said, "I need a good, practical, inexpensive young lawyer for this case. Did Boxer pass the bar?"

By amazing coincidence, on the same day, Miller also received a Boxer resume. Miller invited Boxer in for an interview with him and with Bryan Malloy, who had been an avid golfer and immediately liked Boxer at the job interview. Malloy further liked the fact that his firm could make a nice profit by paying Boxer a low salary and having him work on low-pay insurance-defense cases.

They offered Boxer forty thousand dollars per year. This was way below going rate for new lawyers. It would hardly cover Boxer's two-thousand-dollar rent each month. But Boxer thought the Malloy firm would be a good showcase for his talents. Plus he had no other offers or potential offers. He thought that he could get raises at Malloy in the short run. He accepted.

The Todd Case

Insurance-defense work is usually low-pay, high-volume work. A student from Boalt or Stanford might receive a starting salary of $170,000 per year in San Francisco, more in New York. Traditionally, insurance defense consists of personal-injury automobile cases. The legal issues are straightforward, and the factual issues involve reconstruction of times and distances to determine who entered the intersection first. For a young lawyer who wants to be a litigator and trial lawyer, insurance defense can be a terrific stepping stone. The practice requires many court appearances, many witness interviews, many depositions, and negotiating with very aggressive plaintiffs' lawyers. The defense lawyer has to deal with judges, claim managers, and defendants. He has to cross-examine expert accident reconstructionists. He is responsible for secretaries and paralegals and timely filing of pleadings. Sometimes the stakes are high. Not all fender-benders result in whiplash; some result in brain damage and quadriplegia. Not all those insured are auto drivers; some are drug companies, chemical companies, and hospitals.

Boxer thrived in this world. He learned more about the practice of law in one year at Malloy than he would have learned in three or four years somewhere else. His hourly rates were so low that the insurance companies did not lose money when he won the small cases he tried. Boxer could try to win a case with a hundred-thousand-dollar demand for fifteen thousand dollars in defense costs and fees. He learned to be an articulate, effective advocate.

Women judges, in particular, seemed to buy his creative arguments. He learned how to make billing entries that allowed his bills to be approved and timely paid by the carriers. He introduced Miller Johnson to golf and to golfing claim managers. He wrote briefs and took depositions for Johnson. He made Johnson look good, and Johnson made partner two years after Boxer arrived. Because insurance-defense cases were usually high-volume and low-paying, they were not carefully managed as much as high-stakes corporate commercial litigation. Boxer defended a number of rear-enders. These could be handled routinely. They involved the same interrogatories, the same deposition outlines, similar police reports, the same doctors testifying about the same whiplashes. There was an army of chiropractors to describe the months of manipulations. Boxer had these cases organized and handled them cheaply and efficiently. He had tried twelve cases over two-and-a-half years when the *Todd* case came in. It fit the whiplash mode. It was a low-speed, low-impact, rear-end automobile accident. Boxer told Miller he could handle it without partner help. He said, "I've got this, boss."

Miller reminded Boxer, "Todd's lawyer is tricky. He likes to try cases, and he likes to surprise his adversaries at trial."

Boxer took Paul Todd's deposition a few weeks after the accident. Plaintiff Todd testified, "I have been treated by a chiropractor for whiplash, but the treatment is not helping me with my terrible headaches. Further, I'm becoming forgetful and sleepy all the time." Boxer forgot to follow the Todd deposition with the usual cleanup interrogatories. These were written questions that required written responses. They would have required the plaintiff and his attorney to update the medical status of Todd and identify the doctors he had seen. Thereafter, Boxer could have subpoenaed the new medical records. If Boxer had followed up, he would have learned that after the deposition, Todd was referred to an out-of-state neurologist who diagnosed Todd with a hematoma that resulted in brain damage. According to the Nevada doctor, "All this was caused by the crash."

In the meantime, Boxer had reported to the insurance company, which just happened to be Atlas, that the case had a settlement value of about twenty-five thousand dollars. It took the *Todd* case about a year to wind its way through the system. He was stunned when the pretrial settlement demand came in at a million dollars. Todd's attorney refused to allow a continuance (postponement) of the trial so that Boxer could obtain an update of the medical records, depose the Nevada neurologist, and have a defense medical examination to confirm whether or not there was brain damage.

Boxer could no longer delay telling Miller the situation. Miller was furious. He said, "I told you at the outset that one of the keys to success in this business is no surprises. This is more than a surprise. It's a catastrophe. You should have advised me when the million-dollar demand came in rather than telling me when the postponement was denied. I fear that Atlas will consider this malpractice and we will have to put our malpractice carrier on notice. When word gets out, it will kill our reputation. Atlas will take us off its panel counsel list."

Miller put his head in his hands and thought. Finally, he said, "First, I will immediately tell Malloy, and then I will telephone Atlas and tell them the situation."

Needless to say, Atlas would not let Boxer try the case. Miller was ordered to try the case, and further action was deferred pending the outcome.

Boxer was permitted to "second chair" the case, which meant he was allowed to sit at the counsel table during trial and whisper and pass notes to Miller, who was first chair.

The case did not go well from the start. In his opening statement to the jury, Todd's attorney described Todd's brain damage and sequelae: "Todd lost words, forgot faces, lost his job, and suffered severe headaches." Todd's Nevada neurologist was going to testify that the brain damage was caused by the rear-ender.

In his opening argument, Miller could not flatly deny the plaintiff's attorney's allegations, because his expert neurologist had not examined Todd or received and reviewed Todd's latest medical records. Miller coughed and sniffled throughout his opening.

Todd's first witness was Dr. Vegas, a neurologist from Nevada. Boxer immediately forgot the doctor's name, and the man became "Dr. Nevada" in his mind. At first, Boxer found himself taking mental notes about the way the attorney questioned the doctor. There was a lot to learn, but soon Boxer became too depressed to pay attention. The neurologist was golden on the stand. He dazzled the jury with charts and radiologic images that showed the extent of the brain damage. While the x-rays were just shadows, the neurologist brought them to life with nothing more than his words and a few sketches made with a black marker. It was all Boxer could do to avoid slumping over in his chair. Somehow he kept himself upright and rigid. He wouldn't win any points with the jury by looking defeated on the first day.

Besides, Miller was taking care of that all by himself. Miller looked sick as a dog. Boxer wished they could just call it a day, because clearly Miller wouldn't be able to even start a cross-examination. He was relieved when the judge announced a recess for the day and that the case would begin again in the morning.

Boxer spent the night looking for any way to discount the doctor's testimony, but it appeared that he would be out of luck. Things got worse when the phone rang.

Miller's wife was on the line. She told Boxer that Miller had just been hospitalized with the flu and could not attend trial the next day. Miller's wife agreed to get a confirming doctor's note and fax it to Boxer, who intended to seek a continuance of the trial until Miller could return to court.

Ordinarily, Boxer would have been thrilled at taking over a big case. But this was different. Without updated medical records, Boxer's cross of Dr. Vegas might allow the good doctor merely to restate and reemphasize the severe injuries suffered by Todd as a result of the conduct of the Atlas insurance holders. But a continuance might permit him to update the medical records.

Boxer desperately telephoned his defense neurologist, Dr. Al Purcell, and reviewed Dr. Vegas's direct testimony with Dr. Purcell. Boxer had to train himself to use Dr. Nevada's real name—Dr. Vegas.

Dr. Purcell said it sounded a little suspicious. "From what you say, Dr. Vegas has not seen the plaintiff or looked at the plaintiff's medical records for over a year."

"That's true," said Boxer.

"And you also believe that Dr. Vegas and the plaintiff's attorney are both competent."

"Yes."

"There must be a reason why the doctor has not seen the most recent medical records. My guess is the most recent medical information hurts their case. Get me a subpoena for these records, and I will get them from the hospital tonight. I will also telephone my old buddy who used to be chief of neurology at Nevada General Hospital, where Dr. Vegas practices." Court was to start at 10:00 a.m. the next morning, and Dr. Purcell agreed to meet Boxer in the lawyers' lounge at the courthouse at 7:00 a.m.

The next morning, Boxer met with Dr. Purcell and spent the next three hours learning neurology and the ways Dr. Vegas had abused it. Purcell was explaining the difference between trauma-induced brain damage and disease-induced brain damage when Boxer interrupted and said, "I got it, doc."

Purcell noted that Boxer seemed to catch on very quickly. At 10:00 a.m., the judge took the bench, and Boxer asked for a twenty-four-hour continuance so that Miller could return to the courtroom and cross-examine Dr. Vegas. The judge said, "It's your case, Boxer, and you should try it." The judge denied the motion to continue. Boxer was not as upset as he would have been the previous afternoon. Todd's attorney, hoping to find Boxer unprepared, announced he'd finished his direct and passed the witness for Boxer's cross-examination. Boxer immediately proceeded:

"You're from Nevada, right?"

"Yes."

"And isn't it true you are not licensed in California?"

"True."

"All of Todd's treatment was in California, wasn't it, doctor?"

"Yes."

"Indeed, there are dozens of qualified neurologists right here in San Francisco, right?"

"Yes."

"This is not the first time you have testified in court, is it?"

"True."

"You charge five thousand dollars for a half-day of testimony, right?"

"Yes."

"And you always testify for the plaintiff?"

"I'm not sure. I guess so."

"You made more money testifying last year for plaintiffs than you did practicing medicine?"

"I'm not sure."

Boxer, holding what looked like a tax return, said, "Well, isn't it true you reported to the IRS that your income for testifying last year was five hundred thousand dollars?"

"Yes."

"And you are testifying more this year, right?"

"Yes."

"The last time you saw Todd was in Nevada about one year after the accident. In fact, that's the only time you saw him. Isn't that true?"

"Yes."

"Yesterday, you rendered your expert opinion to the jury based on the medical records you were given by the plaintiff's attorney?"

"Yes."

"And if the plaintiff's attorney did not give you plaintiff's most recent medical records over the last year, you cannot testify as to his present diagnosis, can you?"

"That's partially true."

"In this case, the last medical records you have reviewed were over a year old?"

"Yes."

"And you do not know what entries doctors have made in Todd's medical records in the last year, right?"

"Right."

"And you are not in a position to criticize those medical records?"

"Well, I have to look at them."

"Well, doctor, here they are," said Boxer.

Dr. Vegas evasively said, "I still can't comment on them without examining them."

"To be fair, in order for you to give an accurate medical opinion, you'd have to study the updated medical records, right?"

"I agree."

Boxer addressed the court. "To have a complete record for the jury, I move that we take a break to allow Dr. Vegas to read these medical records."

The plaintiff's attorney started to object but realized it would not play well with the jury. The court allowed the recess, and the doctor was given the updated medical records.

After the court readjourned, the judge said, "Mr. Tate, you may now proceed."

Boxer began, "Doctor, let's put this all in context. Did you actually examine Todd a year ago?"

"Yes."

"And you looked at his medical records a year ago?"

"Yes."

"And based on those first set of medical records, you reached the opinion that Todd had brain damage caused by trauma?"

"Yes."

"And you did not see any head trauma revealed in that set of medical records, did you?"

"True."

"And the head trauma you saw was first listed in the medical records about a month before you saw Mr. Todd, right?"

"Right."

"In the first set of medical records, no one attributed the hematoma to that trauma, did they?"

"No."

"No one attributed that trauma to the low-speed, low-impact rear-ender, did they?"

"No."

"Head trauma does not necessarily lead to brain injury, does it?"

"Right."

"There was no diagnosis of hematoma at the time of the automobile accident, was there?"

"No."

"If the automobile accident caused hematoma, it would manifest itself within twenty-four hours of the accident, right?"

"Yes."

"Did you see any history of hematoma noted in the medical records after the accident?"

"No."

"Right after admission, the admitting doctor took a history from Todd indicating that among the medicines he was receiving was Zoloft."

"Yes."

"And how long had Todd been taking Zoloft before the accident?"

"About one year."

"And, Dr. Vegas, please tell the ladies and gentlemen of the jury what Zoloft is indicated for?"

"What do you mean, indicated?"

"You know that the word 'indicated' means the reason the patient was receiving the medicine, right? My question to you is why was Todd taking Zoloft?"

"I don't know."

"Well, you'll agree with me that *The Physician's Desk Reference* says Zoloft is indicated for anxiety and depression."

"I agree, counsel. That's what it says, but I don't know if Mr. Todd is actually suffering depression and anxiety."

"In rendering opinion here, if Todd did have anxiety and depression, wouldn't that be significant?"

"Yes."

"Dr. Vegas, Did you ask your attorney for the updated medical records?"

There was a long pause. Then Boxer said, "Your Honor, please ask Dr. Vegas to answer the question."

"Go ahead and answer the question, Dr. Vegas," said the judge.

"Yes, I did ask for updated medical records."

"And what did plaintiff's attorney say?"

"Object," Todd's attorney snapped.

The judge leaned forward in his seat. "Overruled—you may answer, doctor."

Dr. Vegas was used to being impeached on cross-examination. Ordinarily, he never allowed his demeanor to change, but this was not the usual; this kid had set it up to inflict maximum pain. He knew both the judge and the jury would hate him and his lawyer. He had no choice but to answer the question. "He said he had read them and there was nothing in there."

Boxer said, "After taking a break and reading these second set of records, you now know there is something in there, don't you?"

"Yes."

"Please read it to the jury."

Dr. Vegas read, "'Todd's latest battery of brain tests show he is not suffering from brain damage but rather has had anxiety reaction unrelated to his automobile accident.'"

"Thank you, Dr. Vegas," said Boxer. "No further questions."

"Call your next witness, counsel for plaintiff," ordered the judge.

"I have no further witnesses, Your Honor."

The judge turned to Boxer. "Counsel for defendant, call your first witness."

But Boxer responded, "At this time, the defense makes a motion for nonsuit and entry of judgment in favor of defendant. It is our view that there is not sufficient evidence for this case to go to a jury."

"Let's take a recess while I consider this motion," said the judge.

After several minutes, the judge returned to the bench and said, "Madam Court Reporter, I'd like this on the record." He then announced, "After reviewing the testimony for plaintiff, I am of the opinion that there is not sufficient evidence of any relationship between the low-speed, low-impact rear-ender and any brain damage. In fact, I'm not sure there is enough evidence to establish that there is brain damage. Therefore, I dismiss this case with prejudice and enter judgment in favor of the defense.

"Ladies and gentlemen of the jury, thank you. The court and counsel greatly appreciate your advice and wish you well."

Boxer maintained his composure. There was no fist-pumping or excitement. He wanted the jury to feel that this was an expected result. He assumed that Atlas would be elated. Not so.

He turned to the back of the courtroom expecting joy, but all he saw was stern faces, cold as stone. Atlas's assistant claim manager, who was in the back of the courtroom, said to Malloy, "I want you to appoint a senior lawyer to review all of Boxer's files at the expense of your firm. Further, he's no longer authorized to manage files without partner oversight."

Malloy briefly considered reducing Boxer's salary but for one problem. Before Boxer's cross-examination, word had spread through the courthouse that a young associate at Malloy's firm was going to get slaughtered by an expert witness in a brain injury case he was trying. The courtroom was packed for Boxer's cross. To the surprise of all, Boxer was great, and the crowd loved it. Malloy wandered into the hallway, which was filled with trial lawyers from other courtrooms who were still buzzing, "Did you see that kid! He's got a gift. His timing is great. He really set up the plaintiff's expert."

Malloy knew that in this free agency market a good trial lawyer was in demand and Boxer would be receiving phone calls from headhunters and partners from other law firms. All of them could easily pay Boxer more than he was making at Malloy. Boxer would have to receive a good raise immediately.

Privately, Fortune Jones was thrilled with Boxer. On the pretext that she was in the neighborhood, she stopped by the Malloy firm and walked unannounced into Boxer's small associate office. Boxer, sleeves rolled up to show his sinewy forearms, looked exhausted but well satisfied. He was clearly elated and made a slight move toward a Hollywood air kiss but stopped.

Fortune saw the movement and touched Boxer's arm. She could not help but look into his gleaming eyes. She said, "Isn't this fun? I wish I could stay and rehash the victory." She turned to the door but said over her shoulder with a bright smile, "We'll have more time to talk, because I'll be throwing more work your way."

Boxer chose to reinterpret. *She thinks I'm a good lawyer, and she wants to spend more time with me.*

Headhunters

Audi Johns remained in her seat for several minutes analyzing what she had just witnessed. Leaving the courtroom, she stopped by to thank the attaché who had suggested she stop in to the see the trial. He said, "Yeah, sorry it didn't go as advertised."

Audi said, "It was more interesting than I had expected." She thought to herself, *Get to know Mr. Boxer Tate. He could be useful in more ways than one.* Audi was known to the courtroom attachés. Her job was to find great lawyers for rich law firms. She was a headhunter. She had just happened to be scouting a superstar trial lawyer when the attaché let her know something interesting was going on in courtroom 2. The word was that a young lawyer named Boxer Tate was going to get his clock cleaned by an out-of-state professional expert witness.

Like other courtroom watchers, Audi proceeded to courtroom 2. She anticipated a young, frightened associate trying to cope with a glib, smooth-talking medical expert. Instead, she found a confident, aggressive, prepared trial lawyer controlling the courtroom. Boxer asked nothing but leading questions on cross-examination so that Dr. Vegas from Nevada was given no leeway to give speeches or sermons. He could do nothing but agree with the carefully crafted closed-end questions. The jury was not looking at the witness but was riveted by the handsome, young trial attorney, Boxer Tate, who was an expert in medical terms.

Audi wasn't sure how Boxer might fit into her practice, but she definitely wanted to get to know him.

Traditionally, law firms were stable places. Corporate clients sent their business to the same large law firms year after year and case after case. A lawyer in a large firm could not leave the firm, because his corporate clients would generally not follow him to another firm. Most big-firm partners spent their entire careers at the same firm. All this changed when the "book of business" concept arose. Corporate general counsel started sending their business to lawyers and not law firms. Lawyers became specialists, not generalists. Patent lawyers handled patents, not automobile accidents. Mergers and acquisitions lawyers could charge hourly rates as if they were investment bankers. Insurance-defense work was considered routine and thus did not command high hourly rates. The insurance companies dubbed it "commodity work" and tried to hire lawyers by the case, not by the hour. They wanted to pay less, and many did. Corporations bought more insurance coverage, and insurance companies defended lawsuits against corporations by hiring insurance-defense lawyers, whom they paid a lot less than intellectual property lawyers. Corporations also retained boutique law firms and specialty law firms.

When Boxer started at the Malloy firm, clients like Atlas were just starting to change their client concept. They were viewing individuals as their attorneys rather than law firms. Thus, if an individual attorney left a law firm, more and more of his clients would follow him. Law firms started keeping track of how much they charged a client per year. Thus, if the Malloy firm charged Atlas a million dollars a year for the hundred cases it worked on, it would be considered a million-dollar book of business. If the book of business would follow Miller Johnson if he left Malloy, it was considered a portable book of business, and headhunters would use these figures to sell lawyers from one firm to another.

Law firms who wanted to offer a wrongful discharge capability to their clients would buy a wrongful discharge lawyer or a small wrongful discharge firm. This new mobility was encouraged by headhunters. Initially, headhunters would act on behalf of a particular law firm seeking a particular lawyer. If the law firm needed a trial lawyer, they'd hire a headhunter to find one. To persuade the superstar lawyer to leave a firm, the acquiring firm would have to allow the lateral to come in as a partner. It would have to offer points, or a percentage interest in the profits of the acquiring firm. As the lateral hiring business expanded, headhunters with no clients would solicit lawyers and then shop these lawyers to acquiring firms. The headhunters tried to charge a percentage of the lateral's salary for the first year at the new firm. Thus, if the salary was five hundred thousand dollars per year, the acquiring firm would have to pay the head hunter an additional hundred thousand. The headhunter fees rose exponentially as they put together lateral moves of not just individual lawyers but groups of lawyers. Lateral incomes were negotiated in part based on the size of the lateral's portable book of business.

Also important in the negotiation was the extent to which the acquiring firm needed the lateral's expertise. Thus, while Boxer had a small book of business that probably was not portable, he was developing a reputation as a trial lawyer. Commercial litigators were good at pretrial strategies, but since few of their cases got tried, they did not have enough in-the-trenches experience to go to trial. Lawyers like Boxer had that expertise.

Audi, who was a decade older than Boxer, had taken up headhunting after a mediocre twelve-year legal career at a midlevel law firm. She made dozens of cold calls every day and had Boxer at the top of her list. She had achieved some reputation as a headhunter who could identify unrecognized young talent. She had placed several lawyers as associates in firms where those lawyers had gone on to become successful partners.

She called Boxer and was impressed that he answered his own phone on the first ring and presented himself as courteous and happy to chat.

She said, "Mr. Tate, I was fortunate enough to see your cross-examination of Dr. Vegas yesterday. I represent several outstanding law firms who I think would be interested in you as a lateral associate."

Boxer replied, "Call me Boxer, please. I'm happy at the Malloy firm. This firm has given me chances that no other law firm could offer. They have allowed me the opportunity to try cases, essentially manage my own case load, take my own depositions, and go to court several times a week. I love what I am doing."

Audi wanted to go slowly, but she could not resist. "At Malloy, your horizons are limited. You will not get to handle complex, bet-the-company cases. Your income is restricted, and the longer you wait, the harder it will be for you to make a lateral move. Also, age is on your side. Larger firms can afford to make the investment of time and money in helping you learn to handle mass torts and class actions. You'll be exposed to exciting and lucrative practice areas. Further, you will be learning from the top lawyers from the top law schools. If you don't move now, you may never get the chance again."

Boxer paused. Audi sensed he was going to try to get out of this conversation. He asked, "What law firms are interested in me?" She had to confess that no law firm had inquired specifically about him, but she said she had wanted to talk to him before shopping his name to law firms. In the same theme, Boxer asked, "What firms would you shop me to?" Audi thought she would have to prepare before speaking candidly and in-depth about the pros and cons of each possible firm and said so. She asked Boxer if he could be free for dinner. Boxer reluctantly agreed, and Audi offered to reserve a private booth with drapes drawn at Sam's Grill two nights hence.

Sam's

Sam's was a San Francisco tradition, not a tourist trap. Patrons were mostly professionals from the financial district. They would meet in the small bar area before proceeding to their tables with starched white linen. On one of the walls were booths with drapes to preserve a private atmosphere beyond. Audi ran into several of the lawyers she knew and recognized Fortune Jones at an open table. Fortune was involved in a conversation with an academic. Boxer arrived and immediately recognized what he believed to be an awkward situation. He really didn't want Fortune to see him at dinner with a headhunter. By Audi's attire, Boxer also recognized that this could easily look like a social evening as opposed to a professional one. He didn't think Fortune saw him enter the private booth.

Inside the booth, Boxer maintained his cool and explained that he did legal work for Atlas and, in fact, the *Todd* case was an Atlas matter.

Audi had the looks to go with her job. Boxer was sure the job-changing lawyers would want to spend time with her. Boxer said, "Do you take all of your clients here?"

Audi replied, "Only the good-looking ones." She added quickly, "That means most of them."

The food at Sam's Grill was great. Audi ordered her usual, Sam's seafood salad, followed by grilled wild salmon. Boxer ordered the shrimp salad followed by sand dabs.

The draped private table, together with the well-chilled Rombauer Chardonnay, lent an air of both conspiracy and intimacy that made it easy for Boxer to share his hopes and dreams with Audi. Audi confessed that she could only get one firm willing to talk to Boxer. None of the firms had ever hired a lawyer from Stephen A. Douglas Law School. They had hired several from the tops of their classes at the second-rate law firms and had been disappointed. They felt that one great cross-examination did not a career make. She explained that the law firm that was willing to interview Boxer had made it clear that they were not really in the market for a Boxer-type lawyer but were agreeing to meet based on the recommendation of Audi. The name of the firm was the Thompson Firm, named after its chairman and senior partner, Tommy Thompson, also known as Tommy Torts. It was a firm of 150 lawyers based solely in San Francisco but acting as national counsel for some California corporations in class-actions, mass torts, and white-collar crime cases. Thompson was forty-four years old and was a graduate of Boalt Hall Law, where he was on Law Review. His first job as a lawyer was as an assistant US attorney in San Francisco. He successfully tried seventeen major cases over a spectacular ten-year period. He left the US attorney's office to open his own shop. He was immediately retained by CEOs and corporate chairmen to defend them individually in white-collar criminal cases. He was successful and developed close relationships with these general counsel and corporate leaders in San Francisco. These corporations retained him for other major cases, and his firm grew steadily over the next eight years. It was on everyone's list to be acquired by one of the thousand-lawyer national megafirms.

Audi and Boxer discussed the pros and cons. Audi said, "Conventional wisdom says growth is good. The larger the firm, the larger the cases, the more the income."

Boxer asked, "Would a lawyer from Douglas fit in at a megafirm, to say nothing of Tommy Thompson's hundred-fifty-lawyer boutique firm?" Boxer went on, "Paper is king at these firms, and I have no paper ... articles ... and have not given any presentations. I have clerked for no judges. Other than the *Todd* victory, I have won no big cases, and I am not a fellow in the prestigious American College of Trial Lawyers."

Audi said, "Tommy Thompson is not a snob. Paper is not as important as performance with Thompson. He has hired public defenders who have had great success representing bums, drunks, and those with extensive rap sheets. Ordinarily, he does not bring in laterals based on their book of business but rather their trial success. He particularly likes to hire assistant US attorneys because of the fact that they have tried intricate, complicated, bet-your-company cases. He believes that these are the lawyers that keep corporate America honest, and Tommy is now using them to help corporate America become dishonest."

Audi said, "I saw your cross-examination on the *Todd* trial. I think you'd fit right in, especially with the women."

Boxer said, "What?"

And Audi replied, "I saw you and how the women jurors watched you so carefully as you moved around the courtroom."

Audi tapped the back of his hands with her fingers to make her point. Boxer left his hands in the middle of the table because he liked the touches.

Audi thought her charm might be working. She asked, "Well, what do you think? Do you want to talk to Thompson?" She squeezed his hand. "I'll fix it up right away."

Audi paid the bill, and on leaving the booth, Boxer saw Jones with what looked like a Stanford professor. Fortune rose and said, "Oh, I know you, Audi. You're a headhunter. You're not trying to steal my lawyer, are you?"

Audi replied, "Oh, I didn't know you owned him. I suspect I won't be the only headhunter who wants to talk to him."

"But the only one who takes him to dinner after a defense verdict," said Fortune.

Audi said, "If you would have been there, you would have been impressed."

Fortune said coolly to Boxer, "We have to talk."

Before Boxer could respond, Audi took Boxer's hand and walked him out of Sam's, saying loudly so Fortune could hear, "I'll call you tomorrow about the Thompson interview."

The Thompson Interview

The next day Boxer decided to confess to Miller Johnson. He said, "Headhunter Audi Johns has been pursuing me. She has talked me into a short interview with Tommy Thompson."

Miller gave a whistle and said, "Wow. We can't compete with Thompson."

Boxer replied, "First, I have no idea what they have in mind. The odds of them giving me a job are *de minimis*. If they offered me a job, I suspect it would not be as a partner-track associate. Finally, I love it here."

Miller was still pleased at how Boxer had salvaged the *Todd* case and saved the Atlas Insurance account. He certainly did not want to lose Boxer, who had saved his ass on other cases before *Todd*.

Boxer and Miller came up with a game plan. Boxer would talk to Thompson and any other firms that Audi might propose. Neither Boxer nor Miller would reveal this to Malloy until Boxer received an offer—if ever. Boxer agreed that he would not accept an offer without first taking it to Malloy, thus giving Malloy first right of refusal. Miller said that he wasn't involved in the firm's long-range planning and there was always the chance that Malloy was working to merge the firm with another firm with greater prospects and more money. If so, it might be worth Boxer's while to remain involved.

The Thompson firm occupied the two top floors in One Embarcadero Center in downtown San Francisco. Boxer arrived at the appointed hour but had to wait twenty minutes before he was ushered into a modern conference room that overlooked Coit Tower, Alcatraz, and the San Francisco Bay.

Thompson arrived apologizing for his lateness and further announcing that he had to be on a conference call in fifteen minutes. Boxer replied that he understood and if Thompson wanted to spend the next fifteen minutes preparing for the conference call, Boxer could come back later. Boxer was hoping to get Thompson's full attention if the interview was only going to be for twenty minutes.

Thompson hesitated and then said, "Actually, I could use the time, but the next hole in my calendar is after five thirty this evening."

Boxer said, "I'll take it," and quickly withdrew from the room.

At 5:30 p.m., Boxer returned. Thompson was already waiting for him in the conference room, and he again apologized for his earlier tardiness.

Thompson was tall, square-jawed, and blond. His shirt collar was loose and unbuttoned in a physical rather than fastidious look. He could have been a lifeguard—or maybe a lifeguard captain. Boxer could see that Thompson was distracted. Boxer asked Thompson how the conference call had gone. Thompson said, "You will be interested in it."

Boxer was taken aback. "Why?"

"One of the people I talked to was Al Purcell."

"I just used Dr. Purcell as an expert. He was helpful in the extreme. Why are you talking to him?" asked Boxer.

"I am being interviewed about defending a series of cases against a Silicon Valley pharmaceutical company called Jonas. Jonas is insured by Atlas, and Al Purcell is its part-time medical director. He told me that you tried the *Todd* case for Atlas using Dr. Purcell as a consulting expert. That is why I agreed to interview you. What can you tell me about Dr. Purcell?"

Boxer said, "I have had many doctors try to teach me medicine. Dr. Purcell is the best. I think he would be great in front of a jury. You would want him to be the face of Jonas at trial. He knows how to translate medicine into English. He has great credentials, and he is very credible. He can make complex neurological principles understandable."

Thompson said, "Let me get right to the point. These drug cases will involve reviewing, summarizing, and organizing thousands of pages of medical records and pharmaceutical records. I would like you to be the paralegal in charge. I will pay you more than you are now making at Malloy."

Boxer immediately replied, "No, thank you! I am a lawyer, and I won't take a paralegal job no matter what the pay."

Thompson did not expect such a vehement response. He said, "Well, maybe it could evolve into an associate position."

Recalling his conversation with Audi Johns at Sam's Grill, Boxer said, "If you were me, would you take this job?"

Thompson paused longer than he should have and said, "I think you should take my job offer. Malloy is a dead-end practice. You will never handle anything but auto cases. The firm won't grow, and the money is bad."

Boxer said, "I want to try cases. I don't see that happening here. I also want to run my own practice, and I don't see that happening here either."

Thompson concluded, "You are probably right. But thanks for coming by." They shook hands, and the meeting was over quicker than Boxer wanted.

10

The Tate-Malloy Deal

Boxer spent the next morning arguing pretrial motions in San Francisco Superior Court, so he didn't have much time to agonize over what he considered a rejection by Thompson. When Boxer returned to the Malloy offices, there was an e-mail on his computer from Thompson. "Please call me soonest. Tommy."

Boxer called Thompson's direct-dial number, and Thompson himself answered. "Boxer, I have been thinking, and I can understand that you could never accept a paralegal title and so I am changing the offer to make it an associate position."

Boxer asked, "Can I have a few days to think about it?"

Thompson said, "You can have twenty-four hours, but I don't want you to shop the offer. I don't want to be used as a pawn in negotiating a raise for you at Malloy."

Boxer did not answer the question but said simply, "I'll get back to you," and hung up.

Boxer sought out Miller Johnson and brought him up to date on the discussions with Thompson. Johnson pointed out the obvious. "While Thompson might give you the title of associate, you will still have the job of a paralegal."

Boxer replied, "True, but I think that I can work my way into the actual job of an associate."

Miller asked, "Is it a partnership track?" Then he said, "If you are thinking of taking the Thompson offer, you agreed to talk to Malloy first."

Boxer decided that he had not replied to Tommy's statement that he didn't want Boxer to shop the offer to Malloy. In his own mind, by not replying, Boxer had not agreed to the restriction.

Boxer wanted to talk to Malloy before lunch, so he immediately walked down to Malloy's office. It was a small office, and there were hundreds of files covering the desk, filing cabinet, and sole chair in the room. Malloy waved him in and continued his telephone conversation with a plaintiff's attorney. Malloy could be very charming with adversaries and clients. He could be rude to lawyers and staff in the office. He had red cheeks and puffy eyes; these forecast an angry man.

Malloy said, "What do you want? I am late for lunch. I have got to get out of here."

Boxer wanted to ask why but decided this was not the time. Instead, Boxer described the Thompson situation.

Boxer said, "I have a job offer from Tommy Thompson. Thompson believes that he will be representing a Silicon Valley drug company called Jonas, and he is going to give me a job to help out on those cases and told me not to shop the offer."

Malloy laughed a little too loudly. He said Atlas also had talked to him about the Jonas drug cases.

Boxer discourteously said, "Malloy, you have never handled a large, complex mass drug tort case or a series of mass tort cases. How can Atlas assign the cases to you?"

"Let me explain Thompson's thinking," Malloy said. "Atlas insured Jonas for two million dollars. Jonas has to pay anything in excess of that, so Fortune Jones is considering retaining two sets of lawyers for these suits: one to handle the routine matters, and another, like Thompson, for the more complex aspects of the case. Thompson, of course, doesn't want to split the money with anybody. So he wants to hire you so he can tell Jonas that he has competent lawyers who have low salaries to work the routine stuff."

Boxer asked, "If I stay here, what are the odds we will get retained?"

Malloy said, "It's just a guess, but I would say about 50 percent and if you go with Thompson, it will probably all go to Thompson. So to answer your question, if the routine business really follows you, we are both offering you less than you are worth."

Boxer said, "I have an idea. I know that this firm has two partners, you and Miller Johnson. Rather than giving me a raise, just make me a partner. If the firm makes nothing, then I make nothing. Further, I am not asking for 33 percent of the profits but only 25 percent."

Malloy responded, "Twenty-five percent sounds steep, but I will talk to Miller about it and we will get back to you."

The next morning, Malloy and Miller offered Boxer a partnership interest in which Malloy would receive 45 percent of the net profits and Miller and Boxer would receive 35 and 20 percent respectively. If Malloy profits remained flat, Boxer would not be receiving as much as Thompson had offered. But Malloy pointed out that Boxer would be more in control of his destiny at an earlier age. Boxer accepted the deal.

Boxer needed someone to celebrate with. He called his friends and said, "Now it is my turn to treat. Let's have a drink before you guys go to work tonight. I have some good news."

Boxer had not been keeping up with his friends. There was a lot of chatter after their draft beers and his Makers Mark arrived. Boxer tried to explain the Malloy deal. Their first response was "We don't understand." Their second response was "It sounds like both you and the Malloy firm will be working for Thompson." Boxer could not understand their dazed looks when he explained the points. Boxer also tried to explain what it was like being pursued by a pretty headhunter. His friends wanted to talk about Buster Posey. One said, "I have got some Giants tickets for next Tuesday. Want to come?"

Boxer said, "No ... I have to be in court."

After he left early again, they whispered, "He hardly ever sees us, and when he does all he wants to do is talk about his job."

Boxer's thoughts turned to how to tell Atlas about the Malloy deal and how to get the Jonas cases.

The Thompson-Malloy Deal

First thing in the morning, Thompson called Boxer and asked for his decision. Boxer said, "I have decided to accept a partnership at Malloy."

Thompson exploded. "You violated our agreement. You shopped my offer to Malloy. I consider this a breach of contract, and if I don't get all of the *Jonas* cases I will seek compensatory and punitive damages."

Boxer calmly responded, "There was no contract. But there was an intentional misrepresentation on your side. You purposefully failed to reveal to me that the reason you were soliciting me was to try to garner 100 percent of the Jonas business, leaving Malloy with none of the work. And don't you think that Atlas will question your loyalty in trying to manipulate the situation so that Atlas would have to pay higher defense costs to you rather than saving money by splitting the work in the most cost-efficient manner between Malloy and Thompson?"

Thompson switched gears immediately. He calmed down and said, "You know neither one of us has the business at this point. Maybe we should make a joint proposal to Atlas and Jonas."

Boxer noticed Thompson's subtle use of anger to try to get his way. He filed that trait away. Boxer said, "I think my partners will agree. I will talk to them and get back to you."

Thompson was impressed at how quickly Boxer had assumed the partnership mantle.

Miller and Malloy were thrilled with the Thompson proposal. There were many reasons that work on the *Jonas* cases would be good for the Malloy firm. Jonas was a trophy client, and representing it in large, complex litigation would be a credibility builder for Malloy. Further, working with Thompson would not only bring prestige, but the firm's size ensured that it would have conflicts and would have to decline cases when one client was suing another. Law firms want to refer conflict work to friendly firms that are not too brilliant and will not become competitors for the work from the conflicted client. Malloy was a perfect conflict referral.

Malloy agreed that Boxer should tell Tommy that Malloy suggested that Thompson and Boxer stage a joint beauty presentation for Atlas and Jonas. Thompson agreed and further agreed for the two firms to enter into a nonaggression and nondisparagement pact and that Malloy would release any claims for Thompson's efforts to solicit Boxer. It was further agreed that Thompson would be overall head of the Jonas litigation but that Boxer would be day-to-day in charge of the work. Thompson and Boxer decided to develop a marketing approach and schedule meetings with Jonas and Atlas.

Boxer was impressed with his ability to make things work out in his own favor. He thought. *Before, I was small-time, with a relatively small pay-out of twenty-five thousand dollars. Now I can even influence a large firm like Thompson.* He enjoyed the power.

The loser in the deal was Audi Johns. She only collected if Boxer went to work at another firm. Boxer told Johns of his elevation to partnership at Malloy, and she offered congratulations. She asked, "What is Jones's reaction to all of this?"

Boxer responded, "I haven't asked. Do you have any suggestions?"

Johns said, "If I were you, I would talk to her during a candlelit dinner." She paused and thought perhaps she shouldn't have said it that way, inasmuch as she wanted to fuse her own future relationship with Boxer over a quiet dinner. He represented future business opportunities and more. Boxer volunteered that if he needed a headhunter in the future, she would get the job.

The Atlas-Jonas Deal

Thompson set up the initial meeting with Jonas, and Boxer did the same with Atlas. Thompson and Boxer decided what they would propose— that Boxer and his team would be in charge of the more routine work, such as collecting, organizing, summarizing, and producing documents.

Further, Thompson and Tate decided to propose that Thompson would be the first-chair trial lawyer and his team would argue the more sophisticated pretrial motions. Jonas would pay the Thompson bills, and Atlas would pay the Boxer bills. They also prepared a proposed budget that detailed all of the work, who would do the work, and how much would be charged for each item of work. The proposal demonstrated forethought and effective strategies.

Thompson and Tate geared the budget to this single-entry beauty contest. They would point out to Jonas and Atlas that the right lawyers would be doing the right jobs. Tommy would not be indexing files. Boxer's team would not be arguing sophisticated motions to dismiss.

Their first presentation was to Fortune Jones at Atlas. They assumed that Atlas would be the easier sell. Atlas would not have to pay the high Thompson bills, and the case would still have the expertise of Tommy Thompson. Atlas would have big-firm depth without big-firm bills. There would be a minimum of double billing because of careful budgetary assignments. The plan was designed to satisfy Atlas's thrifty culture. As anticipated, Atlas accepted the proposal subject to Jonas also accepting. But there was one condition. Fortune wanted Boxer to be designated the second-chair trial lawyer. Atlas remembered the *Todd* case when the first-chair trial lawyer, Miller Johnson, got sick and Boxer had to replace him with little time for preparation. Atlas wanted the security of a prepared second-chair trial lawyer without having to pay the Thompson firm rates to get that lawyer. All agreed.

The meeting with Jonas was equally successful. Jonas's main concern was securing a prestigious law firm that would give comfort to their board of directors, stockholders, and the financial community. No matter how talented the lawyer, if he was not known in the financial community, Jonas's stock would go down.

Further, Jonas's in-house counsel, Kenny Clark, wanted to retain counsel early. He knew it was important to execute and circulate document hold orders. The plaintiff's bar had successfully persuaded some judges that corporations were prone to destroy key damning documents in anticipation of litigation. The courts then issued orders requiring the corporations to hold the key relevant documents. If the documents were not retained, some judges entered issue sanctions or terminating sanctions. Thus, if a pharmaceutical company destroyed records documenting clinical trials, the court could order that the issue as to whether or not the drug caused the type of injury suffered by the plaintiff would be automatically decided in favor of the injured party.

On the way out after the Jonas presentation, Thompson whispered to Boxer, "Go home and learn everything you can about pharmaceutical litigation."

Jonas

Jonas Pharmaceutical was the creation of Patrick Jonas, a pharmacist whose parents had migrated from Germany to California's Silicon Valley, where they created a generic drug empire. Its chief product was a sleeping medication simply called Jonas. Jonas was sold over the counter (OTC) without a doctor's prescription. It was grandfathered through the Food and Drug Administration, meaning that no clinical trials or other testing was necessary because the product was successfully on the market before the regulations were in effect.

Patrick Jonas developed a small sales force that obtained orders from pharmacies throughout the United States. Once a pharmacy purchased Jonas's sleeping medication, follow-up orders came quickly since the product worked. Like most generic companies, Jonas had no research capability.

Patrick Jonas had been happily married for twenty years to his college sweetheart, Jayne. It was a great marriage. The couple was rich, and they enjoyed traveling the world. They particularly liked Africa. The people were different, as was the climate, the culture, and the geography. Jayne was bright, vivacious, and striking.

One winter while they were traveling in Africa, Jayne started feeling bloated. Fluid was building up in her stomach. The couple diverted their plans and went to a doctor in Kenya. After several blood tests and biopsies, Jayne was referred to a cancer specialist who diagnosed her with pancreatic cancer. She was told that the cancer was considered fast-acting, painful, and incurable.

The Kenyan doctor told Jayne that the statistics in the literature projected that she had three months to live. However, her doctor said that the local clinic believed that they had a cure. It was a remedy extracted from the bark of what was called a Nobo tree indigenous to Kenya.

Jayne started taking the Nobo extract, and her symptoms subsided almost immediately. This was four years ago. In the meantime, Patrick Jonas had bought all rights to the extract and set about using independent contractors to perform animal studies, toxicity studies, and clinical trials. He spent ten million dollars. Jonas ultimately obtained FDA approval to market the drug in the US. After a year on the market, there were reports in the scientific literature suggesting that not only did the extract not cure pancreatic cancer, but in some patients it caused brain cancer. Plaintiffs' lawyers around the US solicited clients and began filing lawsuits against Jonas. Most of the cases were filed in Superior Court in San Francisco by the famous San Francisco attorney Dodge Lee. San Francisco was a favorite plaintiffs' venue, because the jurors and judges were liberal and this produced high verdicts. Some called San Francisco a judicial hellhole.

The Lee-Thompson Deal

Thompson's usual ally at the firm was his young partner Bill Dawes. Tommy had been Dawes's champion for years. Tommy, as he frequently did, wandered into Dawes's office. Dawes said, "Well, how is it going in the Jonas matters?"

Tommy Thompson was thrilled and said more than he meant to reveal: "I think there will be gross billings of about twenty-five million in the first year and higher thereafter as more cases are filed and more cases are tried." He said, "The Jonas account will be by far the biggest moneymaker in our history. So far fifteen hundred cases have been filed, and more are anticipated. Each of the cases is for either brain damage or wrongful death. I expect the average case will have a settlement value of about one-point-five million—some higher, some lower. I don't think either side will settle without a number of bellwether trials to set case values.

"Bill, you are going to have to take charge of a lot of things. I think the cost of defense will be about seven million dollars for the first bellwether case, and it will probably take five to six bellwether trials before each side will come to the table with serious money. I don't want to share either the legal fees or the mass tort prestige with the Malloy firm."

Dawes said, "This kid Boxer Tate is going to be a handful."

Tommy said, "I underestimated him. I was surprised that Fortune Jones would be so impressed with him. Malloy was smart to give him a piece of the partnership. If he had kept Boxer on salary, it would have been possible for me to offer him enough money to buy him away from Malloy. But the higher the Malloy profits are on the *Jonas* cases, the more Boxer will make and the less likely he will be enticed away from Malloy."

Tommy went on to say, "We will have to get most of the work to get most of the billing. In this strategy, knowledge is power, and we will have to control the retention of experts and the scientific research and the interviewing and preparation of all Jonas's key employees.

"The smarter we are, the more likely and the more necessary it will be to have us defend all of the depositions, prepare all pleadings and motions, and essentially control the defense of the cases. Certainly we will be doing the trials and the big motions. We have the ability to put together a team of well-educated, experienced, smart lawyers. Malloy doesn't have that capacity. He has Boxer and Miller Johnson. Malloy himself will be of little help, particularly after lunch."

Dawes said, "I don't know Dodge Lee. What is he like?"

"He is a bully, but that could work out well, because he makes outrageous demands, which can lead to higher defense costs and attorneys' fees." Tommy paused and then said, "I am sorry—I just remembered I have to make a private phone call."

That phone call was to Lee. Thompson stepped into his private office and placed the call. Lee and Thompson had been classmates at Boalt Hall but had gone in different directions after law school. Lee had built a national reputation as a plaintiffs' personal-injury lawyer. He was active in plaintiffs' bar association activities and had been referred cases by other lawyers from around the country. Collecting multiple cases against a single corporate defendant gave the plaintiffs' attorneys leverage that an attorney would not have with only one case against that corporation in his portfolio. An attorney with mass cases could spread the costs between cases so that it was economically feasible to spend the money deposing hundreds of corporate officers, directors, scientists, and marketing representatives. This onslaught could virtually interrupt the entire business of a company.

The division of expenses made it feasible for plaintiffs' attorneys to spend money retaining outside testifying experts in addition to retaining and paying separately for private consulting experts.

Just the service of subpoenas requiring production of millions of documents had a punitive impact on corporate defendants.

Thompson did not relish a telephone call with Lee. Lee was smart, aggressive, outspoken, and really was a bully. Lee had obtained some huge verdicts that led to some even higher mass tort settlements. Nevertheless, Thompson made the phone call. In one sense, Lee's outrageous demands were financially helpful to Thompson, since they justified equally extreme defense measures. Tommy wanted to be the defense conduit to Lee. He wanted to talk to him before Boxer.

Lee's secretary put Thompson through the usual hoops. "Your name, please? What file are you calling on? Will Mr. Lee know what this is about?"

Finally, Thompson got through to Lee. Lee said, "Great to talk to you. I understand you will be representing Jonas in these voodoo bark cancer cases. You will be having your hands full." Lee enjoyed denigrating his opponents, their clients, and their defenses.

Thompson replied, "That's true. Look forward to working with you. I called to talk to you about some possible procedures we could agree upon."

"Go ahead. I'm always looking for ways to make life easier."

Tommy said, "Since there are so many cases, I thought that we could agree that all papers would be served on me and I would undertake to circulate them to others."

"Sounds good to me."

Tommy said, "Also, I will accept service of any new complaints. How many do you anticipate?"

Dodge said, "We are culling through the medical records of potential suits. We only want to file meritorious cases. The CDC and the National Cancer Institute estimate that about 5 percent of those exposed to the voodoo bark will get brain cancer. About a hundred thousand patients received the bark extract last year. Thus, there should be about five thousand deaths or brain injuries per year. I would anticipate we will have more than ten thousand total cases over time."

Tommy said, "Since I am trying to make life easier for you, perhaps you can do me a favor. Could you, at my expense, provide me with copies of the medical records you have already collected?"

Lee said, "I think I can do that, but because of privacy concerns, I can only provide you with the relevant documents."

Tommy said, "That would be great, but I worry that our concept of what is relevant and what is not may be different. You might claim that a patient's breast cancer records are irrelevant to her brain cancer, and then my experts would not have the benefit of some very important exculpatory information."

Lee said, "That's true, but don't you want this early discovery?"

"Yes."

Tommy said, "How about you provide the records without prejudice to our later fighting over whether the ones you didn't provide are relevant?"

Lee said, "Explain."

Tommy said, "Suppose the records of a cancer doctor referred to treatment by a liver specialist. We will want the liver records, and you might argue that they are not relevant to the brain cancer."

Lee said, "Who decides?"

Tommy said, "If we can't agree, then it is up to the court to decide."

Lee said, "Deal."

Tommy was pleased with the telephone call. First of all, it made him the main contact with Lee. He would be the first one to receive new complaints. He would have first crack at receiving and analyzing the records, and thus he would have a head start in proposing and implementing follow-up strategies. He would be the one to parcel out the records to the defense consultants and experts. The fact that Tommy had made this telephone call gave him the indicia of access. If the defense wanted information or agreements with Lee, it would likely go through Tommy.

15

Tommy Seeks Control

Tommy's next exercise of control was to schedule a defense teleconference. He sent an e-mail to Fortune Jones of Atlas, Patrick Jonas and his general counsel Kenny Clark, and of course Boxer. The e-mail had an agenda and listed Tommy's call-in number.

The agenda was this:

- phone call with Lee
- communications
- further procedures

Boxer brought the agenda to Miller Johnson and asked if Miller could also participate in the conference call. Miller said he would love to, and then the two discussed strategy.

Boxer said, "Maybe I am paranoid, but I see this conference call as a way of controlling who runs the case."

Miller thought and then replied, "You are right, but remember that Tommy does have overall control, and I think he is right to use conference calls and agendas to exercise his powers."

Boxer said, "True, but I think we should have input as to what is to be decided, and I think now is the time to start."

Miller said, "Have you noticed you are becoming pretty controlling yourself?"

Boxer said, "You haven't seen anything yet." He then grabbed the phone and called Fortune.

Boxer asked Fortune if she had seen the agenda, and she replied, "Yes, it just came in."

Boxer said, "Did Tommy ask you for any input before he sent it?"

Fortune said, "No, but I wouldn't expect that."

Boxer said, "Well, he didn't call me, and I would expect it."

Fortune reminded Boxer that Tommy was the overall lead attorney. Boxer responded that he was day-to-day in charge. Fortune also reminded Boxer that Atlas was only paying for the Malloy team and the more work that Thompson did the less Malloy did. Boxer replied, "The less Atlas and Malloy are involved, the more control Thompson has."

Finally, Fortune pointed out that the last agenda item was "further procedures." "Can't we use that item to push our own agenda?"

"I will be ready," said Boxer.

The Thompson teleconference proceeded as scheduled. Tommy acted as master of ceremonies. Following the agenda item, he described his phone call with Lee and stated how Lee wanted the convenience of serving only the Thompson firm with legal papers.

Boxer said, "Sounds good. Do you mind if I drop Lee an e-mail asking him to add my name to the service list? That will save time and expense of your having to be the middle man."

Not wanting to appear wasteful, Tommy reluctantly agreed.

Boxer was pleased, because he knew he could use e-mails he wrote to Lee as a prelude to additional communication. Also, Boxer wanted to receive legal papers at the same time as Thompson so that he could stay current and in the loop.

Tommy then described the deal concerning the production of medical records. Tommy said, "Initially, they will not be giving us what he determines are irrelevant records. However, we will still get enough to allow us to make an early initial evaluation of those cases."

Boxer said, "Great, and could you ask Dodge to copy me also? We have a very good nurse paralegal who analyzes and summarizes all of our personal-injury medical records for a very low hourly rate."

Again Tommy felt compelled to agree. Boxer did not really think the relevancy deal was great but was pleased to be getting whatever records were produced at the same time as Tommy. The medical records were key to estimating settlement value. They reflected the diagnosis and prognosis of the treating doctors. Boxer suspected that some of the plaintiffs' records would not show any diagnosis of brain cancer caused by Nobo extract. These were the cases Boxer would push for trial even though he was not trial counsel. Boxer was planning for the future. Communications was next on the agenda. Boxer peremptorily said, "I think that we should copy each other on all of our e-mails and correspondence."

Tommy said, "I don't want the Malloy firm communicating with my client Jonas. Tell me, and I will decide what goes to Jonas. I don't want them burdened."

Jonas's general counsel, Kenny Clark, interjected, "It's no trouble. I would like to be copied on everything."

Fortune Jones said, "As would I."

Boxer was delighted that he and Miller Johnson would have the opportunity to show their work directly to Kenny Clark and Jonas.

Tommy announced the last agenda item was further procedures. Tommy said this was merely an invitation for brainstorming. Boxer and Miller were prepared. Boxer said, "While many of the complaints have been filed with the court, not many have been served. I obtained copies online. The complaints are all identical and subject to a motion to dismiss on the grounds of FDA preemption."

Boxer went on to explain, "If the FDA has approved the drug for marketing, Jonas is immune from civil suits. For instance, the FDA totally controls the labeling and warnings, thus preempting a jury's right to rule that the warnings are not adequate."

Boxer could hear Tommy's cough over the phone. Tommy said, "Well, I will have my associate, a Stanford Law graduate, look at these complaints. He clerked with the California Supreme Court and would be able to give us the most up-to-date analysis."

Boxer replied, "Have him look at the preemption issue."

Tommy paused and then announced that the meeting was adjourned. There was some doubt in Boxer's mind as to whether Tommy even knew what the preemption defense was.

16

Nobo Extract

"The anticancer drug that can cause cancer," said Dr. Purcell. "It can cure pancreatic cancer in some cases, but it can also cause brain cancer."

Tommy had organized a teleconference with Dr. Purcell, Boxer, Fortune Jones, and Kenny Clark.

Dr. Purcell had been asked about the background on pancreatic and brain cancer and their causes and cures. He was in lecture mode.

"It is estimated that about forty-four thousand cases of cancer of the pancreas will be diagnosed in the US each year and about thirty-eight thousand will die each year. The median age of death is seventy-one years of age. Because pancreatic cancer is usually diagnosed late in its development, the five-year survival rate is less than 5 percent. The cancer is exquisitely painful."

Thompson asked Kenny Clark to describe Jonas's experience with Nobo extract in clinical trials. Clark explained that Jonas had conducted what are known as double-blind trials. "That is, Jonas selected two hundred pancreatic cancer patients, gave a hundred of them Nobo extract, and gave the other hundred a placebo that looked like Nobo extract but was a nonreactive agent. Neither doctors nor the patients knew who was receiving the real thing or a placebo. Thus the double-blind label. After three months, ninety-five of the hundred patients receiving placebo died. Seventy of those receiving the extract died. Arguably, the extract saved twenty-five lives."

Dr. Purcell asked, "Have the statistics changed over time?"

Clark said, "No. They have stayed the same over time, but after about one year, two of the twenty-five survivors developed terminal brain cancer; and after two years, five more of the survivors developed fatal brain cancer. The warnings have only recently been changed to reflect these statistics."

Thompson asked about the financials. Clark said, "The extract has been approved and on the market for three years. It generates profits of about fifty million dollars per month or six hundred million per year or one-point-eight billion dollars for three years."

Thompson hypothesized that the families of those that had died of pancreatic cancer would seek restitution of all of the $1.8 billion in Jonas profits because the extract had not worked and that the families of more than seven thousand patients who had suffered brain cancer would want at least one million dollars each, totaling seven billion dollars. Thompson concluded, "This is the very definition of a mass tort case."

Dodge Lee

The plaintiffs' bar used to call it the Million-Dollar Round Table, and only lawyers who had obtained a verdict in excess of one million dollars could join. There is no longer such an elite group. Many average plaintiffs' attorneys have obtained jury verdicts in excess of a million dollars.

Dodge Lee himself had twenty-eight verdicts in excess of one million dollars. The highest had been thirty-six million dollars for a quadriplegic brain damage case. In addition, Lee had settled literally hundreds of cases in excess of a million dollars each.

A successful plaintiffs' attorney has to be multitalented. He has to be smart, quick on his feet, and spontaneous. He has to be able to communicate with learned judges and street-savvy jurors. He also needs good writing skills. He needs both charm and toughness. Despite brilliance in the courtroom, many highly successful plaintiffs' lawyers were not at the top of their law school classes. One of the skills that sets them apart is their willingness to gamble. Their legal conventions usually take place in Nevada or New Jersey or the Caribbean or even Monte Carlo.

Between high-stakes jury trials, Lee consumed the casino life. Lee could usually be seen at the craps tables, where the odds were the best. He was well known. The pit bosses took good care of him.

"Mr. Lee, here is the card to your suite."

"Mr. Lee, what would you like to drink?"

Most of all, Mr. Lee liked the Las Vegas ladies.

Occasionally, Tommy Thompson took a plaintiff's case, but he did not promote himself as a plaintiffs' lawyer, because it would have irritated his corporate clients who were the targets of the high-stakes plaintiffs' bar. One thing Tommy had in common with his brethren was his addiction to gambling. A weekend being pampered in Las Vegas was his idea of heaven.

Back in San Francisco, Lee was a consummate business man. He hired good young associates who helped him carefully organize his files. The associates created first drafts of most of Lee's legal briefs. He had a private investigator who carefully identified and interviewed witnesses. He retained the best consultants and paid and prepared them well. Unlike many of his brethren, he wasn't flamboyant or theatrical. When he entered the courtroom, he left his casino persona behind.

To better understand his adversary, Boxer sat in the back of a courtroom to observe one of Lee's trials. Lee did not lecture. When he examined prospective jurors, called *voir dire*, he used a conversational tone. He took the role of teacher, and Boxer could see that the jurors ultimately looked to Lee to explain the issues and the law. Lee conducted himself like the officer of the court that he was. His demeanor caused a big pit to form in Boxer's stomach. The trial judge loved Lee because he adhered to his rulings and did not push the edges of the courtroom rules.

Lee asked one of the prospective jurors, "Do you think juries award too much money?"

The prospective juror said yes.

Lee said, "Because my client was seriously injured and I am going to be asking for a lot of money, do you think that you could be fair under these circumstances?"

The prospective juror said, "I am not sure."

Lee said, "Would you be more comfortable on another case?"

The woman quickly blurted "yes," and the judge excused the woman.

Boxer noted that not only had Lee gotten rid of a probable defense juror (who, if she awarded anything, would award a small amount) but he also had come across to the rest of the jurors as a good guy. There was another prospective juror who sat up straight with arms crossed and a frown during his questioning. He had not behaved in such a fashion during the defense attorney's questions. Lee asked, "If I could know your state of mind, would I take you as a juror?"

The juror said no, and the judge excused that man. Amazingly, several other jurors also volunteered that they too didn't think they could be fair, and Lee thanked and excused them. Boxer thought this was a brilliant way to get unfavorable jurors to identify themselves. A number of jurors would use this as a method of getting off the jury if they didn't feel like serving. Lee was packing the jury box with people who thought they would be fair to Lee's client.

Most of Lee's practice was based on referrals from other lawyers. Trying cases was hard work. Trial lawyers spent months preparing for trial and many weeks in trial. While the court day might consume six or seven hours, preparation consumed late nights and weekends. Referring cases was easy, and referring attorneys usually received about 25 percent of the trial lawyer's fee. Thus, the more successful the trial lawyer, the higher the referral fee. Dodge Lee was very successful, and thus he had his pick of good cases. What plaintiff's lawyers called good cases were really cases with bad injuries.

Lee hated the 25 percent referral fee. One way he tried to ameliorate the fee was to insist on a 40 percent contingency fee whether he settled the case or tried it.

The math was thus: if Lee settled the case for a million dollars, the injured party received six hundred thousand, and Lee's contingency fee was four hundred thousand. But the referring attorney received 25 percent or a hundred thousand dollars of the four-hundred-thousand-dollar contingency fee, and Lee thus netted three hundred thousand dollars cash—still not a bad day at work.

Lee also tried to avoid the referral fee by obtaining cases directly from the injured parties. He sent his private investigator to try to sign up injured parties, also known as ambulance chasing, and he advertised. What he lost in reputation he made up for in money.

Lee also rented billboards. He emphasized his $36 million verdict and his many multimillion-dollar settlements. The Jonas cases opened up new vistas for advertising. In infomercials, Lee described the horrors of brain cancer that occurred in people exposed to Nobo extract imported from the jungles of Africa. He also described the difficulties of negotiating complex scientific issues with "cold-hearted insurance companies."

Lee had to hire extra paralegals to keep track of the new *Nobo* files. He had paralegals do the intake interviews and obtain the executed retention agreements. They also had the so-called victims sign authorizations to obtain medical records.

Since the statute of limitations for these California cases was two years, Lee had already started filing complaints in superior court before all of the medical records were obtained and analyzed. Lee started to realize that some of these cases had flaws.

After some follow-up investigation, it turned out that not all the people who had suffered both pancreatic cancer and brain cancer had used Nobo extract. Thus, the extract could not be blamed as the cause of cancer in those cases.

Many plaintiffs thought their deceased spouses or parents had been diagnosed with brain cancer when they had not. Some of the cases believed to be brain cancer had been diagnosed incorrectly and were not brain cancer cases. And in a few instances, unscrupulous medical examiners encouraged by equally unscrupulous referring lawyers had intentionally identified brain cancer as the cause of death on the autopsy report when it was really some other form of cancer that had caused the death.

Lee also learned from his medical consultants of further problems. There are many people who die from brain cancer without exposure to Nobo extract. Not every brain cancer of a person on Nobo extract was necessarily caused by Nobo extract. Research clinicians at Johns Hopkins were independently trying to find markers that differentiated the brain cancers associated with Nobo extract, if any, and the brain cancers which occurred without Nobo extract.

Lee's head paralegal asked him, "Are we going to produce these bad medical records to Thompson, or are they irrelevant?"

Lee said, "I don't think in good conscience we can say that they are irrelevant, but I wouldn't mind trying to settle these cases before we produce all of the records. For the time being, let's put a slow walk on these record productions." The paralegal said nothing but put a note of the conversation in his personnel file.

18

Keys to Lee's Success

Lee's key to success was to settle the questionable cases early, before defendants knew all of the facts, and to try the good cases. Thus, Lee would work hard to identify the very best candidates to be tried as bellwether cases.

The next key was to select the best venue. The exact same case was worth at least three times more in state court in San Francisco than in federal court in Bakersfield, California.

In Bakersfield, the judges and jurors were tough as nails. They were suspicious of lawyers and their clients. They were particularly suspicious of out-of-town lawyers. A case was worth less money in Bakersfield, because at least some of the farmers on the jury panel had suffered some form of serious physical trauma, and no one paid them. Furthermore, if the case was not in San Francisco, Lee would have to consider hiring local counsel, which would further dilute his contingency recovery.

In most mass tort cases, Lee filed all of the cases in San Francisco Superior Court and the defense lawyers then tried to remove to federal court or filed motions to change venue to more conservative state courts in the San Fernando Valley. This process was called forum shopping. Both Lee and Thompson had fought these forum-shopping battles and knew all of the tricks. At the end of the day, the cases would be filed by the plaintiffs' lawyer in courts throughout the state and then would be coordinated in one court at least for pretrial purposes. The courts did not want to be in a position where different courts would make different decisions on the same legal issues.

Lee was a pragmatist. He did not want to spend time and money on hundreds of pretrial motions. He would rather stipulate to a reasonable venue to avoid the hassle. To negotiate such a venue, he knew he would have to give up having his cases tried in state court in San Francisco or Los Angeles. But he would not agree to having his cases in federal court in the Valley.

A reasonable compromise would be to agree to have the cases heard in the United States District Court for the Northern District of California. The case would be assigned to one judge for all purposes, unlike in many state courts, in which you would get a different judge for every hearing and a different judge for trial. The federal judges were generally smart and fair, and since they were assigned to the case from start to finish, they were familiar with the facts and the issues and therefore usually made quick, consistent rulings.

The jurors in federal court were drawn from the northern coastal cities of California, so there were no valley jurors, but some San Francisco residents were jurors. In general, verdicts in federal court were not as high as San Francisco State Court verdicts and not as low as Bakersfield verdicts. Also, the federal court was located in San Francisco—not too far from the offices of Thompson ... and the offices of Lee.

Before filing these cases, Lee considered the preemption defense. He had confronted it in prior pharmaceutical cases. It was his experience that if the defendant pharmaceutical company had violated any FDA regulations, injured parties could sue. He was also aware that package insert warnings were continuously updated as the company received information of new adverse events. Invariably, pharmaceutical companies received information of new adverse events before there was a change in labels.

By definition, this would occur. When plaintiffs evaluated their cases, the best cases were those in which the adverse event occurred right before the change in labeling, because it could always be argued that the warning should have been made sooner. Tardy warnings were FDA violations.

Judge Earl Max

Thompson, Tate, and Dawes were all sitting in a meeting going over corporate records when Thompson's secretary walked in and said, "Judge Max has just been assigned to handle the *Jonas* case."

Judge Earl Max was appointed to be a Federal District Court judge for the Northern District of California by the president of the United States and confirmed by the US Senate. Ordinarily, race, religion, and ethnicity are important considerations in selecting federal judges. Most politicians and presidents at least give lip service to the proposition that the ethnicity of the bench should be a reflection of the population it serves.

In the case of Judge Max, the appointment was political. Max had been the US attorney for the Northern District of California. Tommy was a former assistant US attorney, and thus Thompson was very aware of Max's reputation. Tommy said, "Max was a great trial lawyer. He successfully prosecuted four California corporation chief executive officers for price fixing. It came out at the price-fixing trial that the corporations involved had also been big contributors to major political parties. The politicians wanted to demonstrate their honesty and purity to the public by elevating the prosecutor, Earl Max, to the federal bench. It would have the added benefit of putting a less aggressive prosecutor in the US attorney's office to fill Max's spot."

Boxer said, "He sounds good if we have a clean case. But I'm not positive we do." Boxer went on, "He is considered a law-and-order judge.

He is tough on lawyers. He demands that they be prepared and that they be scrupulously accurate in their representations to the court. He is capable of making hard calls and difficult decisions. Thus, if standing evidence should be excluded, he will not allow it to be presented to the jury. If corporate officers should be sent to jail, Judge Max imposes the punishment. He follows the law. As he said, 'I'm here to call balls and strikes.'"

Tommy Thompson loved the assignment of the case to Judge Max. While Thompson did not personally know Max, Thompson had been an assistant US attorney before Max was appointed. He thought they would have much in common. Thompson mused, "Most assistant US attorneys present themselves in court in an understated, objective fashion. They are not flamboyant. Their goal is to gain credibility with the judge and jury. They know how to play that role."

Boxer was ambivalent. He worried that Max was a member of a boy's club in which he had not yet been included. He wanted to understand Max's courtroom idiosyncrasies. He had observed Lee in trial, and it seemed that Lee had the same conservative, impressive courtroom demeanor. With little enthusiasm, Boxer said, "Tommy, you know Judge Max better than I do. I'm going to get a copy of one of his trial transcripts—of the price-fixing trial—so I can get a feel for how he applied the rules of evidence. I want to learn what arguments he accepts and which he doesn't."

Tommy said, "Sounds like a waste of time to me."

Max Down the Middle

Judge Max, by e-mail, ordered all parties and their attorneys to attend a case management conference in his courtroom.

A case management conference sounds innocuous and informal, but bad things can happen—rulings that can seriously interrupt the flow of business of a big company. Rulings like the court ordering a corporation to produce all its officers and directors for depositions and further ordering the corporation to search for and produce hundreds of thousands of documents and computer entries.

Most judges hold their case management conferences in chambers and proceed in an informal fashion. They take their robes off and invite the attorneys to be seated. Judge Max was different. He held his case management conferences in open court, and he sat fully robed behind the bench. Lawyers stood when they addressed the court, and a court reporter transcribed all of the proceedings. Max was serious, and he asked Thompson what pleadings he wanted to file.

Tommy had prepared himself for this question and was slowly rising when Boxer quickly stood and grabbed the podium. Without so much as a by-your-leave, he launched into an argument that the first pleading that should be filed and heard was a motion to dismiss based on federal preemption. Tate continued, "Your Honor, all Jonas testing, manufacturing, and labeling was mandated and approved by the Food and Drug Administration, and those regulations preempt any contrary state rules. A jury verdict is a contrary state rule and cannot change or increase the warning or testing requirements. If juries had the power to make such changes, different juries in different states could impose different standards all over the country, leading to impossibly contradictory requirements."

Tommy was not happy that Boxer had taken over the argument, but he could tell that the judge was buying the Boxer rationale. Dodge Lee could see the same thing and strenuously objected to setting a hearing to consider dismissing on the basis of the preemption agreement. He desperately wanted to avoid a preemptive strike that could threaten the viability of all his cases, but Judge Max said, "I think if all of these fifteen hundred cases are barred by federal preemption law, I want to know it now, not two years from now."

Lee quickly switched strategies and argued that if the motion to dismiss was to be heard early in the litigation, he wanted to depose Jonas's medical director, Al Purcell, first. He believed that Purcell may have information that Jonas had violated FDA rules and thus could not take advantage of the federal preemption defense.

Tate argued that Jonas had strictly adhered to all federal regulations and a deposition of Dr. Purcell would thus be a witch hunt. Ultimately, Judge Max ruled that the deposition of Dr. Purcell could proceed and that if Purcell had knowledge of any FDA violations, both the court and Lee should have that information now, but to preclude undue burden on Jonas's counsel or a witch hunt, the Purcell deposition was limited to two hours.

After the case management conference, Dodge Lee was afraid that he wouldn't get any concessions from Dr. Purcell at the deposition and Judge Max would accept the preemption argument and dismiss all fifteen hundred cases.

Secretly, Tommy Thompson was also worried about a quick end to this enormous cash cow. In anticipation of the increasing work, Thompson had already exercised a lease option allowing him to rent fifteen extra offices in his building at One Embarcadero Center. Only Tate was happy. In his mind, only victory counted. He had total confidence in Dr. Purcell, and he thought Judge Max was buying the preemption argument. Of course, Fortune Jones of Atlas and Kenny

Clark of Jonas would grasp at any straws to obtain an early conclusion to what was predicted to be protracted litigation. They were willing to push the preemption defense and push it early and hard.

Tommy Continues to Seek Control

After the case management conference, Kenny Clark, Fortune Jones, Tommy Thompson, Miller Johnson, and Boxer all met at Tommy's office at One Embarcadero. Thompson took control. He looked at Boxer and said, "I thought we agreed that you would be playing a supporting role. You caught me off guard when you jumped into the preemption argument."

Boxer, not to be intimidated, said, "Frankly, Tommy, I never thought you understood the preemption defense, and anyway, why fight? We got just the ruling we wanted." Jones and Clark nodded affirmatively.

Tommy registered irritation but moved on. He said, "Let's discuss the Purcell deposition. It is key, and as lead counsel, I think I should handle it. If Purcell can testify that Jonas fully complied with all FDA regulations, we win. If not, we go to trial on fifteen hundred cases." Tommy, arguing harder than he really needed to, said, "The very reason I was retained was to handle make-or-break matters, such as the Purcell deposition."

Boxer rebutted, "I have already successfully worked with Purcell in the past and should at least be part of the team that prepares him for his deposition. Also, I can help on the preemption issue."

Thompson said, "While I admire your work, it would be more efficient if my team indexed and analyzed the relevant medical records and worked directly with Dr. Purcell."

Ultimately, Kenny Clark accepted Thompson's position, and Fortune Jones was forced to agree. It became obvious that Fortune Jones of Atlas and Kenny Clark of Jonas were the clients and would have the last word on important decisions.

Boxer then said, "Since I have already argued the preemption issue before Judge Max, I think he will expect me to argue the preemption motion to dismiss itself."

Tommy took the gloves off. "I think the judge will not take the motion to dismiss seriously if proffered by a junior lawyer, so I intend to make that argument myself."

The silence was deafening, and Boxer realized he had lost this argument also. The usually ebullient Boxer left the meeting in brooding silence.

IIII IIII IIII IIII IIII IIII IIII IIII

Woodshedding
Purcell

Thompson selected partner Bill Dawes, associate Karen Klein, and paralegal Mary Smith for the Purcell deposition team. Smith was assigned the task of researching all medical articles concerning pancreatic cancer, brain cancer, and Nobo extract. Karen Klein was to review and analyze all relevant FDA regulations, and Bill Dawes was to review and index all Purcell publications and transcripts of past Purcell testimony. Tommy would consume all of this information and, with the help of his team, would prepare Purcell for his testimony. In litigation parlance, deposition preparation is called "woodshedding" as in "taking the witness to the woodshed." There is a suggestion of influencing the testimony. Tommy was an expert at this.

In particular, the preparation of an expert like Purcell is a bit of a balancing act. On the one hand, the attorney does not want to feed the expert information that will be harmful to the case. The expert may reveal this adverse information on cross-examination. On the other hand, the expert should be ready to explain away harmful information if confronted with it. Thompson was fully aware of the risks. He had prepared and presented hundreds of experts for deposition.

The area that Dodge Lee would examine most closely would be whether or not Jonas had complied with FDA regulations. FDA regulations required that the pharmaceutical companies advise the FDA of adverse events associated with the drug in a timely manner. Here the adverse event was brain cancer. Even though it might not be proven that Novo extract caused brain cancer, the fact that brain cancer occurred at the same time the patient was taking the extract had to be reported to the FDA within thirty days of the drug company becoming aware of the adverse event. In reviewing the adverse event, the FDA could require the manufacturer to make a change in warnings.

The Thompson team found that a treating physician had orally told a Jonas sales representative, also known as a detail man, that one of his patients on the extract had developed what the treating physician thought might be brain cancer. Jonas had never told the FDA of the oral communication, thus creating an argument that Jonas had violated the thirty-day rule. Thompson's team learned of this oral notification when it interviewed the detail man who had the conversation with the treating physician. The title arose because these salesmen know all of the details about the drug. There was no written confirmation of the oral communication with the treating physician. Two months later, the patient's oncologist gave written notice to Jonas of the possible brain cancer, and within thirty days, Jonas passed that written notice to the FDA. Thompson and his team met and weighed the question of whether they should tell Dr. Al Purcell of the conversation. Thompson wanted Dr. Purcell to testify that Jonas had fully complied with all FDA regulations, including timely reporting of adverse events. To support the testimony, Purcell would have to testify that he, or others at his direction, had researched whether Jonas received any adverse event reports. If that research had been effectively done, it would have revealed the oral request. Tommy hypothesized, "Purcell can argue that the oral report of the treating physician does not trigger the need to report to the FDA."

Dawes, who tended to be more ethically driven, said, "If Purcell does not reveal the oral statement of the doctor and if through further discovery and investigation the fact of this oral communication is obtained by Lee, he would attack Purcell's credibility and Jonas's credibility, also arguing a cover-up. Lee would also argue that Purcell has not done the research to allow him to say that Jonas made no FDA violations. If Purcell had done such research, he would have found out about the oral communication."

Dawes said, "If Purcell reveals the oral communication himself at deposition, he can explain that Jonas did not know of an adverse event until the expert brain cancer doctor made his final written report. Jonas, it can be argued, fully complied with the regs by passing the brain cancer doctor's report to the FDA within the appropriate thirty-day limit. In fact, they reported it within fifteen days."

Thompson said, "If Purcell reveals the oral report himself, it will also give greater credibility to his testimony and add support to our argument that Purcell has performed the necessary investigation to allow him to testify that Jonas did not violate any FDA regulations."

Thompson decided—without consulting with Boxer, Fortune, Clark, or Jonas—that he would tell Purcell of the oral communication and, of course, the brain cancer expert's written report. Tommy was of the view that a judge and jury would believe that Dr. Purcell, as the medical director of Jonas, should know this information, and Purcell could tell the story in the most exculpatory fashion.

Thompson and his internal team met with Dr. Purcell to prepare for the deposition. They took Dr. Purcell through all FDA regulations, all written communications with the FDA, and through the medical literature. Finally, they came to the oral communication of the treating physician. Purcell was of the definite opinion that Jonas did not have to notify the FDA until the brain cancer expert, not the treating physician, had actually diagnosed the brain cancer. In Purcell's opinion, Jonas did not have to notify the FDA of the oral possibility of a future diagnosis of brain cancer.

After the preparation session, Tommy, as an aside, said to Dawes, "I think we have done everything we can, but I'm still nervous."

Dawes nodded yes.

The Purcell Depo

The deposition of Dr. Purcell was taken by videotape at the office of Dodge Lee. Dr. Purcell had testified a number of times as a treating physician but never as an expert witness or as a party witness as he was now doing as the medical director of Jonas.

Lee cut to the heart of the deposition. "Do you know of any violations of FDA regulations by Jonas?"

Dr. Purcell responded with confidence, "No. But for completeness, you should be aware that one of our detail men was told by a treating physician that his Nobo extract patient had been seen by an expert cancer doctor for possible brain cancer. Jonas did not report this information to the FDA until after a diagnosis had been confirmed by the cancer doctor. Jonas reported this written diagnosis less than thirty days after receiving it, thus complying with the FDA regulation."

Lee asked for the name and contact information of the treating physician, the cancer doctor, the patient, and the detail man. Dr. Purcell gave the information concerning the doctors and detail man but refused to give the name of the patient based on doctor-patient privilege and privacy grounds. Lee asked Purcell, "Have you talked to the doctors, the patient, or the detail man about this matter?"

"No."

"Have you looked at the medical records?"

"No."

"How did you get this information?"

"From my lawyer, Tommy Thompson."

"What did Tommy tell you?"

Tommy interjected, "Objection. The question asks for attorney-client and work-product privileged information."

Lee then turned to Tommy. "Did you talk to any of these witnesses?"

Not wanting to look like he was trying to influence independent witnesses, Tommy said no. Soon Tommy would regret that strategy.

Lee concluded, "I have no further questions."

Boxer was not at the deposition, and he received no reports from the Thompson team about the deposition. He called Bill Dawes, who said that Dr. Purcell had testified that Jonas had violated no FDA regulations and the Thompson team was preparing a motion to dismiss based on preemption.

Boxer was still concerned. He wanted a more complete description and ordered a copy of the deposition transcript directly from the court reporter.

24

Motion for Dismissal

Thompson filed his motion to dismiss based on Dr. Purcell's testimony that Jonas had violated no FDA regulations. Dodge Lee waited until the last day to file his opposition. In it, he included an affidavit of the treating physician, who said that forty-five days before Jonas reported the brain cancer to the FDA, he had told the Jonas detail man that the patient had brain cancer caused by Nobo and he expected this would be confirmed on tests. Lee also argued that the FDA regulations did not allow Jonas to wait for proof positive that the extract actually caused the cancer before notifying the FDA of the adverse event.

Boxer received the opposition at about the same time he received the Purcell deposition transcript. Lee had sent copies of the opposition to the news media, claiming a cover-up. Boxer's initial reaction was that Purcell was hung out to dry. Boxer was further of the belief that Thompson or Jonas should have interviewed the treating physician, the brain cancer doctor, the patient, and the detail man before the deposition of Purcell, if for no other reason than to confirm the facts. Boxer thought about calling Atlas and Jonas with his concerns but decided to first confront Thompson. He reached Thompson and exploded. He told Thompson that the deposition of Purcell and the handling of the preemption issue were a disaster. "If you don't advise the client," he said, "I will. We have to move fast. We have to depose or interview the doctors, the detail man, and the patient before the hearing on the motion to dismiss. We'll likely have to file a surrebuttal if these interviews help us."

Tommy shouted, "All of these problems were caused by your pushing a preemption defense. You think you're so smart, but you really have no strategy sense at all."

Boxer was well aware that Tommy was much more experienced, but in Boxer's opinion, he was just winging it here.

Boxer said, "The die is cast. We are making the defense, and we should do the best job possible. We shouldn't just roll over."

Tommy said, "The preemption argument is not ripe. We should take it off-calendar and reset it when we are more prepared."

Boxer, with no respect to the older firm chair, said, "The lack of a good preemption argument will result in a huge expenditure of time and money in defending depositions and producing hundreds of thousands of documents. Tommy, if you don't set up a client teleconference within the hour, I will."

Tommy said he would … but he wasn't happy.

Tommy's
Teleconference

Thompson started off the conference call. He recited the facts that his team had prepared Dr. Al Purcell for deposition, that Purcell had testified that Jonas had not violated any FDA regulations, that Tommy had filed a motion to dismiss based on preemption, and that the plaintiffs had filed opposition based on affidavits contradicting Purcell's testimony.

Boxer heatedly interjected, reminding Fortune Jones and Kenny Clark that he had been instructed not to participate in this phase of the case, not even as a member of the team. The media reports had caused him to review the Purcell deposition transcript and motion-to-dismiss papers. Boxer said, "It appears that the Thompson team made a decision to inform Purcell about an oral notice from a treating physician to a Jonas detail man reporting a possible brain cancer case. This adverse event was not reported within the thirty days required but rather within forty-five days, after a written report by the brain cancer expert was received." Boxer said, "The oral notice created a possible rebuttal to our preemption argument. I think that the client and I should have been advised of the strategy. Further, the strategy was not properly implemented as is illustrated by these questions and answers given at Purcell's deposition." Boxer pointed to the part of the deposition where

Lee asked whether Purcell had talked to the doctors, the detail man, or the patient.

Boxer said, "These questions revealed that Lee probably was going to interview these key witnesses looking for discrepancies. We should have interviewed the witnesses before Dr. Purcell's deposition and certainly after these questions were asked at the deposition."

Tommy interrupted, "You know, I was never a big fan of the preemption defense. I always thought the causation defense was better. It's true that the plaintiffs' cover-up argument has seriously reduced our chances of winning preemption at this point. Therefore, I think we should take our motion to dismiss off calendar and refile it if the facts get stronger."

Boxer spoke with passion. "Rather than essentially waiving the preemption defense, why not give it to me? There are fourteen days until the hearing. Let me borrow Bill Dawes, Mary Smith, and Karen Klein, and we will devote ourselves to this part of the case for the next two weeks. If we win, the case is over. If we lose, we are no worse off than we are right now."

Kenny Clark said, "On behalf of Jonas, I'm in favor of Boxer's idea. I also am very concerned about the lack of communication. I, for one, want to be kept in the loop on all strategy decisions, and I also want Boxer in the loop."

"Ditto," said Fortune.

Boxer said, "Everyone will receive e-mails from me no less than twice daily. Questions and suggestions are welcome."

Tommy Thompson said nothing.

Boxer Inquest

Boxer asked the Thompson-Purcell team to meet at his offices precisely at noon. But Dawes, a good Thompson soldier, said, "All of the papers and pleadings are here, and it would be easier to meet here."

Boxer replied, "I want you and the files near me. I will assign filing spaces and offices to the team right away. I want the move to be completed by noon today, when we'll have our first meeting."

Dawes said, "Shouldn't we clear this with Tommy?"

"No."

The Purcell team arrived precisely at noon except that Dawes came two minutes late. Boxer said, "Dawes, you kept us waiting. Don't let it happen again." Boxer then asked, "Everybody moved in?"

Dawes said, "We are moved in, but we still have work to do back at Thompson."

Boxer said, "This is more important. I will tell Tommy to reassign your other matters." Dawes was dubious, but Boxer continued, "Now, let's get started. Dawes give me an overview."

Dawes started with a history of the preemption defense. Boxer intervened, "I know all of that. Tell me how we are going to handle the opposition pleadings."

Dawes proceeded: "Associate Mary Smith has reviewed the medical literature and says there is nothing in the literature suggesting any association between Nobo and brain cancer before the date of the oral report."

Paralegal Karen Klein said she believed that the FDA regulations allowed an argument that adverse events did not have to be reported until there was actually an event, not just the suspicion of event.

Dawes said, "I have reviewed Purcell's prior publications and testimony. There's no question in my mind that he is honest and objective."

Boxer said, "I have reviewed Judge Max's price-fixing transcript, and he is highly critical of testimony that does not include the whole truth. He abhors half-truths and tends to strongly favor the side that opposes the half-truth tender. And right now, the credibility of Purcell is not good."

Boxer decided to divide up the work as follows: "Mary Smith, you will reinterview the detail man and try to interview the treating physician. Bill Dawes, you will try to interview the expert oncologist. Paralegal Klein will seek the medical records, which she will review and index. We will meet again this afternoon at three."

Results of Inquest

Precisely at 3:00 p.m., with all present, Mary Smith reported that the detail man was clear that the treating physician never had said the patient had brain cancer. She was only being tested to see if she had brain cancer. Mary also learned the name of the patient, who turned out to be a client of Dodge Lee and a plaintiff in the *Jonas* cases. The treating physician, not surprisingly, had refused to talk to Smith, but the brain cancer expert had agreed to talk and said that ultimately he told the patient and patient's lawyer, Dodge Lee, that the oncology tests for brain cancer were negative!

Boxer immediately scheduled the deposition of the treating physician. Boxer did the cross-examining of the treating physician. After repeated questioning, the treating physician admitted that Lee had given him ten thousand dollars in consulting fees for executing the affidavit and agreeing to consult with Lee. The physician went on to reveal that Lee had said if they defeated the motion to dismiss, he would have many more cases and would need to hire the treating physician as consultant on those cases. Lee had gone on to tell the treating physician that he would retain him to read the literature and become a testifying expert on causation, for which he would receive a payment of five thousand dollars per half-day.

Dawes, Smith, and Klein were all at the deposition. Dawes whispered to his compatriots, "This guy is good."

Smith said, "I thought you said he wasn't very smart."

"I was wrong."

Dawes proceeded to construct a scathing surrebuttal for the court, pointing out that Lee's treating physician's affidavit was bought and paid for and was disingenuous at best and outright fraudulent at worst in its failure to reveal the financial relationship between Lee and the treating physician. Boxer thought the surrebuttal was brilliant and so informed Dawes.

Max Hearing

Max's courtroom was filled for the *Nobo* hearing. The press was there. The Jonas team was there—including Dr. Purcell, Fortune Jones, Miller Johnson, and even Patrick and Jayne Jonas. Tommy sat at the counsel table, but other than to identify himself, he did not speak. Since he was not arguing, he had not read the treating physician's depositions or the Dawes brief. But he listened to Boxer whispering instructions to his courtroom team at the counsel table.

Boxer told his team to be prepared for questions from the press and to make a statement that would be essentially the same whether they won or lost. "Say, 'Jonas is a conservative pharmaceutical company. It plays by the rules. It is aware that all drugs have side-effects and that its job is to label its products so that the medical profession is aware of those side-effects.'"

Tommy was watching and listening to every word, silently seething not only at how Boxer was handling things but at the fact he was handling things.

Judge Max entered the courtroom as his bailiff commanded, "All rise," and they did. Then Judge Max said, "Please be seated," and commented that he had read all of the papers and invited Boxer to argue first.

Boxer rose and walked to the podium. "May it please the court," he began. He then carefully reconstructed how Jonas had received, reviewed, and timely reported all adverse events of brain cancer. He further argued, "With the help of the FDA, the warnings and statistics were changed to allow the medical community and patients to evaluate the risk of brain cancer and make an informed decision on the use of Nobo extract. The warnings were not changed until after additional information justified the changes."

Tommy found himself rooting against Boxer. The judge had no questions for Boxer, and Lee took the podium. Tommy couldn't help nodding affirmatively when Lee argued that Jonas had an obligation to report even a possibility of brain cancer to the FDA. Judge Max was stone-faced for a few seconds, and finally Lee asked, "Is something the matter, Judge?"

"Mr. Lee, the affidavit and pleadings you filed are so tainted, I don't have to get to the legal merits of your argument. You have not been candid with the court. The financial incentives you have created were not revealed. The treating physician, in my opinion, has committed perjury. His testimony is not worthy of belief, and I will turn his affidavit over to the district attorney. I hereby rule that Jonas's motion to dismiss all fifteen hundred Nobo extract cases is granted with prejudice. Cost to Jonas."

Thompson could feel his financial world crumbling and blamed it all on Boxer Tate.

Jonas and Fortune booked the presidential suite at the top of the Bank of America for lunch. The view symbolized the occasion. It was the highest point in San Francisco. It was a crystal-clear day, and one could see all the way across the Golden Gate Bridge to Mount Tamalpais in the north and across the Bay Bridge to Mount Diablo in the east. Fortune said to Tommy, "The luncheon location seems appropriate." Tommy tried to nod, but his face was frozen. Fortune noticed for the first time how wasted Tommy looked.

Tommy did not want to be at the celebration but had no choice. He had not succeeded in the law by making the same mistake twice. He was pulling himself together and realized this was his time to be modest. He saw Boxer and the preemption team and congratulated them on a great victory. He admitted he had not properly pursued or executed the preemption strategy. He further admitted that he should not have excluded Boxer, the originator of the strategy, from his team. Tommy publicly restated these admissions in a toast to Boxer. Everybody then cheered and stood, acknowledging a Boxer team victory.

Boxer rose and thanked Thompson for loaning him some of Thompson's superstars, who really had done all of the work in obtaining the dismissal. Boxer also thanked Atlas and Jonas for allowing him and his firm to work for these ethical, innovative, and honest corporations.

Malloy, who was now slurring his words, wanted to make a toast also, but Boxer put a hand on his shoulders and kept him in his chair.

After lunch, Jonas, Thompson, Fortune, Purcell, and Malloy each approached Boxer separately and asked for individual private meetings or dinners. Boxer agreed to all. Interestingly, the Thompson group of Bill Dawes, Mary Smith, and Karen Klein also asked for a meeting.

A euphoric Boxer returned to his office. Boxer had scheduled a round of golf at Harding that afternoon with some of his 1906 friends. But he had become so consumed by the *Jonas* case that he canceled the golf so as to continue working the room with his clients and legal compatriots.

At the firm, champagne was flowing, Malloy was staggering, music was playing, and Boxer's phone was ringing. The media was seeking quotes and interviews. Boxer did not refuse to comment but rather employed another theme: "The brilliance of the pharmaceutical companies and the vigilance of the FDA have allowed new and powerful drugs to increase the life expectancy of people not only in the USA but also around the world. Jonas is proud to be part of these advances."

In the middle of the party, Boxer received a call from plaintiffs' attorney, Dodge Lee. Boxer put Lee on hold and shouted to his entire group, "Dodge Lee is on the phone. You might want to hear this." He hit the speaker button.

Lee congratulated Boxer and told Boxer that he would be seeking a rehearing before Judge Max based on surprise. He said, "I did not receive your papers in time for proper preparation. Also, Judge Max misapplied the law of preemption." With his hand still in the air, Boxer replied, "If you move for a rehearing, I will file a cross-motion for monetary sanctions based on your efforts to buy testimony from the treating physician." When Lee hesitated, Boxer went on, "Frankly, if I was you, I wouldn't want these cases to remain active. The state bar might start looking around. But I have a way out for you. While I do not have authority, I would consider asking my clients if they would accept a dismissal of the complaint and a waiver of appeal in return for Atlas and Jonas waiving their right to costs."

Lee rejected this compromise out of hand. Boxer then dropped his hand and, the office started cheering and clapping. Boxer said over the phone to Lee, "I guess my people are thrilled with your decision to pursue a losing strategy."

By the end of the afternoon, Boxer was still on a high, but he was now alone. He wanted to talk, but his social life was so barren he had no one to talk to. His buddies were still on the golf course. He thought of Audi Johns. Perfect. She would be able to put the victory into perspective and would keep all discussions confidential. Besides, she was not hard on the eyes. He called her, and they agreed to meet at Sam's Grill.

Thompson Defeat

After the victory lunch, Thompson returned to his office and shut the door. The Boxer victory was the worst defeat of his legal career. While the general legal community would call the Jonas dismissal a great success, Thompson knew his own legal grade was an F. He should have deposed or at least interviewed the key witnesses and participants. His level of preparation was unsatisfactory. Thompson had not believed in the preemption strategy. Thompson had communicated his lack of commitment to the strategy by renting fifteen more offices expecting that the motion to dismiss would be denied. Worse still for Thompson, his legal team and his clients knew he had gotten an F. They knew he had wanted to take the preemption motion to dismiss off calendar and abandon it. They knew he had underestimated the legal ability of Boxer. They also sensed that he had been trying to overshadow Boxer's talent by excluding Boxer from any participation in preparation for the motion to dismiss. Finally, he had committed the unpardonable sin of failing to keep his sophisticated clients in the loop. They hadn't been told of the oral notice from the treating physician to the detail man. Only later had the clients become aware of the fact that this oral notice had been fed to Al Purcell by Thompson without verifying the accuracy of the situation either before or after Purcell's testimony. If Purcell's sworn version of the oral notice had not been verified by the Boxer team, not only would Judge Max have denied the motion to dismiss, but also the reputation for honesty and accuracy of Jonas and its medical director,

Purcell, would have been undermined. In the ethical pharmaceutical industry, honesty and accuracy are keys to stock value and success. Al Purcell; Fortune Jones; Patrick Jonas; and his general counsel, Kenny Clark, were all aware that Thompson had put their fragile reputation at risk without their knowledge. They were also aware that Boxer had saved the day. He had taken the interest and initiative to investigate the status of the motion to dismiss. He had had the guts to confront Thompson and to bring the situation to the attention of the stakeholders. He had led the Thomson lawyers in putting together winning briefs and affidavits. Finally, his oral argument had persuaded Judge Max to grant the motion and award costs to Jonas.

In many respects, Tommy's firm was like a large solo practice. There was no management committee. There were no heads of practice groups. There was no chief executive. Thompson was it. He was the king. On the one hand, this management structure was very efficient. Thompson did not have to report the Jonas situation to anyone. But on the other hand, he had no confidant to brainstorm with to try to salvage the situation.

While he and Dawes worked together, that relationship was not enough to save the day. Tommy thought, *I guess I relied too heavily on Dawes and not heavily enough on Boxer. Really, should I have turned the most important issue in a case over to a Douglas Law School graduate? The problem really started when I allowed Boxer to participate in the beauty presentation. Trying to save money for clients is not a good idea. Also, I should have gotten closer to Fortune Jones from the very beginning. How could I have let this happen? I was not at the top of my game. What was wrong with me?*

One solution Thompson considered was to try to hire Boxer again. Jonas and Atlas now had enough confidence in Boxer that they would retain him without the need to also hire Thompson as first chair. Thompson could foresee Jonas and Atlas becoming part of Boxer's portable book of business. Thompson had first tried to hire Boxer as a paralegal and then as an associate. Now he knew Boxer wouldn't come without being made partner. Thompson did not think he could keep Atlas and Jonas's business without Boxer. Thompson also could see that his own lawyers were attracted by the Boxer charisma. If Thompson lost two large clients and several lawyers, he would have even more empty offices. This concern raised the possibility of merging with Malloy to help fill the offices. Thompson did not like this solution, because he thought the Malloy paper was weak and would dilute the Thompson prestige. Indeed, Thompson did not like Boxer's paper, but Boxer was so good he could overcome the lack-of-paper issue.

After hours of turning the problem over in his mind, Thompson decided that his best option was to talk candidly with Boxer Tate. This was not going to be easy, but he had to save his career.

Sam's Again

Boxer got there early and secured the same table they had eaten at last time. He also ordered the same Rombauer Chardonnay, chilled and kept in an ice bucket by the table. Audi arrived on time, and the couple exchanged Hollywood air kisses. Boxer raised his glass and said, "To us."

Audi raised her glass and said, "To Judge Earl Max." Audi wanted to talk about the victory. She was excited. Boxer told Audi about the requests for meetings and dinners. Audi said, "Your stock at the bar is high. It may never get higher. Any decision you make now may impact your career for years to come. I would be pleased to represent you."

That was not exactly what Boxer wanted to hear. He was flustered. He had not been thinking about a professional relationship but really wanted Audi's advice as a friend, and he told her so. He said, "I really thought this could be about date night." He said that Audi might have a conflict representing him as his agent because her interest would be best served by placing him where his new salary would be highest. Then Audi would receive the largest commission. He also said that one of his options was to stay at Malloy, in which event Audi would receive no commission. Audi said, "I was the one who introduced you to Tommy Thompson, which, in turn, made it possible for you to become a partner at Malloy."

Boxer said, "Yes, but I was the one who won the Jonas case and created the present demand for my services."

Audi said, "True, but your present prospects are only the Malloy firm or the Thompson firm. I can introduce you to other firms and further broaden your horizons."

Boxer jousted, "Give me names and details."

"Give me time."

Finally, Audi said, "Okay, tonight is for free. We'll just talk, but in the long run, this is a friendship I cannot afford."

Boxer said, "Here's a question I learned from you. What would you do if you were in my position?"

Audi paused and then said, "Okay—I'll try to answer your question seriously. First of all, you probably should not stay at Malloy. It's just not a good enough firm for you. But if you do stay, you would probably have to take over the firm. You would have to rename the firm as your own. You'd have to hire better lawyers to handle bigger and more complex cases that would generate higher hourly rates. But of course you would have to pay those lawyers more money.

"It might be easier to just open your own firm. But there would be client payment delays. You'd need to pay your associates for at least six months before your invoices start coming due, and then there's rent, and recruiting, and insurance, and benefits—and the list goes on.

"The next obvious option is Thompson. He has to come after you again if he wants to save the Atlas and Jonas accounts. As always, money will be an issue. Jonas and Atlas will balk at the Thompson rates. They will like the Thompson prestige and the fact that you will have this strong legal support, so some compromise will be possible. However, Thompson is unlikely to give up any control. It's his firm, and he runs it exclusively. The only exception is if he is bought out by a thousand-person firm that gives him lots of money. All of these scenarios impose a new big firm culture on your practice.

"Finally, you could go to market and see what's out there. Your law credentials will hurt you, but there will be firms that need a quality trial lawyer and will also be interested in your ability to bring Atlas and Jonas as clients. While we call them portable books of business, Atlas and Jonas will not see themselves as commodities and will look carefully at where you are going, including going out on your own."

Boxer said, "One more question. Hypothetically, if I decide to open my firm, would it be a good idea to bring you along to help me run it?"

"The answer is yes, it would be a good idea, but I'm not sure I would do it."

"Why?"

"Because I already tried the law, and I like being a headhunter better."

"I suppose if I open my own firm, you would not get a commission."

"Yes, I would. Remember you promised that when you became a partner at Malloy you would use me to recruit and hire."

"This is true. That's maybe why I should just retain you as the hiring partner wherever I go."

"I'm still not sure I would take the job."

"Why?"

"I'm not sure I could handle a job in which the boss wants to see results and romance."

The evening went by too quickly for Boxer. He loved the repartee and exchange of ideas. He was convinced that they could have a romantic relationship at the same time as having a business relationship. He believed he would get Audi's most candid ideas whether she was going to get a commission or not. He said, "You're hired." He didn't list the details of the job, and she didn't ask. Both of them understood the benefits of negotiated ambiguity.

"Now, what do I do tomorrow?" asked Boxer.

Audi said, "Get the lay of the land. Start with Purcell and thank him for his work. If you continue to represent Jonas, you will need his testifying assistance in the future.

"Then call Fortune Jones, then Kenny Clark. You want to be able to tell them, honestly, that you have made no plans. They may have some suggestions you have not considered. Then call Malloy to hear what he has to say.

"Lastly, call Thompson. If he wants to talk business, share with him the concerns about him that I raised.

"Finally let's talk at the end of the day."

31

|||| |||| |||| |||| |||| |||| |||| ||||

After Boxer's Victory

The first thing Boxer did when he reached his office the day after his victory was to turn to the financial pages of the *San Francisco Chronicle*. A headline read, "Jonas Avoids Potential Billion Dollars in Lawsuits."

In addition to using quotes by Boxer, the article quoted Dodge Lee: "We will seek a new hearing, and if that is not successful, we will appeal." Most concerning to Boxer was Lee's further statement: "We also intend to file more suits out of California in states where courts won't be bound by Judge Max's misinterpretation of the law of preemption." The article ended by saying, "It was a good day for Jonas, whose stock went up 3 percent."

Boxer's first telephone call of the day was from Fortune Jones, who was with Patrick Jonas and his general counsel, Kenny Clark. They congratulated Boxer effusively but quickly turned to the possibility of future litigation. Boxer reminded them that he had predicted this possibility and said that while Judge Max's ruling might be persuasive authority in other states, it would not be binding authority.

Fortune took the lead in the discussion. She said, "We have talked, and we want you to be our lead counsel going forward. We want you to develop a plan for handling the litigation."

Boxer asked, "What kind of a plan?"

Fortune said, "We want you to select local counsel and describe their roles—who will be first-chair trial lawyer in each case, who will be local counsel, and who will be on the trial teams."

Boxer, thinking out loud, said, "It seems there will be plenty for Tommy to do."

Fortune said, "What's your recommendation for inclusion of Tommy?"

Boxer was torn. He said, "I know the financial community has confidence in Tommy, but I have some doubts." Boxer privately had some doubts about himself. He had some success in the courtroom but had never been lead national coordinating counsel.

Fortune, almost reading Boxer's mind, said, "Atlas has selected and worked with national counsel on a number of occasions. Frankly, I think Tommy has gotten too arrogant to build a national team. He also did a poor job of building a team for the motion to dismiss." Boxer was hoping that Fortune would deliver the final blow, but she finished by saying, "We would like you to get back to us with your recommendations."

Thompson called while Boxer was on the phone with Fortune and Jonas. But Boxer had to return Purcell's call first. Boxer thanked Purcell for his help in winning the Jonas preemption motion. He also told Purcell about the risk of more lawsuits and how he was going to need Purcell's expertise going forward.

Purcell said, "I don't love testifying but realize that as the medical director of Jonas, I have some responsibility to tell their story in court. However, I must insist that I deal with you and no one else. For your ears only, I felt underprepared and underrepresented in the deposition I gave in this case."

Boxer said he thought he could make Purcell's desire come true.

Before Boxer could handle any more calls, his secretary announced that Bill Dawes, Karen Klein, and Mary Smith were in the waiting room. Boxer had them ushered into his office, and they again shared high fives and fist pumps. Boxer told them, "Honestly, this victory could not have happened without your great ideas and hard work."

Dawes, acting as spokesperson, said, "We really loved working with you. We felt like real lawyers and real contributors. You listened to our ideas and used them. We suspect there will be more of these cases, and we want to use the expertise we have gained and keep working on them."

Boxer said that he too would love them to be the core of the Jonas team in the future. He asked, "Have you approached Tommy about this?"

"No," said Dawes, and the others nodded. "We are concerned that he won't be hired again, and even if he is, we prefer working with you."

Boxer said, "I couldn't pay you as much as the Thompson firm does."

Dawes said, "We would be willing to take pay cuts, but frankly, we couldn't take the amount you are presently paying your lawyers. However, we suspect if we came over, you could charge higher hourly rates than you do now and thus afford to pay us more."

Boxer thanked the group and said vaguely that the information they had given him would be extremely helpful in the decisions being made.

Dawes backed out of Boxer's office with a final request to keep him apprised of his plans. Boxer said that he would, and as he started to close the door, his secretary, Laura Flood, caught it before it latched.

"Thompson is on the line for you again," she said. She had a look in her eyes that told Boxer he had better take the call this time.

"All right, tell him I'll be right with him." Boxer sat back down at his desk. This was it. With a deep breath as if he was about to dive into the deep end, he picked up the phone. "Mr. Thompson, thanks so much for getting back to me."

Thompson got right to the point. He wanted Boxer to come to Thompson as a partner.

He thought he could triple Boxer's income. Boxer said, "I think we should talk in person. Why don't you come over here, and I'll have some sandwiches brought in." Boxer did not want to meet on Thompson's turf. He did not want to eat at Thompson's clubs or Thompson's overwhelming offices. He wanted Thompson to treat him like an equal, although he frankly never thought that could happen.

Thompson said, "Please, be my guest."

Boxer said, "I really don't have time for a fancy lunch. I've got a lot of balls in the air."

Tommy said, "Great. I'd love to see your offices."

Boxer, feeling somewhat paranoid, thought, *Way to slap down my offices.*

Boxer and Thompson met in one of Malloy's modest conference rooms outfitted with ham and swiss on rye and coffee. Thompson's arrival caused some commotion. Laura Flood insisted on bringing him water and telephone notes, and finally both Bryan Malloy and Miller Johnson came in the room to say hello. Privately, they hoped the meeting was about the handling of the Jonas-Atlas account but realized that Thompson might still be trying to poach Boxer.

Finally, Boxer and Tommy got down to business. Tommy looked somewhat uncomfortable in these surroundings. His three-thousand-dollar suit looked out of place among the dented metal and worn wood, to say the least, but that was nothing compared to the look on Tommy's face. As he sat down and sized up the sandwiches, he looked like he was about to change a dirty diaper.

Tommy candidly acknowledged that Boxer's stock had gone up and Tommy's had gone down in the last several weeks. He was aware that Boxer might get more of the Jonas work in the future, but he said, "I think they have to keep me and my firm on the cases, because they still need the Thompson name and the Thompson bench strength." Then a light seemed to go off in Thompson's face, and he said, "You've already talked to them, haven't you?"

Boxer acknowledged that he had talked to the clients and, at Thompson's request, told him the details of the conversation.

Thompson said, "My analysis of your need for my firm still prevails."

Boxer nodded but asked, "At what price? If I came over there, would I get my choice of your lawyers to work on the file? Would I have input on paychecks and promotions? Would I be an equity partner? Would I be involved in management?"

Thompson said, "Boxer, you've only been out of law school for about four years."

Boxer said, "Yes, but do you have any other four-year lawyers—or ten-year lawyers, for that matter—who generate fees totaling possibly twenty-five million per year? Do you have any other lawyers who have tried seventeen cases in three years? Don't you think your lawyers will want to work on my cases?"

Thompson groaned. "Don't tell me you have talked to my lawyers."

Boxer said, "No comment." Then he added, "Don't you have some vacant offices also?"

Thompson realized that he had been had again, and he asked: "Okay, give me a list of all you want. I'm not saying I'll do it, but I'll look at it."

Boxer said, "I don't have a list, but if I did, what would you suggest I put on it?"

Rather than answering, Thompson said, "By the way, we do have other lawyers who have been national coordinating counsel for large mass torts cases, and we do have written proposed plans for organizing that type of litigation, and we do have terrific lawyers to work on such cases."

Boxer said, "Could they work with me?"

Tommy replied less positively than Boxer expected, "If I insist."

Audi opted out of dinner with Boxer, as she had another dinner with a client that night, but she chatted with Boxer by phone. Audi said, "You are in a position of great strength. No one of Tommy's options is perfect, but all are good." She went on to say that she was leaning toward the Thompson firm but was worried that Jonas-Atlas might not want to go the Thompson route again. She might have to see the plan to help her analyze the situation. If Boxer put Thompson in the plan and Atlas-Jonas rejected Thompson, becoming a partner at Thompson might not be the right strategy.

Finally, Audi said, "I think you should have some off-the-record contacts with Fortune about the Thompson partnership offer." Fortune took Boxer's call late that night and loved the details of the cold swiss-cheese-sandwich lunch at the Malloy firm.

Lee to West Virginia

Lee had twenty days following Judge Max's ruling to file notices of rehearing or notices of appeal. All was quiet. Lee had not called, and Thompson had not communicated further. Boxer was handling his caseload and thinking about the Jonas plan. Part of the plan depended on what strategy Lee employed. If Lee appealed, things might be quiet. The cases might be inactive during appellate briefing and arguments.

Three days before appellate notice was due, Boxer received an e-mail from Thompson: "My partners have decided they're against bringing you in as an equity partner; any offer is withdrawn." Boxer was curious. He suspected that Thompson's partners had little input into the details of any partnership offer to Boxer. Boxer decided to ignore the e-mail. On the final day for Dodge Lee to file his appeal, Boxer received not only a notice of appeal of the California cases but also was served with an additional three hundred summons and complaints against not only Jonas but also against Dr. Purcell and Atlas Insurance Company. All of the cases were filed in West Virginia. This was a jurisdiction that had denied preemption defenses in prescription drug cases in the past. At least one West Virginia court had ruled that the FDA labeling requirements did not preempt a drug company from adding additional warnings if the circumstances justified it.

The complaints were identical. They all alleged either brain damage or wrongful death caused by Nobo extract. They alleged all of the causes of action set forth in the San Francisco cases but added causes of actions against Purcell and Atlas for conspiracy, fraud, and $100 billion in punitive damages. They claimed that the defendants including Purcell and Atlas had conspired to hide the true dangers of Nobo extract from the medical profession, consumers, and the FDA.

Boxer's first reaction was that Thompson had withdrawn any partnership offer because he had somehow learned that Lee would be filing these new cases. Thompson probably assumed that Atlas, Jonas, and Purcell would be so intimidated by the three hundred new West Virginia cases that they would want the Thompson firm to remain as their counsel. Boxer wasn't sure that he didn't feel the same.

Deep down, Boxer believed that Thompson was pleased by the influx of new cases. He further worried that Thompson could now say that while the San Francisco victory was important, it only caused Lee to work harder to find a way to shake big money out of the Nobo litigation. Lee increased the pressure by hiring a retired West Virginia Supreme Court justice as local counsel.

Not wanting his clients to learn of the new cases from any other source, Boxer quickly e-mailed the summons and complaints to all, scheduling a teleconference call in one hour. It turned out Boxer's e-mail was minutes behind Thompson. Boxer was concerned that events were getting by him. The national plan was needed yesterday. He needed the Thompson firm, but he had lost faith in Thompson.

All defense interests were on the conference call including Thompson, who aggressively started laundry-listing all of the problems these new cases created and possible settlement scenarios.

Fortune interrupted and said that the group had asked Boxer Tate to create a proposed national plan for handling the Nobo cases. Thompson shot back, "Tate never asked for my input."

Kenny Clark said, "Because the plan may not include you." After a few seconds of silence, Clark said, "Boxer?"

Boxer calmly proceeded: "This latest ploy by Mr. Lee is not unexpected. He has been soliciting plaintiffs for many months. He has contacted plaintiffs' lawyers from around the country. The quickness with which he was able to get three hundred complaints on file shows that he anticipated defeat in San Francisco. I suspect he will try to slow the San Francisco appeals down and speed the West Virginia cases up in hopes of getting some success in West Virginia before any more adverse rulings in California."

Boxer continued, "One possible defense strategy would be to hire separate counsel for Atlas, Jonas, and Purcell, but I recommend against that. On the one hand, having the same lawyer for all three defendants gives some visceral support to plaintiffs' conspiracy theory. But on the other hand, it reduces the risk of division in the ranks. Lee will try to turn one lawyer against the other—he will tell one lawyer that the other revealed something negative about his clients. Also, it will cost more to have three lawyers for the three defendants. Lee believes that the more expensive it becomes to defend these cases, the more the defense will be willing to pay to settle."

"What do you recommend with respect to assignment of legal responsibilities?" asked Kenny Clark.

Boxer paused and then proceeded slowly, "By way of full disclosure, I will have to breach some confidences, but I believe the client's interest must come first. I have been approached by Tommy about becoming a partner there. I know some of you have become disenchanted with Thompson. I have not revealed this to Tommy but believe he has a general sense of this. For reasons not stated, Tommy has withdrawn from those partnership discussions. I have considered talking to Malloy about assuming authority and retaining more legal talent at the Malloy firm.

"I've also hinted to Tommy that some of his lawyers have approached me about the possibility of joining me in the defense of these cases."

Tommy was red in the face and fuming and said in a loud tone, "Boxer, I know you are a fighter, but your comments are inappropriate and constitute slander."

Fortune, who had been secretly kept up-to-date on the discussions between Tate and Thompson, asked, "Tommy, why did you withdraw from these discussions with Tate? I would have thought it would be a good marriage."

Thompson said, "The reasons were internal, privileged, partnership issues, and unlike Boxer, I intend to keep them confidential."

Fortune said, "Well, don't you agree the client's interest should come first?"

Thompson responded with restrained anger, "First? Ahead of what? We're not going to take the fall for your mistakes."

Fortune, taking a gamble, asked, "Well, Tommy, what do you recommend?"

Tommy could see that his attorney-client relationship was rapidly deteriorating. He decided to try to salvage the situation as best he could. He said, "I still think having the Thompson name on the pleadings adds value. I think it will have a calming influence on the financial community. Further, I have many friends around the country who are great lawyers, and I could introduce Boxer when he is searching for outstanding local counsel. And I know many judges.

"I sense that I have hurt my own credibility in this case, but I can also help Boxer to identify and work with outstanding lawyers at my firm who have already worked their way through mass tort cases. All Thompson lawyers working on the cases would be instructed that Boxer is first chair and lead lawyer. He would be in charge."

Fortune asked, "Boxer, what do you think?"

While the Thompson solution did not give him a raise in salary or change his status, it was a great client solution and gave Boxer a structure that would help him defend the Nobo litigation. Basically, Boxer was thrilled, but he responded in a contained manner: "I think Tommy has outlined an excellent team approach. His cooperation will stand us in good stead. I suggest that each of you call me separately with either your agreement or disagreement with this arrangement. It is important that each of the clients is individually satisfied that you are well represented under this proposal. Thereafter, I will prepare a retention letter for each of you to sign, and then we will have a brainstorming session.

"Tommy said it will be almost impossible to find effective defense counsel in West Virginia. The plaintiffs' bar and bench are like a revolving door. They switch places every couple of years and take turns ruling for each other. The local defense bar practices in fear. We will have to go there ourselves with guns blazing, prepared to expose blatant misdeeds."

Jim Rocky

Dodge Lee belonged to the San Francisco Roundtable, a group of plaintiffs' trial attorneys that met informally Friday afternoons in the back room of the Deco Club. Lawyers went to get ideas on how best to handle sticky legal issues. Lee wanted to crystal-ball what to do with his Nobo extract cases. The first thing that one of the lawyers said was, "California is good for plaintiff jurors and plaintiff judges, but the law of preemption here is terrible."

Lee said, "I know that. I know that I have to go to another and better plaintiffs' venue. But where?"

An old warhorse sipping his first Manhattan of the day said, "West Virginia is the best plaintiff venue in the country. The plaintiffs' lawyers and trial judges are joined at the hip."

Lee said, "I've thought of that. Who are the big hitters?"

The old guy mentioned a few names and then said, "Jim Rocky."

Lee raised a fist in triumph. "Why didn't I think of him? You're absolutely right. He would be perfect."

Justice Jim Rocky retired from the West Virginia Supreme Court after eighteen years on the bench, first as a trial judge and later as a supreme court justice. At fifty-eight, he returned to private practice, and in recent years he had built a successful law firm. He knew most of the judges and lawyers throughout the state. While he was a capable courtroom advocate, his greatest strength was ex-parte advocacy— advocacy without the presence of the adversary. He belonged to two country clubs and three eating clubs where he could be seen most afternoons and evenings buying drinks and meals for members of the legislature and judges. He was careful not to talk about cases, specifically, but if he could drop a dismissive hint about a dishonest expert, lawyer, or party, he would do it. His wife played bridge and golf with the spouses of many of the judges.

Sophisticated users of the legal system retained Rocky for their cases in West Virginia. As much as Lee hated to share contingency fees, he believed Rocky was worth the money. Many plaintiff lawyers around the country chose West Virginia as their favorite venue just to be able to use Rocky's contacts with the judges in the state. Lee was aware that many West Virginia judges opposed the concept of governmental regulations preempting state courts and legislators.

Lee called Rocky and gave him the history of the Nobo extract litigation. He said Dr. Al Purcell was a good witness for Jonas Pharmaceutical and Atlas had deep pockets. Rocky said, "Thus we should add both of them as defendants. Purcell's testimony will seem less credible if he has a stake in the cases. Atlas will hate the additional defense costs created by defending two new clients." Repeating himself, Rocky mused, "Having Dr. Purcell as a party defendant will weaken any perception of scientific impartiality when Purcell testifies. Besides, there is virtually no malicious prosecution cause of action here."

Having Atlas as a named defendant would inject more money into the case and result in less science in the courtroom. Further, the conspiracy theory would broaden the scope of discovery and allow them to seek documents and testimony about communications between the three defendants and their principals and embark on a so-called fishing expedition. Rocky went on: "Finally, as the financial risk to each defendant gets higher, they become susceptible to agreeing to a settlement for not just money but an agreement to cooperate with the plaintiffs and testify against the nonsettling codefendants. The likelihood of the defendants turning against each other is reduced if they are all represented by one counsel, but that counsel puts himself in a conflict posture if there are disagreements by the defendants about facts or strategy." Justice Rocky knew just how to take advantage of these thorny problems.

Rocky was retained and immediately started searching for plaintiffs. He filed and served new complaints naming the additional defendants. Boxer immediately reviewed the new complaints, and his awareness of the conflict problem was now front and center. Boxer had not actually handled any conflict problems in his own career. He decided to reach out to Thompson. In a firm like Thompson, conflicts were a way of life. In many of his cases, Tommy was asked to represent codefendants. He had thought through and drafted many retainer agreements raising the conflict issues and obtaining waivers from the clients. Thompson agreed to take the role of conflict counsel even though that role created the highest risk of legal malpractice suits if things went wrong. Thompson agreed that having all defendants represented by one set of lawyers was the best and cheapest defense, and Thompson was confident in his own ability to manage such a strategy. This also gave Thompson the best way of reinjecting himself into this lucrative litigation.

When Boxer reiterated the strategy to the individual clients the next day, they all worried about Tommy resurfacing, but Boxer's confidence in his ability to remain in charge persuaded them that Thompson could become conflict counsel without jeopardizing Boxer's leadership role. Boxer said, "With Tommy involved in managing conflicts, it will be hard for him to also participate in defense strategy on the merits."

|||| |||| |||| |||| |||| |||| |||| ||||

Boxer's Strategy Meeting

Boxer's secretary, Laura Flood, set another defense teleconference after all defendants individually agreed to hire Boxer.

Boxer presided. The first item on the agenda was the announcement that Tommy would be conflict counsel. Any conflict issues would be referred to Thompson, but Boxer would be available to handle issues that could not be resolved. The next item was the announcement that Karen Klein would handle plaintiff's appeal from Judge Earl Max's ruling. Miller Johnson would handle all discovery propounded by plaintiffs, and Boxer would handle pretrial hearings and discovery propounded to plaintiffs.

Finally, Boxer announced that he was concerned about there being too many lines of communication between plaintiffs and defendants. He was worried about different lawyers sending different signals, and therefore, for the present, he, Boxer, was the only one authorized to communicate to plaintiffs' attorneys. Thompson shifted uncomfortably in his seat but said nothing. Boxer secretly wondered if somehow Thompson was talking to Dodge Lee out of school. If that was the case, Boxer hoped this admonition would close the door.

After the announcements, Boxer asked all to stay and participate in a brainstorming session. Boxer was particularly interested in the standing of the individual plaintiffs. In other words: Did each individual plaintiff have a right to sue? Had they really been exposed to Nobo extract (the exposure issue)? Did they really have brain cancer (the damages Issues)? How had they been recruited to be plaintiffs? Had they given both Rocky and Lee authority to represent them?

One way to determine if each plaintiff had standing was to depose each one individually. Boxer did not have the time, and his clients did not have the money to depose all three hundred plaintiffs. Boxer proposed that they retain a West Virginia private investigator to do a public-records search to identify those plaintiffs who had police records or had filed lawsuits or were unemployed. "Find the ten least attractive, least educated plaintiffs, and I'll depose them." He put paralegal Mary Smith, who had reviewed all of the medical literature on Nobo extract, in charge of finding these unattractive plaintiffs. Boxer said, "We will try to push these to trial first."

Boxer realized that as he raised issues, he tended to resolve them himself without input from the others. He raised one issue that he didn't have the answer to. How should he respond to the three hundred complaints? A motion to dismiss on preemption, while successful in front of Max, would probably be unsuccessful in West Virginia, as would a motion for change of venue or an attempted removal to federal court. No one came up with a great solution, and it was decided to revisit the question in twenty days, ten days before a responsive pleading was due to be filed. At the last moment, Bill Dawes suggested, "Why don't we have our private investigators look into the public records on Jim Rocky and our trial judge, Bobby Waco? It would be fabulous if we could somehow get Rocky as plaintiffs' attorney and Waco as the judge of our case recused."

Boxer adjourned, having announced a weekly defense strategy meeting for every Monday.

After the conference call, Fortune telephoned Boxer. She said, "I hate to complain about costs, but at each conference call, someone comes up with a new idea, and each idea costs money. The idea about trying to get Rocky and/or Waco recused from the case is great, and if it works, it will make all of the other strategies unnecessary. Why don't we just work on the recusal strategy and delay all of the other work?"

Boxer said, "For one thing, when you start out, you are never sure which argument is going to be the winner, if any. If you try to argue each one in a row, you will run out of time. Further, the information we obtain using one approach may end up reinforcing other arguments we are making. Finally, Boxer said, "I am very suspicious about the relationship between Rocky and Waco. I think the legal system in West Virginia is so corrupt that only a lawyer coming from out of state could take it on. I think I am that lawyer, and I don't intend to lose. I see the Nobo extract litigation as a vehicle to do great good for the legal system entrenched in this state. I think a victory for Jonas here will be a victory for corporate America around the country."

Rocky at Home

Jim Rocky scheduled the depositions of Fortune Jones, Al Purcell, and Patrick Jonas in Wheeling, West Virginia, ten days hence. Ordinarily, witnesses cannot be compelled to travel out of state to be deposed, but there is an exception—named parties can be compelled to travel to the trial venue, in this case West Virginia.

Boxer was well aware that Rocky intended to try to cross-examine these witnesses in confidential areas ordinarily not subject to questioning and was further aware that he, Boxer, would get little relief from the West Virginia judges.

Boxer called Rocky and asked him for more time before he had to produce his defendants for depositions. Ordinarily, adversaries give each other more time as a courtesy. Rocky felt no compunction to show any courtesy to out-of-state counsel and said, "All you want is more time to prepare."

Boxer acknowledged this was true but said, "You're going to want to change court dates and times, and I will show you the same courtesies you show me."

Rocky said, "You're in West Virginia now, and you'll do things my way. No change in the deposition dates!"

Boxer was not surprised at Rocky's attitude and was further aware that he would probably get no relief from Judge Waco. Boxer had two immediate goals concerning his clients' depositions. One, he wanted to spare his clients the rigors of what promised to be nasty cross-examinations, and two, he wanted to delay the depositions until he could get the benefits of private investigation of the plaintiffs. Thus, after consulting with his clients and team, Boxer filed and served objections to the depositions and also noticed the depositions of each of the three hundred plaintiffs over the course of the next two years. Boxer did not really want to take the depositions of all three hundred plaintiffs at this time, but he needed leverage.

Rocky did not call Boxer to negotiate a discovery schedule or change of dates, but within several days Rocky filed a motion seeking assistance from the court in working out mutually agreeable schedules. Boxer filed a similar motion and asked that all deposition dates be stayed until after a discovery conference. Waco, without having oral arguments, postponed all depositions until after he could hold a discovery conference, which he set thirty days hence. Boxer got what he wanted, a delay before the depositions of his people.

Almost Heaven

"Almost heaven, West Virginia—mountain mama bring me home." If you're high on marijuana, West Virginia may be heaven. But if you're trying to make a living off the local economy, it can be hell. On one of his trips to West Virginia on other matters, Boxer had first had to go to New York before going to Wheeling. Breakfast in his New York hotel had been fifty-four dollars. Breakfast in his hotel in Wheeling had been $4.50. Poverty abounds. But one of the ways to get rich quick is at the courthouse. West Virginia judges and juries view the trial system as a means of redistributing wealth. This is particularly so when a non-West Virginia citizen is the defendant. Lawyers advertise for plaintiffs, and Jim Rocky's face and phone number were on billboards throughout the state.

When Dodge Lee associated Jim Rocky on the Nobo cases, Rocky was all over it. He ran TV ads soliciting anyone who had consumed Nobo extract and suffered headaches, depression, visual disturbances, anxiety, or any possible signs and symptoms of brain cancer. He even had a doctor who would give you a free examination and counseling.

Rex Annex saw one of the Jim Rocky TV ads while at his local tavern. Rex was just the audience the ads were intended to attract. He had all the symptoms anyone could ask for but no way to get medical treatment. He had been dishonorably discharged from the Marine Corps after fourteen months in the Gulf War. The discharge had followed several AWOLs, which precluded him from obtaining Veteran's Administration benefits. His health insurance had been canceled after he was fired from his job as a coal miner. And Rex's chances of getting another job were slim, as Rex had built up a history of drunk and disorderly arrests. Rex called the Jim Rocky number and was greeted by a professional, friendly voice, who announced, "This is an attorney-client privileged communication," and asked for preliminary background information. Rex confirmed that he had received Nobo extract but couldn't recall the name of the prescribing doctor or the reason for the prescription. He could not remember if he had been diagnosed with pancreatic cancer but insisted that he had received Nobo extract.

He had plenty of signs and symptoms of brain cancer. He had depression, anxiety, headaches, double vision, dizziness, stress, and nausea.

The friendly voice set up an appointment with a legal consultant the next day. Rex arrived at the office, which looked like a storefront with a large waiting room. There were probably thirty other clients, all reading the forms that had been created by the confidential friendly voice the day before. Rex was told to review the form and, if it was accurate, sign it. The form stated, "I have taken Nobo extract, and I now have the following signs and symptoms," and listed the signs and symptoms Rex had recited the day before. Rex signed in the appropriate spot. And within a half-hour, Rex was brought into a small, sparsely furnished office where he was greeted by a nice-looking young man who talked like a lawyer but, unbeknownst to Rex, was a paralegal. The young man gave Rex another form that was labeled a retainer agreement. The professional-looking man explained that if Rex wanted to hire the Justice Jim Rocky firm to represent him in seeking monetary compensation for his injuries, all he needed to do was sign the form and the young man would notarize it. Rex signed.

Rex asked when he would see a doctor and was told he would be contacted. Rex said he was very concerned that he had brain cancer. The young man said he understood.

There was no effort to obtain the identity of prior treating physicians, or prior hospitalizations, or prior prescriptions. There was no effort to seek an education history, or a job history, or a military history.

Within ten days, plaintiff attorney Justice Jim Rocky (retired) had three hundred new Nobo extract clients. Rocky rationalized the filing of these lawsuits with such skimpy evidence because of his intention to have each plaintiff diagnosed by a doctor he had already hired for this purpose.

Needless to say, Rocky was not ready to present Rex Annex or his coplaintiffs for deposition at this time, and Boxer's notice of three hundred depositions caused some panic. Rocky's strategy was not necessarily to find valid claims but rather to collect as many colorable claims as possible and, out of these, find the best plaintiffs and use them for a bellwether show trial first. Assuming the first trials were successful, Rocky would then settle the rest of the cases on an inventory basis, trying to get settlements by presenting basic unverified fact sheets.

The ethical rules in most states and in West Virginia require an attorney to sign the complaint, thus verifying to the best of his knowledge that the factual allegations are true and accurate. All of the complaints alleged that plaintiffs had brain cancer. Rocky considered this a technical, minor ethical issue, because he intended to have the allegation of brain damage verified by his medical consultant in the future. Thus, Rocky signed each of the complaints.

The friendly voice received more calls similar to the Rex Annex call. One was from a slightly argumentative party who called himself Craft Smith.

37

Woody Wilson

Boxer called Fortune Jones and asked her who Atlas used in West Virginia to do background checks and perform private investigations. He said, "Not only do I want to find grounds to recuse Waco and Rocky, I also want to start developing a standing defense to show the lack of cancer, lack of causation, lack of injury, lack of diagnosis, and other defense arguments."

After checking with Atlas's head of claims in West Virginia, Jones recommended Woody Wilson, a retired Wheeling police detective. Woody had built a small, private, lucrative investigation firm. Woody worked for criminal lawyers and civil trial lawyers. He was a lifelong resident of West Virginia and had gone to school at the university. He had a network of law-enforcement colleagues, which permitted him broad access to information on virtually anyone. He charged by the hour and required payment upfront. Woody found that with enough investigating, almost everyone has a few warts, and Woody loved uncovering them.

Woody had a personality and demeanor that he could adapt to the situation. In the past he had presented as a businessman, a laborer, and even a doctor. He could appear older or younger with only slight changes in his voice and attire.

When interviewed by video, Woody assured Boxer that he would do a background check on both Rocky and Waco without contacting or tipping off either.

Woody and Boxer agreed that the first order of business would be for Woody to run the names of the three hundred plaintiffs and Rocky and Waco through the usual databases. Then Woody proposed that he call the telephone numbers that Rocky had set forth in his TV commercials and see what happened.

Boxer invited Woody to report at the next Friday-afternoon videoconference. Woody did. He first described the results of his database search. So far there were about fifty of these plaintiffs who had prior arrests, prior accidents, DUIs, lawsuits, or had been fired from jobs. Woody further reported that Waco and Rocky had a friendship that went back generations. They played golf together and had handled cases together.

Bill Dawes commented, "This is not enough for recusal in many jurisdictions. In smaller towns, this is business as usual. Unlike San Francisco, most of the lawyers know most of the judges and jurors, and getting hometowned is the reason hiring local counsel is so important. Appearing without local counsel is a recipe for defeat."

Boxer asked both Woody and Tommy to look for a good local lawyer.

Woody said, "Next, I called the Rocky billboard telephone number and was greeted by a nameless friendly voice. I was asked for preliminary confidential information, and I supplied fictitious information but agreed to an appointment the next day. I arrived at the storefront, signed the information sheet using false information, and was interviewed by the friendly voice. When presented with a retainer agreement, I carefully read it word for word and asked some questions: 'What is the name of the doctor I will see? What is his specialty? When will I meet Jim Rocky? Will I receive a copy of the complaint before it is filed?' Also, I told them I wanted a copy of this retainer agreement.

"The friendly voice turned cool. He said all of these concerns would be addressed in the next several weeks but it was important to get the complaints on file because the statute of limitations was running. I then asked, 'What if turns out I don't have brain cancer and there is a complaint on file that says I do? Can I get in trouble?'

"The young man answered, 'No, we will just dismiss the complaint.'

"I finally said I would have to think about it and turned to leave with the retainer agreement in hand. The friendly voice tried to get the agreement back from me, but I had already tucked it in my pocket where it was too awkward for him to retrieve.

"At this point I said, 'I assume you are a lawyer?' and the man said yes. The real answer, I presume, is no.

"By the way, I've e-mailed each of you a copy of the retainer agreement."

Bill Dawes interjected, "I have read it, and it is not only unethical and illegal, it is outright fraudulent."

Finally, Woody said, "As I was outside of the storefront building, I was approached by a poorly dressed, poorly spoken man who said he had overheard my questioning of the Rocky team. His question to me was 'How soon will we get our money?' Wearing my investigator's hat, I invited him to have breakfast with me. He did, and he told me his story. In short, he has no case but was still signed up by the Rocky group. At the end of our conversation, he agreed to sign a written statement. I also have it here. His name is Rex Annex."

On the video, in front of the group, Boxer thanked Fortune for identifying and approving the retention of Woody.

Boxer invited the group to propose follow-up courses of action, "inasmuch as Atlas is receiving new complaints daily and the stakes continue to rise." Woody suggested that Fortune talk to Atlas's local West Virginia lawyers to seek more background on Rocky and Waco and that she talk to any attorney who was adverse to Rocky in front of Judge Waco. Fortune also asked Boxer to have his team scour the police reports and the military records of Rex Annex.

Bobby Waco and Jim Rocky

Woody's initial investigation of Justice Rocky and Judge Waco only scratched the surface. Indeed, Bobby Waco and Jim Rocky had practiced law in Wheeling, West Virginia, for years, and their fathers had practiced there before them. They had been in each other's weddings and had referred cases back and forth. Waco had supported Rocky in his successful effort to become first a trial judge and then a supreme court justice. And Rocky had supported Waco when he ran for trial court judge. When Rocky had gone on the bench, he had referred all of his open files to Waco and vice-versa. Each had paid the other referral fees when the cases closed. These referrals had continued when either was on the bench. It was a casual but lucrative arrangement and not so unusual in small towns in West Virginia. Indeed, small-town lawyers in West Virginia have a joke: "When I was the only lawyer in town, I starved. When a second lawyer came to town, we both got rich."

It became particularly lucrative when Rocky secretly referred a mass tort to Bobby Waco before the cases were filed and before Rocky went on the bench. After Rocky went on the bench, as each case was resolved, Waco sent Rocky a referral fee that was one-third of the fee Waco received. Rocky received these fees while on the bench and while Waco appeared before him on other cases. Rocky never disclosed the fees and never recused himself from a Waco case. While it was never discussed, both lawyers knew their friendship was financially rewarding.

Now that the Nobo extract cases were coming before Judge Bobby Waco, like Rocky before him, Waco did not recuse himself. Basically, Rocky and Waco were sending each other referral fees while one was an attorney and the other was a judge ruling on his friend's lawsuits. But each privately reasoned that he would rule in the best interest of the State of Virginia.

After the Nobo extract complaints were filed, Rocky casually stopped by the chambers of his good friend Judge Waco and said he looked forward to appearing in front of him on these cases and that he did not want to ex parte on the facts or law but just to warn Judge Waco that defense attorney Boxer Tate from San Francisco had a reputation of using obscure technicalities to rob deserving injured parties of their recoveries.

Judge Waco replied, "I'm well aware of the preemption defense, and it won't happen here." Rocky went on to reveal that Boxer Tate was renowned for attacking the integrity of his adversaries. Judge Bobby Waco said, "Jim, you know this is not California, and those shenanigans won't be tolerated in my courtroom."

Rocky went on to reveal that Boxer Tate was renowned for violating the bar association's civility rules.

In searching through prior lawsuits filed by any of the three hundred Nobo plaintiffs, Woody and his team found four in which the minor plaintiff had been represented by Waco and later Waco had withdrawn to take the bench, at which point Jim Rocky was substituted as counsel of record. Rocky's plaintiffs still had been minors at the time the case was settled. When a case was settled for a minor, it had to be approved by the court. Not only did the court have to approve the amount of the settlement, but it also had to approve the amount of the attorney's fees.

Woody suspected that Waco, on the bench, had approved these sums, which would go back into his pocket. Woody expected that the court file would contain papers seeking such approval of any referral fees. Woody had a suspicion that the files might reflect the payment of referral fees to Justice Waco. The approval documents had to be filed with the court clerk.

Woody went to the clerk's office, waited in line, and filled out the paperwork and requested the files from the court clerk. The clerk went to look for the files. Woody waited for what should have been a two-minute search.

After fifteen minutes, the clerk returned and said, "The files are out."

Woody asked, "When will they be back?" The clerk said he didn't know, and then Woody said, "Who has them?"

"I don't know."

Woody then asked to speak to the politically appointed chief clerk and was told that he was out.

Woody reported the missing records to Boxer, who said, "Add the chief clerk and the former minor plaintiffs to our deposition list. Let's also subpoena the minors' compromise files from the clerk, from the plaintiffs, and from Bobby Waco." Woody wanted to interview the two former minor plaintiffs, but Boxer said, "No. They are represented by counsel, and it would be unethical."

Meanwhile, Tommy and Woody searched to find local counsel with some favorable connections with Judge Waco. There were many, but when they were told that they would be representing Nobo extract before Judge Waco, they all declined. Ultimately, Boxer hired Atlas local insurance-defense counsel who was competent but not as connected as Jim Rocky.

Atlas local counsel searched all local databases for the names of cases in which Rocky had appeared before Waco or Waco had appeared before Rocky. Preliminary investigation revealed that there were dozens of such cases, and neither man had ever ruled against the other.

Victory in West Virginia

The thirty-day stay imposed by Judge Waco expired, and both sides immediately demanded information from the other.

Amazingly, Rocky filed a lawsuit on behalf of Ralph Craft, the fictitious name used by Woody Wilson, and on behalf of Rex Annex. Boxer decided not to demand discovery of these two or from the last ten plaintiffs. Boxer wanted to save revealing these gaffes for a later date.

Boxer also scheduled early depositions of the chief clerk of the court and the four minors whose settlements and compromiser had been approved by Judge Waco, who well might have received a referral fee from Rocky.

Boxer also sought the identification of the friendly voice and all documents created or collected by the friendly voice. He also went after all of the medical records of treating doctors; the minors' compromise records, which should have been in the court clerk's files; copies of the executed retainer agreements of the three hundred plaintiffs; all Nobo extract prescriptions obtained by the three hundred plaintiffs; and copies of all records confirming plaintiffs' diagnosis of brain cancer or diagnosis of prostate cancer.

Rocky rescheduled the depositions of Patrick Jonas, Fortune Jones, and Al Purcell. He also sought copies of all clinical trial records and the names and addresses of all individuals who had any complaints against

Nobo extract. He further sought all FDA records concerning Nobo extract and all Jonas internal memos regarding Nobo extract.

Not surprisingly, both sides filed objections, and a hearing was set before Judge Waco.

Because of the importance of the hearing, Boxer came to the courtroom early. He wanted to get a sense of Judge Waco's courtroom style. He saw that Waco was smart and ran a tight ship. When Waco entered the courtroom, his bailiff demanded, "All rise," and everyone stood respectfully.

The first lawyer to speak said, "Judge—"

Before he could finish, Judge Waco said, "Please address me as Your Honor, not Judge."

That same lawyer, who apparently wasn't from Wheeling, then walked up to the bench through the well to hand Judge Waco an exhibit. Waco's clerk ordered, "Please don't come toward the judge without first asking, 'May I approach.'"

When the court attachés instructed the lawyers, they did not address them as "Mr. Jones" or "Mr. Smith" but rather "Counselor" in a somewhat dismissive manner.

At the outset of each new matter, Judge Waco would say, "Counselor, I have read your papers, so there is no need for you to repeat what's in them."

Boxer intended to recite this phrase back to the judge when he was arguing. He would say, "Your Honor, I know you have read the papers, so I don't have to tell you …"

Waco moved the calendar along and did not allow prolonged arguments. He announced his rulings at the end of each hearing and permitted no arguments after rulings were announced. Boxer worried that he used this tactic to support autocratic and perhaps incorrect rulings. A casual observer would have been impressed by what appeared to be an intelligent and neutral forum. Boxer knew better, but he also knew that exposing Waco and Rocky could get him in big trouble in West Virginia.

That afternoon when the clerk called the Nobo extract cases, all the lawyers stood behind the counsel table and announced their names and who they represented. In addition, Boxer introduced Fortune Jones, Dr. Al Purcell, Patrick Jonas, and cocounsel Bill Dawes.

No one was invited to sit down. Judge Waco announced, "I have read all the papers, and all plaintiffs' discovery requests are appropriate and any objections are overruled. All documents produced are to be Bates stamped and given to the other side in sixty days or less. All depositions will take place in Wheeling within thirty days."

Then Judge Waco turned to Boxer and said, "I have some concern about your requested discovery. It appears to me," he went on, "that the request for any papers created or collected by the friendly voice are protected by the attorney-client privilege."

Boxer responded, "I know you have read my papers, and you have seen my authority that these papers were created before any attorney-client relationships were entered. And it appears no attorney was present."

Waco said, "They were created in anticipation of litigation by representatives of attorneys."

Boxer said, "I have a good-faith belief that these documents might impeach the allegations of brain damage in the complaints."

Judge Waco sternly responded, "Who are you accusing of fraud? We do not take these charges lightly."

Boxer said, "I don't pursue them lightly. That is why I am seeking the documents to determine if these plaintiffs actually have the brain cancer alleged in the complaints or merely have signs and symptoms which might or might not be cancer."

Judge Waco abruptly announced, without one word from Lee or Rocky, "I have read these papers carefully, and plaintiff's objections to this discovery are sustained."

Boxer was not totally surprised and asked for leave to seek this discovery later if facts so justified. Local defense counsel would not have had the guts to make such a request.

Waco, more hotly, said, "Counsel, I have ruled." Judge Waco then said, "Let's get to the minors' compromise requests. You want court documents from other cases, and you want to depose plaintiffs who were the minors in those cases?"

Boxer said calmly but clearly, "Frankly, Your Honor, I'm not sure you should be the judge hearing this matter. Candidly, we are seeking to learn if you paid referral fees to Mr. Rocky while he was a judge and presiding over cases in which his rulings could have an impact on those fees."

The courtroom grew silent, and everyone looked stunned but was secretly delighted. Boxer was not attacking by innuendo. It was direct, and this lawyer from San Francisco was running the risk of being held in contempt. The courtroom was expectant.

Waco exploded. He ordered the courtroom cleared except for the attorneys. He even had the court reporter leave so as not to make a record. He then turned to Boxer and said, "Mr. Tate, I have been forewarned that one of your tactics is to attack the reputation and integrity of your adversaries or the judge you appear before. I won't have it here."

Boxer said, "Thank you for clearing the court, because I think the situation gets worse. It is my belief that after you became a judge, you received referral fees on many cases taken over by Mr. Rocky, and I believe that in some of those cases, minor compromise fees were going to you. I also believe that you and Mr. Rocky have tried to cover up your ethical violations by removing these minor compromise files from the clerk's office.

"When the court reporter returns, I will make a formal motion to have both you and Mr. Rocky recused from all three hundred cases." Turning to Rocky, Boxer said, "By the way, Mr. Rocky, in one of those cases you mistakenly sued my investigator, Woody Wilson. I can assure you that he has neither brain cancer nor pancreatic cancer, nor has he taken Nobo extract."

Judge Waco was shaking. He said, "Mr. Rocky, may I have a word?" Rocky approached the bench, and the two talked in whispers. Then Judge Waco said, "I'd like a private conference with Mr. Rocky in chambers. Mr. Tate, it may be to your benefit."

The defense team and parties gathered in the back of the courtroom. Boxer said, "If I know these two, they're trying to think of a way out of these cases that will not result in an investigation into their practices. I'll bet there is more."

After about fifteen minutes, Judge Waco appeared and invited all counsel into chambers. In chambers he said, "I don't think any harm has been done. In all of the cases in which I received referral fees, the clients have been well represented. The cases, in which I approved attorney's fees including referral fees to me, were pro forma, and any judge would have approved them. But to avoid publicity, which would not only be harmful to me and Jim Rocky but also to the judiciary, we have a proposal."

Boxer could not wait and interjected, "Before I forget it, through our investigation we have obtained a copy of your standard contingency fee, which is 50 percent of what plaintiff recovers. Even in West Virginia, this is too high. But go ahead—let us hear your proposal."

Rocky said, "We propose to dismiss all three hundred complaints without prejudice to another lawyer, who will refile for these particular plaintiffs if he so desires. Our retainer agreements permit this. The defendants have to waive costs, which are minimal, and have to agree that everything said in this courtroom will remain confidential as will the results of any private investigation by the defense. We agree not to take any more Nobo extract cases, and if any other attorney seeks to file on behalf of any plaintiffs, we will agree that the preretention client forms will be turned over to you."

Boxer said, "What about you, Dodge Lee?"

Lee was rocking back and forth. He had seen shady conduct by lawyers but never any so blatant as Rocky and Waco's. The judges in San Francisco held the lawyers to very high standards. *Of course,* Lee reminded himself, *that is why I came to West Virginia.* Lee said, "I will withdraw from the California cases. I doubt my clients will seek other counsel, because I think that the preemption defense is a winner for the defendants in California, and I will so inform my clients. But Boxer, you and your clients also have to waive costs. Since the costs are chargeable to the plaintiffs personally and most of my plaintiffs don't have the money to pay costs, attempted collection would be futile."

Boxer thought, *What really is happening here is that Rocky and Waco are selling their clients down the river to save their own necks. But since they're not my clients, I couldn't care less.* Boxer also worried that he might have some responsibility to report Waco and Rocky to the West Virginia Bar Association. Nevertheless, the deal was so good he accepted it on the spot. He'd have to worry about the technicalities later.

IIII IIII IIII IIII IIII IIII IIII IIII

Audi and Boxer

On the plane from West Virginia, Boxer was still euphoric. He had heard Bryan Malloy say, "The more wins you have, the shorter the post-victory euphoria. But after defeat, the longer the agony lasts." Specifically, Malloy also said to Boxer, "If you play in the street long enough, you're going to get hit."

Boxer dreaded that day. It was a dread that drove many successful trial lawyers. Boxer was determined to revel in the latest success, and the one he wanted to revel with was Audi Johns. On his arrival at SFO, he telephoned Audi, who had already learned of the dismissals in West Virginia while watching the Bloomberg report. Jonas Pharmaceutical stock had already gone up another 11 percent.

Boxer suggested to Audi that they celebrate in Carmel. Audi agreed but chilled the call by saying, "Yes, we need to do some future business planning. I'll make the reservations at La Playa, where I have a favorite room. I'll make the reservations for you too. Do you have a favorite room?"

Boxer said, "Get me a suite. We can use it for our meetings."

Boxer knew there would be many postmortem discussions and wanted to vet with Audi first to prepare for those discussions, so they decided that Boxer would go to Carmel directly from the airport and Audi would meet him there. It was about a two-hour drive. They would dine at Clint Eastwood's Carmel Mission Ranch and then meet in the morning and be back in San Francisco by early afternoon.

The Mission Ranch view was beautiful. They sat outside and looked over the meadows to the Pacific Ocean. The sheep were starting to gather in the pasture and eat their way toward the barn. The sun was starting to set, and a red glow was burning at the horizon. Audi and Boxer sipped Ketel One on the rocks with olives. Life was good. Audi looked sensational. She worked out every day and had a body hard as a rock ... and Boxer was partial to blondes. He wasn't sure the feeling was mutual.

At Audi's urging, Boxer recounted the West Virginia episode. While the result was great, they both had some ethical concerns. Boxer said, "Basically, Rocky sold his clients down the river. But the law is an adversarial business. Each side vigorously represents its client's interest, and justice will out.

"I am convinced that most of the plaintiffs were not injured by Nobo extract, and those that were injured were not entitled to recovery, because they were injured after the warning about brain cancer was added to the labeling and this provided an absolute defense."

Audi said, "Yes, but there probably were at least a few who were injured before the warnings were added. They had legitimate failure-to-warn claims and a chance at success in the courtroom before their cases were dismissed. You know, Rocky and Waco could privately talk to other plaintiffs' lawyers and refer what they think are the most meritorious cases to these other lawyers, who could then file new complaints since the cases were dismissed without prejudice."

Boxer said, "My clients wouldn't be too happy if that happened."

They both agreed that the West Virginia plaintiffs probably were totally unaware that the real reason their cases had been dismissed was that Rocky and Waco did not want their illegal fee-splitting violations revealed.

Audi said, "If these violations by Waco and Rocky were committed in California, wouldn't the California Bar rules have required you to report Waco and Rocky to the California State Bar Association?"

Boxer said, "Waco and Rocky are not members of the California Bar, and thus the bar has no jurisdiction over them."

Audi reminded Boxer that Tommy Thompson was ethics counsel for the defendants and Boxer could discuss these concerns with Tommy.

Boxer said, "Do I really want Tommy to get so deeply into these cases at their present status?"

Audi just sighed.

Boxer also brought up his own aggressive behavior in front of Judge Waco. He said, "It was my very obvious strategy to get Rocky to voluntarily dismiss the cases, and it worked. But I was concerned that Judge Waco might report *me* to the West Virginia Bar Association, which had jurisdiction over me because I was practicing in their courts. I'll bet Waco and Rocky were discussing just such a strategy in chambers. I could see Waco returning to the courtroom, holding me in contempt, and entering terminating sanctions against our client because of my conduct. I could also see the reviewing court in West Virginia affirming such a decision."

Audi said, "Let's talk about it in the morning."

Audi and Boxer walked back to La Playa and parted with a Hollywood air kiss. Not exactly the ending Boxer had hoped for. Audi herself was conflicted but chose not to reveal it.

The next morning they met for breakfast on the La Playa patio overlooking Carmel Beach.

Boxer said, "Let me recite the present status, and then I would like your analysis of where I go from here. You are on the clock, and I will pay for your time and expenses going forward. As you know, I am presently an equity partner at Malloy. Malloy has a 45 percent interest, Miller Johnson has a 35 percent interest, and I have a 20 percent interest in the profits of the firm. Tommy Thompson has offered me a partnership but has withdrawn the offer. He still has vacant offices and still needs me. I suspect he is subtly trying to show Dodge Lee the way to file more Nobo lawsuits. Bill Dawes, Karen Klein, and Mary Smith are all at Thompson but are interested in continuing to work on the Nobo cases and would consider working with me if the cases continue and I remain as national counsel. There is now a lull in litigation, but I expect there may be more Nobo cases and/or other cases."

Audi asked, "Where do you want to be in ten years?"

Boxer replied, "I don't think Tommy did a good job on the Nobo cases. It's such a shame, because he used to be so potent on these sorts of cases. Nevertheless, in ten years I would love to have his firm and his reputation. I would like to be handling significant cases with lawyers I respect and trust. I want control over my destiny. And frankly, I want to make a lot of money."

Audi said, "When Tommy opened his firm, he had a bigger reputation, a better resume, and more contacts than you do now."

Boxer said, "He was also older than I am now."

"True," said Audi. "Do you want to spend the next ten years getting to where Tommy was when he opened his office?"

"No. I suppose one strategy is to become a partner at Thompson and take over that firm. I don't see that happening without a huge fight."

"Right," said Audi. "Another strategy is to stay at Malloy. But as I said last time we discussed this, Malloy isn't good enough, and further, it has an insurance-defense reputation that will be hard to overcome in the boardrooms of America, and it is not a good foundation on which to build a prestigious law firm."

Boxer said, "I like a third option. Open the Boxer Tate firm and hire Dawes, Klein, and Smith. I would offer Miller Johnson a job, but not as a named partner; he is too connected to Malloy. Finally, I would hire Malloy as of counsel with a caveat that he would have to join AA. Miller and Malloy would still attract Atlas volume business, which would help us through the lulls. Our firm would be made up of ex-Thompson lawyers and our Jonas affiliation, which would give us a complex litigation panache.

"I realize that to offer this capability, we have to grow fast. Thus, I would be the chairman, and you would be the managing partner/hiring partner. Your first job would be to find a suitable merger candidate. This will not be easy, because the candidate will have to have significant talent and reputation and accept me as the chairman."

Audi said, "The most likely candidate would be a small young practice group in a large firm that has become disenchanted with the large firm. There might also be a group of associates who are being terrorized by a tyrannical partner or a group whose senior associate was passed over for partner." Audi took a sip of her bloody mary before continuing. "We now live in a free-agency world, and young lawyers in particular have figured that out. That means we may have to overpay to get who we want. This also means your lust for money may have to wait—as will mine."

Boxer said, "Does that mean you're coming with me?"

"Yes. But that also means no romance."

Boxer said, "Most women find me attractive."

Audi replied with a smile, "Is that why you're still not married?"

Boxer said, "Touché."

Audi said, "We need staff, we need space, and we need equipment. I suppose those are going to be my jobs—you, Boxer, will have to talk to Bryan Malloy, Miller Johnson, the Thompson lawyers, and Tommy, and our two clients, Jonas and Atlas, to say nothing of Al Purcell. After these arrangements are made, we will have to get out press releases and try to generate some publicity, and don't forget—when you talk to Thompson, run the West Virginia ethics issue by him."

The Boxer Firm

Boxer and Audi were back in the city by 2:00 p.m. They didn't need to use the suite for their meetings—or anything else.

Boxer went to his offices and immediately went into Miller Johnson's office. He said, "I want to start my own law firm, and I'd like you to come with me."

Without asking for any details, Johnson accepted on the spot. He confided, "I think my future will be brighter in a new, revitalized firm." Boxer then asked Miller his thoughts on approaching Malloy. Miller said, "If Malloy would just stop drinking, he could run a strong insurance-defense group. This could be a good stepping stone to more sophisticated insurance work. If you are patient, I think ultimately he has to take your offer."

Boxer then went to Malloy. The minute Boxer used the phrase "of counsel," Malloy became hostile and defensive. He said, "This is an insult. Basically, you want me to give you my firm for nothing."

Boxer said, "No. I am leaving your firm but offering you a job at my new firm. I hate to say it, but without me, your firm won't survive. For one thing, I think your use of alcohol is interfering with your practice. If you come with me, I will insist you go into alcohol rehab. Indeed, the new firm would pay for it.

"Further," Boxer pointed out, "I will be taking Miller Johnson with me, and without us, you will have vacant offices, which you will still have to pay the rent on. If you come with our new firm, we will initially work out of the Malloy offices and pay the rent for the duration of the cases."

Malloy asked, "When will I have to start rehab?"

Boxer said, "Now."

Malloy's look changed almost immediately from anger to relief. He said, "I accept the deal and will check into the clinic on Pine Street tonight. I have tried rehab and wasn't successful. I figure I have to make it this time or it's a death sentence for me."

Boxer said, "We need you to make it, because we want you to lead our insurance-defense group."

Boxer then called Tommy Thompson's secretary and asked for a meeting that evening. He was told to come right over. Boxer walked into Thompson's office, and the chill was palpable. Thompson did not invite Boxer to sit down but said, "What can I do for you?"

Boxer got right to the point. "I'm starting my own firm, and I wanted you to know right away. I have not told the clients, and I have not told your team."

Before Boxer could say any more, Thompson said, "Boxer, you're a greedy and selfish man. You're used to getting your own way but not with me. I knew this was coming and called Judge Sheppard's chambers. They have scheduled a hearing tomorrow to consider my request for a temporary restraining order to stop you from stealing my lawyers and my clients. Ultimately, I will be seeking a permanent injunction. Further, I will be seeking damages for the legal fees I have not received because of your conduct."

Boxer thought to himself, *Well, I guess this is not a good time for me to bring up the West Virginia ethics issue.* Boxer also privately assumed that Thompson would be in a conflict position with Jonas and Atlas now that he was adverse to Boxer.

Out loud, Boxer said, "I guess that means you don't want to join my new firm. I know you have a number of empty offices, and I predict there will be more."

Thompson said, "I will just add that to the damages you will owe me."

Boxer said, "You know, Tommy, litigation between us will hurt your aura. We will have to rebut your claim for lost legal fees with the evidence that your practices and procedures were so substandard that they hurt rather than helped the Nobo cases. Your lack of knowledge of the preemption defense was below the standard of care for a lawyer handling complex litigation. Your preparation of Dr. Purcell for deposition was downright malpractice. Your representation does not justify any legal fees on your part. Maybe we will have to cross-complain to get a return of the legal fees you obtained from the Nobo defendants. Finally, I suspect that if we do any discovery against you and your firm, there will be multiple instances in which you took practice groups and their clients out of other firms. You won't like the publicity, and you really won't like it when I depose you and your practice group heads."

This was it. Boxer studied Thompson's face carefully, trying to see through the façade. Thompson had to be outraged. Nobody had stood up to him like this before, and if Boxer knew anything about Thompson, he was sure that his youth—not to mention his tactics— were getting under Thompson's skin.

But Tommy remained calm, quickly reversing field. He said, "Okay, Boxer, you win again. But I really think instead of opening a small under-armed law firm you should join my firm. You would have a great platform to attract more mega-lawsuits. You would make a lot more money, and you could surround yourself with more of the great talent we have here."

Boxer replied, "Tommy, you have done a great job building this firm, but frankly I worry that you are no longer afraid of losing and maybe have lost your edge. But the real reason I won't come is because it's your firm, not mine. When you're ready to change the name to Tate and Thompson, give me a call.

"By the way, Tommy, are you still going to pursue the litigation against me?"

"No, I'll take the TRO motion off-calendar and dismiss the claim for damages and, by the way, great job in front of Judge Waco. I despise Jim Rocky and loved seeing him go down."

That reminded Boxer of the ethical issue, and he decided to seek Thompson's thoughts.

Thompson said, "I've already thought of this, and I think if Rocky ever seeks to be admitted *pro hac vice* in California, we can oppose the motion with the evidence we have in this case. In reality, I think Rocky knows he would not be very effective outside of West Virginia. While one might argue we should report Rocky to the West Virginia Bar Association, I am sure it would result in no sanctions against Rocky and would only enmesh us in proceedings in a state we can't win."

Boxer said, "One of the reasons we took the West Virginia cases was because we didn't think there was any lawyer in West Virginia who could stand up to the self-dealing and downright fraud of the entire bench and bar. But you are correct. I don't want to go back."

Lateral Hiring

The next morning, Audi and Boxer met with Dawes, Smith, and Klein. The Dawes group was excited about the new firm concept, but they were concerned about the lack of business and low salary structure. The existing insurance-defense practice could probably cover rent, expenses, and a modest income in the short run. But at present, Boxer Tate did not have a big book of business or a big reputation. Tate was optimistic, but he realized he was asking people to give up secure jobs for an uncertain future.

That evening at cocktails at Sam's Grill, Tate and Audi came to the conclusion that without cash they were going to have to sell part of their future. They would have to give an equity interest to the Dawes Group and Miller Johnson. They would defer on Malloy pending the success of his rehabilitation. In return for receiving a percentage of the profits in the new firm, the new partners would have to put their signature on any new leases. These signatures would act as soft handcuffs. If headhunters tried to steal any new partners from the new firm, signing a lease usually required the signatory to guarantee timely rental payments. If the signatory left the firm, unless the landlord waived the guarantee requirement, the departing partner still would have to make the payments. Thus, if by leaving the firm the departing partner put the old firm in financial jeopardy, he would have to pay any default out of his own pockets. Thus he would be handcuffed to the firm he wanted to leave.

By law, only lawyers were permitted to have an ownership interest in a law firm, so paralegal Mary Smith could not have any points.

Audi and Boxer could avoid giving away points by just borrowing the money. But empty offices, employee turnover, and debt are the major downfalls of most firms. Ownership is one key to stability, and Boxer and Audi wanted to build a legal institution on a solid foundation.

In the meantime, Tommy was making his own plans. But rather than talking to his clients or his legal team, he called his adversary, Dodge Lee. Lee knew that frequently he could obtain more information from informal sources than from legal discovery and readily consented to lunch in Tommy's private dining room at the firm.

The Thompson firm had a main cafeteria on the thirty-first floor, but off the cafeteria was a small oak-paneled private dining room with a view of the Bay Bridge to the east and the Port of Oakland to the south. Tommy found the setting was perfect for closing deals or soliciting new cases. He also liked the layout because his own suite of offices was right off the private dining room.

Lunch was at twelve thirty, and both men arrived precisely on time. Both started with iced tea. No alcohol. And both knew that the agenda was Jonas. Lee had been thrilled when he got the phone call from Thompson because his intuition was that Tommy was anticipating more cases—indeed, hoping for more cases. And Dodge's first comment on arriving was "Procedurally, what do you think I'll do next, Tommy?"

Tommy replied, "You're going to look for a jurisdiction that does not accept the preemption defense."

Dodge decided to push it further. He said, "We're thinking of filing cases in all states that do not allow the preemption defense. Would you accept service for Jonas in all of those new cases?"

Tommy said, "As you know, if I was in charge I would agree to accept service, but Tate runs the show. When you added a conspiracy count against Al Purcell and Patrick Jonas, I was surprised you didn't include Boxer Tate as a codefendant; that probably would have conflicted Tate out as counsel of record."

Lee said, "Well, Tommy, if you and I were the only lawyers on these cases, I suspect we would get them resolved without wasting millions of dollars in discovery and trial. It would save money for everybody."

Tommy nodded approval.

Dodge Lee said, "As you know, one of the problems I have is identifying victims who have been exposed to Nobo extract and also have brain cancer."

Thompson said, "If you want an early victory against Tate, either subpoena the adverse event reports or get them through Freedom of Information Act. This will help to identify strong plaintiff cases early, and you can still advertise to pick up the other cases."

Lee said, "Tommy, I am sure you already have these AE reports. Can't you produce them to me directly?"

Thompson said, "No. And Dodge, you have to agree that this conversation is absolutely confidential and is not to be repeated."

Lee said, "Yes, and the same goes for you."

The lunch with Lee gave Tommy the confidence to approach the Dawes group. Even if he could not keep them at Thompson, he could drive the price up to make it more expensive for Boxer to hire these people. Further, even if Thompson lost the Dawes group, Tommy believed, based on his lunch with Lee, that the Jonas litigation would explode and he would be able to fill his empty offices. Tommy immediately whispered to his secretary to ask Bill Dawes and Karen Klein to come to his private office. They arrived just as Lee was leaving. Tommy said, "Boxer told me he was going to talk to you about starting a new firm. I assumed that has happened. I am anxious to make plans for the future and would like to know where these discussions stand."

Dawes said, "Yes, we have talked. It is hard for Boxer to make plans because he doesn't know where the Nobo extract litigation is going."

Tommy replied, "I think the two Jonas victories will have a chilling effect on any future filings. This lack of Nobo cases will hurt Boxer a lot more than it will hurt me. Fortunately, Thompson has a number of mass tort cases that will be heating up, so we will need talent and can afford to pay for it." And then Thompson used an old ploy that usually worked on everyone except Boxer. He said, "If you stay here, you will each get a 10 percent raise. I don't want you shopping this offer, and I want a response by the end of the week." All grudgingly agreed.

Boxer Named Defendant

The negotiations about a Boxer Tate firm stalled. The Dawes group got more time to respond to the Thompson job offer. But the litigation flared up when Lee filed a new complaint in Cook County, Illinois. In addition to Jonas Corporation, codefendants were listed as Al Purcell, MD; Patrick Jonas, individually; and Baxter Tate, Esq. The next day, Tate and Purcell were also served, and Thompson received a courtesy copy. Dodge Lee was named as cocounsel for plaintiff subject to a petition to be admitted *pro hac vice* in Cook County.

Boxer immediately convened a war counsel. All defendants and counsel were present as was Tommy Thompson. Tate presided. He said, "Lee is trying to remove me as counsel. In one sense, that's flattering. But it is his way of avoiding a decision on the merits. The new complaint says I conspired to defraud the FDA by counseling Jonas to submit false information, thereby misleading the FDA with respect to the extent of the dangers of Nobo extract."

Thompson, as ethics council, said, "I think that Tate now has a conflict of interest inasmuch as he is named as both a defendant and as attorney for the defendants." Further, Thompson counseled that Boxer should have his own attorney, independent of the attorneys for the other defendants.

Since Boxer was being accused of both a crime and a tort, Thompson was of the view that these were ethical violations that should be reported to the California Bar Association. Thompson warned that the conspiracy charges alone could lead to disbarment.

Boxer was shaken by the allegations and the consequences described. Instinctively, he asked Thompson, "Did you see this coming?"

Thompson said, "What coming?"

"The naming of me as a codefendant."

"Your overly aggressive nature makes this somewhat predictable," said Thompson.

Purcell inserted, "It was Boxer's overly aggressive nature that made our victories possible."

Boxer said, "They haven't seen the real aggressive Tate yet." Boxer repeated the old saw, "He who represents himself has a fool for a client. Nevertheless, I recommend that I petition the Cook County court to appear for both myself and all of the named defendants."

Dr. Purcell said, "I agree. We had a similar discussion in the West Virginia cases about Boxer not representing both Jonas and me because we had a potential conflict. I like the way that case worked out, and I say we do it again."

Thompson said, "I think I have an ethical duty to send a copy of this complaint to the state bar."

Patrick Jonas's in-house counsel, Kenny Clark, said at once, "You do that and you're fired. We have a right to counsel of our own choosing, and we choose Boxer Tate."

Boxer said, "I will represent myself and the defendants, and the first thing I will do is start discovery to see what facts Lee has to support these bogus allegations. Today courts require attorneys to double-check the veracity of the allegations in the complaint, and if they don't and the allegations are untrue, the charging attorney can be subject to serious sanctions."

After the meeting, Boxer received a phone call from Dawes. Dawes said, "I don't know what to think of this, but yesterday after lunch Tommy called us into his office suite. As we were arriving, I saw Dodge Lee leaving Tommy's private dining room."

Boxer asked Dawes, "What do you make of this?"

Dawes said, "I know Tommy is frustrated because he is not lead counsel and he thinks he can do better, but this is strange."

Boxer entered an appearance in the Cook County case and simultaneously submitted a petition to be admitted *pro hac vice.* He also noticed the deposition of Dodge Lee for forty-five days hence. He wanted to find out what Lee and Thompson were talking about at Tommy's office. Ordinarily, courts don't permit one lawyer to depose the lawyer representing an adverse party, because most of the testimony of the attorney would be privileged by both the attorney-client privilege and the attorney-work-product privilege.

The work-product privilege holds that all of the research and investigation either done by the lawyer or on behalf of the lawyer is confidential and protected from discovery by the other side.

Lee cross-noticed Boxer's deposition, and each side sought an order from the Cook County Court quashing the other's deposition. The motions were assigned to the Honorable Homer Frank, who scheduled a hearing sixty days after service of the complaint. Lee appeared and argued for plaintiff. Boxer appeared and argued for the defendant and himself. Judge Frank said, "Mr. Tate, You may proceed."

Boxer immediately took the initiative and said, "Plaintiff Attorney Lee has been trying to turn individual pharmaceutical injury cases into mass torts. Having lost in California and West Virginia, he is now trying a third forum. He is also trying to intimidate the defense by suing not only the pharmaceutical company but also its president, its medical director, and its outside counsel—me." Boxer argued that he was the lawyer most knowledgeable about the legal and factual intricacies of this litigation. "Lee is trying to get an advantage by naming his adversary as a defendant and witness and trying to disqualify me."

Lee rose and replied, "Boxer is an advisor to Jonas and is involved in telling Jonas when to apply for labeling changes and what language to use in those changes. I believe there will be evidence that the actual damages caused by Nobo extract are greater than reported to the FDA, and further, I believe that Boxer helped Jonas delay labeling changes because the changes would reduce Nobo sales. I think Boxer helped Jonas convince the FDA that Nobo extract is safer than it really is."

Tate stated in rebuttal, "I did not represent Jonas before the FDA. I do not belong to the FDA Bar. Before there could be discovery against me, Lee should be obliged to reveal the foundation for his including me as a defendant. Lee should disclose the names of all witnesses and documents Lee consulted about making his decision to add me as a defendant."

Involuntarily, Tate glanced at Thompson, who was sitting in the courtroom as an observer. In the back of his mind, Tate realized that Tommy Thompson could greatly benefit from Tate being disqualified from representing the other defendants. But he hoped he was wrong about Tommy.

Judge Frank announced that because of the sanctity of the attorney-client and work-product privileges, he was quashing the depositions of both Lee and Tate. But because plaintiff had not produced any actual evidence of liability on the part of Tate, he was going to grant Tate's *pro hac vice* and allow him to represent both himself and the codefendants in the Cook County proceeding. Furthermore, he was going to allow Tate to seek any nonprivileged evidence supporting plaintiff's allegations against Boxer Tate.

After the hearing, Lee talked to Thompson about the proceedings. Lee was becoming more presumptuous with Thompson. He asked, "Are there any documents I can find through FOIA request that would reveal Tate's name as a signatory or participant in Jonas's meetings with the FDA regarding delaying the placement of warnings on Nobo extract?" Lee was hopeful of finding evidence that Boxer was involved in trying to persuade the FDA not to add brain cancer warnings to the Nobo extract labels.

Thompson suspected that there might be but responded, "Dodge, I don't know, but if I did know, I couldn't tell you."

Lee said bluntly, "Okay, I see. You'll give me enough information to tempt me to sue Boxer and enough information to help you become chief trial counsel for Jonas, but you won't help me get the right public records?"

Tommy was starting to realize he had gotten in bed with the wrong person.

Bill Dawes, Superstar

Bill Dawes joined the Thompson firm after completing a clerkship for Judge Bruce Friendly. Judge Friendly had a national reputation as a brilliant jurist. He was known as a feeder judge in that he passed his best clerks along to clerk at the US Supreme Court.

Judges wanted to become known as feeder judges. It enhanced their ability to attract the very best law students for their clerkships. One of the most likely students to become a clerk on the US Supreme Court was the editor-in-chief of the Yale Law Review. One summer, Thompson hired a Yale second-year as a summer associate. During the summer, the clerk was elected to be the editor-in-chief of the Yale Law Review. Thereafter, the clerk received telephone calls from judges around the country who frequently offered him a clerkship over the phone with no application or interview. The summer clerk was put in the position of either not accepting the phone calls or turning down offers made by the federal judges. These federal judges did not take rejection well. They wanted to become feeder judges, and they knew hiring a Yale editor would enhance their chances.

One of the benefits of clerking for a feeder judge was the possibility that you could be recommended to clerk for one of the Supreme Court Justices. Even if you were not hired by the Supreme Court, you became in great demand at the best law firms around the country. Those Bruce Friendly clerks who went on to clerk at the Supreme Court usually then went on to become academics, jurists, or government lawyers at the justice department or at the solicitor general's office. The rest were hired by the biggest and best law firms in the country.

Dawes did not make it to the Supreme Court, but he had multiple job offers around the country. He accepted the Thompson offer not because it was the biggest or best firm but because it had the potential to reach those heights, and Dawes could be in on the ground floor.

Dawes had been exposed to the best minds in school and in the courtroom. He had seen Thompson argue appeals before Judge Friendly, and Thompson was brilliant. Tommy was one of those advocates who was more of a teacher than a lecturer. Most lawyers had a set script. They merely recited their notes. Many judges asked the lawyers questions to help them decide the issues raised by the case. Many lawyers hated questions, because they then had to deviate from their speeches. The good ones invited questions that allowed them to propose answers that allowed the judges to write outstanding opinions. Thompson talked without notes and encouraged inquiries. He could recite precedents with no briefs or copies of statutes or cases in front of him.

As a clerk, Dawes read Thompson's briefs, and they allowed the clerks and judges to quickly become experts in whatever field was the subject of his arguments. Thompson was equally facile in torts, contracts, intellectual property, or constitutional law.

One of the things Dawes liked best about Thompson was his respect for the clerks and courtroom attachés. During argument, Thompson included the clerks as part of his audience, looking in their direction on occasion. When responding to questions from the court, he referred to the justices by last name. He repeated the questions in a fashion that showed respect and understanding, treating each question as if it was brilliant.

The Thompson firm paid first-year lawyers New York going-rate salaries. Generally, all first-years in the firm made the same salary, as did second-years. Some firms paid bonuses based on excess billable hours, usually in excess of 1,900 hours per year. Traditionally, clerks with one year clerkship experience were brought in and paid as if they were second-years. A Supreme Court clerk would be frequently paid as much as a fourth-year with a bonus.

At the end of the clerkship, Dawes sent a résumé to Thompson. Thompson received a number of résumés from judicial clerks, but the Dawes résumé stood out. Friendly was a great jurist and teacher, but more importantly, Thompson had a number of cases pending before Friendly. While Friendly had too much character to tilt the ruling toward a past clerk, Dawes could give Thompson insights into what arguments Friendly would find most persuasive.

Dawes accepted the Thompson offer and quickly became a favorite of the chair. Not only did Dawes write persuasive briefs on the Friendly cases, but Dawes adopted the approach of reading opinions written by the judges he was appearing before in order to capture the tone and tenor that the judge would find most acceptable. The Thompson partners and clients wanted Dawes on their cases. Dawes made partners look good while helping them analyze the pros and cons of their strategies. Dawes acted like a partner years before he made partner. He became an equity partner several years early because he became such a successful rainmaker. He brought in high-priced business that other partners and associates could work on. He was a profit center for the whole firm. The bottom line was better for all because of his success. His partners did not begrudge him his seven-figure income, because they too profited. Dawes's favorite legal challenges were class actions and mass torts. He was good at delegating and organizing teams of lawyers and paralegals. The leverage was good. That is, one partner could direct as many as twelve associates, unlike some more esoteric work that took two partners and one associate to handle.

The one problem with Dawes was his financial attractiveness in the open market. Other law firms wanted a Dawes. By hiring one Dawes, a firm could create work for twelve or more lawyers.

For Thompson, if Dawes left and took twelve lawyers and four paralegals, Thompson lost sixteen billers but still had to pay the rent on sixteen offices. Even worse, if Dawes left and took no billers, Thompson was left with fourteen bodies to pay but no cases from which to cover both the salary and the office rent.

Thompson and Dawes had worked well together from the start. Each admired the other's abilities. Dawes made Thompson more profitable, because Thompson didn't need to edit or change Dawes's briefs. He could sign them and file them. The client assumed most of the work came from the mind and pen of Thompson. As happens over the careers of successful junior and senior collaborating attorneys, each began to think the other was taking too much credit and too much money. Ultimately, the junior does not want to be seen as working for the senior. The senior thinks the junior has forgotten who taught him and who made him the lawyer he is today. The senior becomes the mentor for new juniors, but the junior too creates a band of brothers with whom he now achieves and celebrates new victories for new clients. So it was with Tommy Thompson and Bill Dawes. In the Jonas litigation, Tommy was overshadowed by the contributions of Dawes and Boxer supported by associate Karen Klein.

Dawes had thought about leaving Tommy and starting his own firm. He knew he would lose money in the short run, but he would be out of the shadows of the domineering and dominating Tommy Thompson. Like Thompson, Boxer also had his weaknesses. He was young and somewhat immature. He did not have the reputation of Thompson. He did not have a large book of business, and he did not have the legal pedigree of Thompson or Dawes himself. Boxer had great strengths, however. Boxer was a fearless, ferocious advocate. He craved victory. He was collaborative and wanted to build a powerful firm. He recognized he had to share success to create success. Dawes liked brainstorming with Tate. He liked the way Tate brought others into the creative process. Tate even included the clients in the strategy sessions.

But if Dawes was going to make a move, he wanted it to be the last one. He wasn't going to leave one Thompson type for another. He wanted meaningful coownership of any new enterprise.

45

Dawes Fired
by Tommy

Thompson's strategy of getting Boxer out of the litigation by naming
him as a codefendant, thereby creating a conflict, had not worked. Judge
Homer Frank had allowed Boxer to remain as the defense lawyer in the
Cook Country case.

Tommy was also well aware that Boxer's creativity had closed down
statewide Nobo cases in California and West Virginia.

Tommy had hinted strongly to Dodge Lee that if Boxer was out of
the litigation, Tommy would work toward settling the cases. Lee got the
signal. He called Tommy and said, "I assume that when you received the
Cook County complaints naming Boxer as a defendant, you forwarded
them to the state bar. Have you?"

"No."

"Why not?"

Tommy said, "I can't tell you."

"Why not?"

"It's privileged."

Lee said, "You can't hide privileged information that would permit
a person to violate the law. Furthermore, while the Cook County judge
stopped us from deposing Boxer in the Cook County case, if we file a
California State Bar complaint against Boxer, the California Bar can
depose Boxer and make it hard for him to both defend Jonas and himself

at the same time." Finally, Lee said, "I assume that the reason you can't notify the state bar is because your clients have said they would fire you if you did. Further, the clients wouldn't want discovery against Boxer, because that probably would get into communications he had with the FDA about the timing and content of the warnings on the Nobo extract labeling." Lee went on, "Since much of the communication with the FDA is obtainable through FOIA, why can't you just give it to me?"

Tommy replied, "No comment."

Lee paused and then said, "I am agreeable to filing a complaint with the California State Bar against Boxer, but you have to give me grounds. All we need is enough to provoke the state bar into opening an investigation of Boxer's efforts to hide information about the dangers of Nobo extract."

"I'll get back to you," said Thompson.

Thompson thought, *How can I put Lee on the right track without getting myself in trouble?* He considered calling Boxer and asking him about communications with the FDA but knew that Boxer probably wouldn't talk to him. Then he decided to talk to Bill Dawes.

He told his secretary to have Dawes come to his office. When Dawes arrived, Tommy asked, "Did Boxer represent Jonas before the FDA?"

Dawes knew that the answer was yes, but he was becoming suspicious. "Why do you ask?" he said.

Tommy said, "Because I think we have an ethical obligation to report any fraud on the FDA perpetrated by Boxer or Jonas."

Dawes said, "Report to whom? Dodge Lee?"

Tommy was taken aback. In fact, he was ashen. He said to Dawes, "Bill, your comments are insulting and insolent. How could you suggest such a thing?"

Dawes asked, "Why was Lee in your office the other day?"

Tommy replied, "None of your business."

Dawes next said, "Did you tell Boxer or any of our clients about your meeting with Lee?"

Tommy was not used to his juniors cross-examining him. He was furious but scared. He finally said, "In fact, we were talking about possible fraud on the FDA by Boxer."

Dawes said, "That is preposterous—to discuss possible fraud by your cocounsel with an adversary. It is becoming obvious that you are trying to get Boxer knocked off the case because you want all of the business."

Tommy said, "You're fired!"

Dawes said, "The partnership agreement does not give you the power to fire me without due cause and without an affirmative vote of 50 percent of the partnership." Dawes was tempted to say, "I quit," but he was worried that if he quit on the spot Tommy would have security escort him from the building, and Dawes wanted to maintain access to his Jonas files.

Dawes went directly to his own office and called Boxer. Boxer said, "Don't quit. Tommy will probably call a partnership meeting and try to get the votes to fire you immediately. You should get notice of the meeting and attend and give your side of the story. Tommy will probably have enough votes to fire you, but you should argue that you are being wrongfully discharged because you are objecting to Tommy's malfeasance in the defense of Jonas." Boxer added, "Also, if you have time, start boxing up your personal files and we will send a service to pick them up. Finally, try to inventory all of the Jonas files, and I will recommend the Jonas defendants fire Tommy and direct the files be sent to me."

No sooner had Dawes hung up the phone than he received an e-mail from Thompson giving notice of a partners' meeting in the large conference room at 3:00 p.m. The subject of the meeting was the removal of Bill Dawes from the partnership forthwith.

Within the hour, Dawes received a copy of an e-mail from Jonas, Atlas, and Tate to the Thompson firm firing Thompson and removing him from the Nobo extract cases and further giving notice that Boxer Tate would have movers over to retrieve the files the next day.

In a separate private, confidential e-mail, Boxer invited Bill Dawes to join him and Audi Johns for dinner in one of the private booths at Sam's Grill that evening.

46

Dawes Fights Back

Tommy Thompson presided over the partnership meeting. Fifteen of the sixteen partners were present. It soon became apparent that before the meeting Tommy had met privately with each of the partners except Dawes. No one smiled. No one looked at Dawes or acknowledged him.

Tommy announced that he had called the meeting to obtain the necessary 50 percent vote to confirm the removal of Bill Dawes from the partnership. Summarily, Tommy said, "Do I have a motion?"

Before anyone could speak, Dawes rose to his feet and looked individually at each partner. They still did not return his gaze. Quietly, he stated, "If there is cause for my dismissal, no one should fear spending a few minutes hearing my side of the story." He paused again. There was no comment. He continued, "I am the highest billing partner in the firm. I have twelve associates working for me. I have been dedicated to the firm for nine years. Today I learned that Tommy Thompson has been working with our adversary's attorney, Dodge Lee, to try to have our cocounsel, Boxer Tate, removed from a series of cases against our client Jonas. I believe that Tommy encouraged the naming of Tate as a codefendant with our client Jonas to create a conflict that would require the removal of Tate from the litigation.

"I have notified Tate of these matters, and he has removed the Thompson firm from the files immediately. I believe that when all of the facts come to light it will be a huge embarrassment for the firm. It will put us at risk for a very large legal malpractice suit and might even put us at risk for an inquiry from the state bar."

The room was still silent, but the downcast eyes were now focused on Dawes.

One of the partners asked, "How do you know Tommy met with Lee?"

"I saw Lee come out of Tommy's office."

"How do you know what they talked about?"

"Because I asked Tommy, and he said he was talking about possible fraud on the FDA by Boxer Tate. Tommy said he had responsibility to notify the bar association of a possible ethics violation on the part of Boxer."

One of the younger partners commented, "Should we get an outside opinion before we report Boxer?"

Another partner said, "I heard from our own Karen Klein that our client said they would fire us if we reported Boxer to the bar association."

Dawes said, "I am circulating copies of an e-mail firing the Thompson firm. We had budgeted legal fees of ten million dollars a year on Nobo cases for the next three years. The publicity in defending such large cases would have been terrific."

Finally, Tommy spoke. "I am the chairman and senior partner of this firm. I say Dawes should go. He has accused me of malpractice in front of the clients, and he has teamed with Boxer to help Boxer become the lead on the cases. He is not a team player and was using these cases to promote himself over others."

One of the more senior partners cleverly asked Dawes, "If we do not fire you, will you resign?"

Dawes said, "I won't quit, and if you fire me I will sue the firm for wrongful discharge. If you fire me, it will only be because I called out our senior partner for violating the firm's duty of utmost loyalty to its clients."

Tommy shouted, "Call the question. Should Dawes be fired? Say aye if yes, nay if no."

The first three partners abstained. The next two said nay, and the next two also abstained. The next said aye, but when the ninth partner abstained, it was now mathematically impossible to get the eight votes required to carry the motion.

Thompson was humiliated, but rather than accept defeat, he volunteered, "There are only two nays. I say let's retain an outside independent ethics counsel and meet again after his report."

Tate, Dawes, and Johns

It was Ketel One on the rocks with olives all around that night at Sam's Grill. Boxer, Audi, and Dawes huddled around a table in one of the small private rooms in the back of Sam's.

Boxer and Audi wanted details of Dawes's day. They were amazed at Tommy's clear violation of his duty of loyalty by meeting with Dodge Lee and in essence discussing defense strategy with the enemy. Thompson was now fired from the case. But the trio was looking for ways to also get Lee off the case. They could think of none at the time.

Boxer said, "Let's get to the real reason we're here. I think we should start a new law firm."

Audi and Dawes said, "Here, here."

Dawes said, "I have come to the conclusion I cannot work at Thompson. Tommy has not done a good job defending Jonas to date, and his ethics are a serious issue."

Dawes decided to be candid about the pros and cons. Neither Boxer nor Audi had world-class resumes. Dawes did. Boxer and Audi insisted that they too wanted it to be their firm. Boxer said, "Dawes, while you are an equity partner at Thompson, in reality everyone at Thompson worked for Tommy."

Dawes said, "I want to be an owner in the new firm." Dawes agreed that the new firm needed an infusion of excellent young lawyers and agreed that Audi was the person to make it happen. Dawes also agreed that Audi could be the managing/hiring partner. He agreed it would be best if he and Boxer stuck to the practice of law.

Boxer was willing to yield on his demand for complete control. He proposed that the firm name be Tate, Dawes, and Johns, and that he, Boxer, would carry the title of chair. All agreed.

Tate described a phone conference he had had that afternoon with the Jonas clients. All supported the new firm. All wanted their cases to be taken from Thompson, and all were pleased that Dawes was joining the firm. They hoped that Karen Klein would join, and Dawes expected she would come.

Cook County, Judicial Hellhole

The plaintiff's attorney commences a lawsuit by filing a complaint in the forum of his choice. But if he selects an improper venue, the defense can move to dismiss or move to a proper forum. If the defense picks an improper venue, the process continues.

Forum shopping is one of the most important ways of winning lawsuits. In general, state courts are better than federal courts for plaintiffs seeking damages. In general, city judges and jurors are more liberal than country judges and jurors.

Also, the laws are different in different jurisdictions. Some jurisdictions recognize the preemption defense. Others do not. Cook County does not.

State court in Cook County, which includes the City of Chicago, is very liberal. Judges tend to mirror the philosophy of their electorate.

Cook County ranks up there with West Virginia as a judicial hellhole. That's why Lee filed his next Nobo lawsuits in Cook County.

While Boxer did not like Cook County, he was pleased with the assignment to Judge Homer Frank. He was disappointed that Frank did not allow him to depose Dodge Lee but thought Judge Frank understood the arguments and carefully considered the issues. His ruling quashing both motions to take depositions of the lawyers was reasonable. Boxer knew he could have done worse. And he did.

Judge Frank was reassigned to the criminal docket, and the presiding judge assigned the Nobo cases to Judge Charlotte Higgins. Boxer checked with Fortune Jones and was put in contact with an Atlas Chicago attorney, Francis O'Neil. Boxer was told that Higgins had been a plaintiffs' attorney before she took the bench. She still socialized with plaintiffs' attorneys and frequently spoke at their professional meetings. In front of jurors, she would comment on the credibility of witnesses. She always attacked the testimony of defense witnesses and praised the testimony of plaintiffs' witnesses. She freely exercised her role as gatekeeper of the evidence and many times allowed admissibility of junk science when presented by plaintiffs' experts but struck reliable science presented by defendants. Jurors in her courtroom had returned verdicts in excess of $100 million in serious, single-plaintiff brain-damage cases.

Judge Higgins set her first case management conference in the Nobo case for ten days hence.

Boxer immediately scheduled another war council, which included Atlas Chicago counsel. Boxer said, "What should we do about Judge Higgins?"

Plaintiffs' Judge Charlotte Higgins

In the next war council, Dawes reported on the Higgins public records search. He said, "Our local counsel, Francis O'Neil, had a case in front of her. He said she is terrible. This looks like a replay of state court in West Virginia."

Higgins had been a plaintiffs' personal-injury lawyer before she took the bench. She brought many cases against insurance companies and their insurance holders. She always overevaluated her cases and was thus forced to try them. For her, it was like Russian roulette. In reported decisions, she had lost fifteen cases but had obtained million-dollar-plus verdicts in three cases. She was active in the plaintiff bar association and had testified before the state legislature in favor of liberalizing tort law. She was in favor of reducing plaintiffs' burden of proof in punitive damage cases. The judiciary committee, which was dominated by liberals, had encouraged her activities and ultimately recommended to the governor that she be appointed to the bench. In her years as a judge, she had presided over twenty-one personal-injury jury trials. The plaintiff had won every trial, many times for enormous sums of money. She never reduced a large verdict. But sometimes she would put additions on plaintiffs' small verdicts so they would get more money. She never granted a defense motion to exclude junk science. She never granted a defense motion for summary judgment. She rarely denied plaintiffs' proposed jury instructions, and she frequently denied defense-proposed jury instructions.

Atlas found transcripts of eight speeches she had given to plaintiff bar association groups in which she attacked the integrity of defense lawyers and insurance companies.

Of the twenty-one plaintiffs' verdicts returned in her courtroom, the court of appeal had reversed eight of them and entered judgment for the defendant. They had granted new trials in six other cases. Several appellate decisions had explicitly criticized the legal reasons she employed in trying to support her plaintiff-oriented rulings.

It was becoming clear to Boxer that just one or two bad judges could create a judicial hell hole.

In the next two days, Dodge Lee filed fifteen new individual Nobo cases and also asked the court to strike the preemption defense and asked that all of the cases be consolidated for discovery and trial. The presiding judge assigned all of their new cases to Judge Higgins.

The team decided there was no way Jonas could win in her courtroom, and thus all agreed that all grounds for appeal should be preserved.

Boxer said, "I have asked Dawes to look at the possibility of disqualifying Judge Higgins. Bill, what have you found?"

Bill said, "In Illinois state court, a judge can be recused for bias. The problem is that it is the judge who is being accused of bias who hears the arguments and rules on the bias motion. The odds of winning such a motion are remote, because it is a rare judge who will concede bias. Some judges are intimidated by a recusal motion and try to bend over backwards to demonstrate impartiality. Other judges are angered by a recusal motion, and they take their anger out on the attorney and party making the motion." It was decided that Atlas, working with Dawes, would do a public records search on Judge Higgins.

Boxer to Jail Again

CMC stands for case management conference. At the outset of a case and periodically thereafter, judges have CMCs. Many judges permit the lawyers to attend via telephone, but if there are important items on the agenda, smart lawyers feel they can communicate more effectively in person. Judges frequently forecast their inclinations with their body language, which can't be seen over the telephone.

Both Lee and Tate appeared in person, and Tate asked that the conference be transcribed stenographically.

Tate was surprised when Higgins mounted the bench. She looked to weigh three hundred pounds and had difficulty walking. It took her almost a minute to ascend the three steps to her chair. Her first order of business was to demand to be told why Tate was having the proceedings transcribed. Tate said simply, "Because I want a complete record for the court of appeal."

Judge Higgins said, "I have read your papers and your motion to recuse me, and I am prepared to rule."

Tate said, "I have some things to add to the record."

Higgins said, "What?"

"I have marked as exhibit next in order transcripts of your testimony before the state legislature and would like them admitted into evidence."

"The time for filing more exhibits has passed, and the request is denied," said Higgins. "Further, I will not permit these papers to be marked as exhibits. They are hearsay and not authenticated."

Tate argued, "I still need them marked so they can be part of the record on appeal. And further, I demand that all proceedings be videotaped so I can show your demeanor to the appellate court."

Judge Higgins snapped, "Mr. Tate, please sit down—now!"

"I haven't finished, Judge," Tate responded. "I also have marked transcripts of comments you have made on the record about the integrity of defense counsel for insurance companies."

Higgins said, "Denied. Mr. Tate, your reputation precedes you. I am aware that you don't defend cases on the merits but rather engage in character assassination. You try to intimidate judges into ruling your way. You use private investigators to unearth embarrassing private incidents. You do anything to keep your cases from going to a jury. Your major goal is to keep your cases from being heard on the merits. Your motion to recuse is denied."

"Your Honor," said Tate, "I have more evidence of bias to offer."

"Denied," said Higgins. She continued, "I am also recommending to plaintiffs' counsel that he seek certification of a medical monitoring class. That is, I am proposing that everyone exposed to Nobo extract at Atlas's and Jonas's expense should be monitored monthly by a medical doctor to see if they are suffering any signs and symptoms of brain damage. If they are, they will be entitled to treatment at the expense of Atlas and Jonas. If their symptoms develop into actual cancer, they will be entitled to file their own personal-injury lawsuits."

Tate replied, "Judge, you have no authority to propose or order medical monitoring at this stage. You are acting as if you are a plaintiffs' attorney. You are not supposed to be an advocate but rather an umpire calling balls and strikes."

Higgins said, "Mr. Tate, stop shouting. I don't like your tone of voice, and I don't like this outburst. One more time and you will be sanctioned."

Tate said, "Judge, I would like a short recess to set up a videotape."

To no one's surprise, Judge Higgins said, "I warned you, Mr. Tate. I'm now holding you in contempt. The record will reflect that Mr. Tate has used an insulting tone and has not only disrespected me but the judicial office I hold. Bailiff, handcuff Mr. Tate and take him away and hold him in the city jail until Mr. Tate prepares a written apology withdrawing his recusal motion."

After Tate was gone, Judge Higgins announced that the preemption defense was stricken in all pleadings. She then ordered that the record was to be sealed. Lee said nothing during the proceeding. He was worried that Judge Higgins had committed reversible error that would put any favorable result in jeopardy of reversal on appeal. Thus Lee could invest huge amounts of time and money and even obtain a successful trial verdict only to have it taken away by the court of appeal due to reversible errors. He was starting to worry about his hellhole strategy.

With his one phone call, Boxer called Dawes. He told Dawes that he wanted to file an emergency writ to the Illinois Court of Appeal seeking release from his jail sentence and granting recusal of Judge Higgins. He had Dawes's secretary get on the line, and he dictated an affidavit to her setting forth the proceedings before Judge Higgins in detail. Boxer had been worried that his written motion to recuse was not strong enough to win on appeal. Boxer believed that his odds of having the court of appeal consider the Jonas writ had gone up because of Judge Higgins's misconduct at the hearing and because he was in jail. Boxer gave Dawes authority to sign the affidavits and encouraged Dawes to see if the team could find any other recusal motions against Higgins filed by other defense counsel. He would add those to the papers.

51

Dawes's Departure

Dawes worked all night and electronically filed the emergency writ with the Illinois Court of Appeal at 2:30 a.m. A copy went to Dodge Lee. The writ clerk was not at the courthouse until 8:30 a.m., at which time Dawes called the clerk immediately to explain the situation. The writ clerk said he would take the papers to the presiding judge at the court of appeal, who would decide whether the petition was worthy of review by the other appellate judges.

In the meantime, Dawes had to attend a Thompson partners meeting at 9:30 a.m. The purpose was to hear the report from the outside consultant and vote whether or not to expel Dawes from the partnership. Dawes had been interviewed by the consultant but had received no feedback. Further, Dawes had not lobbied his position but assumed Tommy had.

Dawes's reception before his partners was again chilly. Dawes looked at the faces of his partners, but none looked back. He found a seat between two of his friends, and Dawes felt they moved away. Thompson said confidently, "Now that Dawes is here, we can get started." He called the partnership meeting to order. He asked for a report from the consultant.

It became apparent that the consultant was going to cut the baby in half. The consultant said there was nothing wrong with a lawyer meeting with the lawyer for the other side and candidly discussing the strengths and weaknesses of their cases. "A lawyer wears two hats—one the adversary hat and the other the consultant hat," said the consultant. "Most cases are settled and most settlements involve compromise. A lot of what is said is hypothetical—e.g., 'if you do this, I will do that.' Thus, while Thompson was acting unilaterally, on balance at least he believed he was acting in the best interest of the client."

The consultant said most firms had intramural sparring over whose clients were whose, and there was politicking and maneuvering to try to capture the good graces of a client. Since Thompson had been appointed ethics counsel for the Nobo defendants, his comments and analyses were within the bounds of his authority. Finally, the consultant did not consider the handling of the Al Purcell deposition or the handling of the preemption issues malpractice. Indeed, many qualified lawyers would have done the same thing.

The consultant was excused with no questions. Tommy asked if there were any questions or comments. Dawes considered resigning on the spot. He did not like the idea of being fired, but being fired relieved him of any restrictions of the noncompete clauses in the partnership agreement. If he was fired, he could immediately start a new competing firm. He could even solicit Thompson lawyers and employees to come to the new firm. He also had a wrongful discharge suit as an option, although he was disinclined to get into any personal litigation.

Dawes announced, "I will make it easy for you. I will waive my right to sue for wrongful discharge if you will waive the noncompete clause in the partnership agreement and if you will give me my share of the financial value of the work in progress and accounts receivable to date. Both sides will agree in writing to not disparage the other side. I won't solicit your lawyers, but they are free to come practice with me if they so choose."

Tommy said, "Bill, you and Tate have already made a deal, haven't you?"

Dawes said, "When you said I was fired and asked the firm for a confirming vote, I had no choice but to talk to Tate. I was constructively discharged at that time."

Tommy continued, "I don't like your proposal, Dawes, and I vote to confirm your firing."

One of the more senior equity partners rose and said, "Well, I don't care what the consultant said, Tommy, I think your handling of Boxer and the Jonas business is well below the standards of any firm I want to work in. I never thought you would want to drag your firm name so low. If we fire Dawes, we are begging for litigation and a public hearing of our disreputable conduct." Several other partners agreed.

Dawes said, "Can I have a vote in response to my proposal?"

Tommy said, "I have a counterproposal." Dawes, for the first time, noticed how haggard Tommy looked. His facial creases were deeper. His eyes were hollow, and his complexion was sallow. Dawes could not tell if he was hungover, but he appeared on the verge of collapse. He said in a cracking voice, "All of those who are in favor of Dawes's proposal, leave the firm. The rest stay with me. Those who vote to leave will have to remain responsible for their share of the lease—meaning the new firm would have to share the office space for some period."

Dawes said, "Okay, if that means we get our work in progress and receivables."

Tommy agreed.

Bill Dawes said, "I like the idea. You should know the Jonas litigation in Cook County is exploding."

Tommy continued, "All those who want to leave, raise your hands."

Eight of the sixteen raised their hands. One of them said, "My vote is tentative; it depends on whether we can work out a satisfactory partnership agreement with Dawes and Tate." All agreed.

More Investigation

Boxer learned that he was not the first lawyer Judge Higgins had sentenced to jail for contempt. The jailers had housed other attorneys compliments of Judge Higgins. Boxer was given a blanket and pillow but no bed. The beds were all taken.

In the morning, Boxer was told by the jailer that the court of appeal had not ruled. Atlas Chicago counsel had entered an appearance and would probably be the first to receive any ruling. Within an hour, the court of appeal entered a cryptic order.

The emergency writ was granted in part. Boxer Tate was released from jail.

The court of appeal then ordered Judge Higgins to conduct a further evidentiary hearing on the motion to recuse. The court stated that the record was incomplete, and Judge Higgins was instructed to admit the evidence submitted and attach the now-admitted evidence to the record so the court of appeal could evaluate the validity of the rulings with a complete record. The court of appeals entered a stay of all other rulings made by Judge Higgins pending the new recusal decision. The court emphasized the need for a complete record, and it invited Dodge Lee to submit any evidence or arguments he deemed relevant.

Boxer borrowed some space from Atlas Chicago offices. He called together what he now called his war counsel. He had Dawes explain the status.

Dawes said, "The court of appeal has given Judge Higgins another opportunity to recuse herself. If she recuses herself before the new recusal hearing, the evidence of bias will not be filed, and Higgins will be spared the public airing of her bias. If she denies recusal, the court of appeal has the option of accepting the recusal matter for review or denying review, which will have the same impact as affirming Judge Higgins's denial of recusal. If she denies recusal, Judge Higgins is in the awkward situation of allowing us to create a complete public record of her biased career. If she denies recusal, she could hire an attorney to represent her before the court of appeal, but that, in and of itself, would make her look biased."

Dawes continued, "Most trial judges file nothing and rightly assume that the court of appeal will work hard to not find bias. A finding of bias undermines public confidence in the judicial system, to say nothing of what it says about the integrity and impartiality of the judge in question."

Boxer stated the obvious: "We have been given an opportunity to be even more aggressive in attacking Judge Higgins. We should hire a private investigation firm and dig deeper, and we should prepare and file a more thoroughly briefed recusal motion attaching exhibits to the brief. We want to get before the trial court and the court of appeal as much actual evidence of bias as possible. I suspect Higgins is reeling now, but she will recover soon and probably set a new CMC. She won't want us to have much time to improve the record."

Boxer said, "Bill, I will stay in Chicago so I can attend any hearings Judge Higgins sets on order, shortening time. I also want to direct the investigation."

Dawes volunteered, "I will organize the briefing from here, but we should have another phone call with Audi to talk about my meeting at the Thompson firm. Can we reconvene after this call?"

Tate Takes Over

Bill Dawes reported on the Thompson meeting. Dawes said, "If there is one thing Tommy did well, it was hire excellent people. I think this presents us with an opportunity."

Boxer thought and then said, "I agree. Ideas on how we should proceed?"

Bill said, "I think first thing is that Boxer, you should meet with the eight who are seriously considering leaving and tell them we want them. Some of these are very strong people and may resist you as chair and will want to know their roles in a new firm."

Audi said, "I know what young lawyers want. We will have to assure them that risks are low and rewards are high. Tell them we are building a nationwide, bet-your-company defense firm. They have an opportunity to be owners and to get in on the ground floor. They will be involved in future planning, goal-setting, rainmaking, and growth. Governance will be transparent, but great lawyering and rainmaking will be more highly rewarded than administration or committee work. The firm will be run for the lawyers. They will have great associates and great support. The new partners will be involved in writing the new partnership agreement."

Dawes and Tate responded simultaneously, "Great."

Tate said, "It sounds like a good mission statement. We have to move fast. I would like to talk to the eight today. Will they be offended that it will be by videoconference?"

Audi said, "No. They'll be impressed that you are working on a case in Chicago and further impressed that you are taking time out to address them. You should tell them a few words about the magnitude of the matter you are working on; that will impress them too. Also, I think you should tell them that Bill and I will be arranging private meetings to discuss their individual issues. Also tell them that the word will leak quickly and they should try to get to their associates before the rumor mill does. Tell them there is a nondisparagement agreement in place and neither they nor their associates should dishonor it."

Boxer said, "I got it."

Audi continued, "I will start working on banking and insurance issues. We also have to make public-relations arrangements to properly publicize the new firm. I will also start collecting partnership agreements used by other firms in hope of drafting what works best for us. I already have a few such agreements gathered from when I was representing candidates for lateral partnership."

Boxer said, "Also, we have to worry about office space. We have committed to both Thompson and Malloy to take care of the rental on our share of those spaces. I hate to have offices all over town."

Audi said, "I am already looking into subleasing the space and trying to find an office that will consolidate our firm into one place. I think if things work out we might be able to make a profit on the subleases and get the consolidated space at a favorable rate. Although I think you, Boxer, should talk to Fortune Jones at Atlas about using its office space around the country. That might help us to get business in other cities from not only Atlas but other San Francisco companies who are sued around the country."

That afternoon Tate talked to the eight. He briefly described the Jonas litigation and said, "The future of litigation is nationwide mass torts and class actions. In order to be eligible for that work, you need offices and lawyers around the country. You also need great trial lawyers—that's where you come in."

One of the eight interrupted and said, "I went to Georgetown and passed the DC bar. I'd love to go back."

Another said, "I grew up in Chicago and have a lot of connections there."

Ideas kept coming, and the brainstorming became more productive. There was an air of excitement that one said they had never had at Thompson. Dawes and Audi got caught up in the moment and made their own pitches. The lawyers started volunteering for projects. One represented a PR firm that he thought would be great for the new firm. Others started promoting cross-marketing strategies. They all said they could not wait to talk to their associates. Several made suggestions to Audi about new space. Others proposed lawyers and practice groups that they could steal from other firms.

Audi got volunteers to help her with her projects. Boxer was exhausted from his night in jail and was still in the same suit but was thrilled with the response of the eight. He was pleased that he had identified Dawes and Audi as his core team. In many respects, they had more brain power and experience than he did. At one point he had told them it was their job to make him look good, and they were doing it.

Before he ended his day, Boxer called Fortune Jones and brought her up to speed. He especially wanted to talk to her about his desire to use Atlas offices around the country. She said, "Let's talk in person. I'll fly to Chicago and we can have dinner tomorrow night." Boxer agreed. He had not seen Fortune in a while and was looking forward to it. He thought he detected, for the first time, that she might be looking forward to it too.

Fortune and Boxer

Boxer reserved a private room at Mike Ditka's restaurant in Chicago. He ordered an Opus One cabernet sauvignon and was halfway through his first glass when Fortune arrived. She wore a form-fitting, pencil-thin deep purple business suit. She was striking, and she greeted Boxer warmly. Fortune said, "You should really try to stay out of jail. It ages you."

Boxer replied, "For some reason my jail time only makes you look better."

Fortune flirted back, "Well, that's because you haven't seen or talked to a woman in a while."

They continued to hold hands, and Fortune nuzzled Boxer again and said, "You want a merger—is that it?"

Boxer replied, "I want a business deal that I think will bring us closer together."

Boxer took a seat on the booth side of the table, and Fortune slid in next to him.

Fortune said, "Sounds exciting. What do you have in mind?"

Boxer answered, "Because of you, I am on my way to building a firm that will specialize in defending class actions and mass torts nationwide. You insure a number of major corporations who will be hit with these cases. I think I can build a firm that will provide excellent results at reasonable prices. One of the strategies will be to keep overhead low. I don't need offices and lawyers in every city in the country—but periodically I will need competent local counsel in out-of-the-way places. Atlas panel counsel can fill this role at prices lower than the silk-stocking big-city lawyers. Depending on the case, I will use expert, experienced national counsel who can fly in for big court appearances, depositions, and trials while the lower-price local counsel help keep us from getting hometowned by local judges. Since we will only try a few of these cases a year, we don't need to have local counsel to be trial ready. We will have five or ten person trial teams who will work with our experts and be fully educated in the science and the law. To build this powerhouse, I will need Atlas committed to the Tate law firm as your first choice to defend these cases."

Fortune said, "What do I get out of this?"

"Better service at lower prices. Companies will know that Atlas-Tate will provide a great defense. Excess carriers will be willing to sign on knowing that Atlas, as the primary carrier, together with Tate law, provides the lowest risk of the excess coverage being invaded."

Fortune said, "Several things I think I should get. One, if there are multiple cocarriers insuring the defendants in a case, I want first right of refusal to hire you and your firm. Two, periodically you should provide us with updates on the relative law and science, which I can circulate to the appropriate counsel and excess carriers. Finally, while I know you can't try all of the cases, I want you and me to decide which cases you will try, and in return you can use all Atlas offices and personnel around the country. We will charge you the lowest rates, and you can include that charge as an expense on your bills to me. That way I can accurately measure your structure to determine if we are really saving money. I want you to be rich and happy and be mine."

Boxer did not know if Fortune meant romantically or in a business capacity but decided not to clear up the ambiguity as Fortune leaned in, clinking glasses and saying, "A toast—to us."

Boxer said, "Hear, hear," and poured more cab.

Even More on Higgins

At the direction of Boxer, the investigator interviewed defense lawyers who had represented corporations before Higgins. Many lawyers agreed to talk off the record. They all hated Higgins but also feared her. They were thrilled that Boxer had the guts to take her on. They were willing to share trial transcripts, which were public records anyway, but all pointed out that Higgins did most of her damage off the record. She was the mistress of intimidation, and the investigator found three other defense lawyers who had been held in contempt and jailed for opposing her rulings and reasoning.

The investigator said, "There are rumors that Judge Higgins received extravagant gifts from plaintiffs' lawyers who appeared before her. Reportedly, a group of plaintiffs' lawyers paid for her to go on a week-long cruise on which she gave a half-hour CLE speech. At the time, two of the plaintiffs' lawyers had cases pending before her."

Boxer subpoenaed the records of the plaintiffs' lawyers in question. Copies of the subpoenas were filed with the court; Boxer hoped that Judge Higgins would become aware of the investigation and fear the outcome and the publicity she would receive. One way for Higgins to stop the Boxer investigation was to recuse herself. Another judge would be assigned to the case, and the investigation of Higgins would become irrelevant to the Jonas litigation.

Judge Higgins improperly telephoned Dodge Lee and asked him why he had been so silent at the recusal hearing. Lee said, "Your Honor, there was no chance to speak." In reality, Lee did not want to publicly endorse Judge Higgins's actions.

Judge Higgins said, "Well, Boxer is subpoenaing records of plaintiffs' attorneys in Cook County and Chicago, and I want you to move to quash them."

Lee said, "Why aren't the lawyers themselves moving to quash?"

Higgins said, "They are, but I am concerned that they may have destroyed the relevant records, and we don't want that to come out. You're not privy to that information and can support the propriety of my CLE activities and agree they have nothing to do with the recusal motion. Besides, if you support me, it will put you in good stead with the other Cook County judges if you should ever end up in front of them."

Lee was uncomfortable with this ex parte communication. If somehow Boxer found out about the conversation, he would make it public and seek sanctions. Lee's license was much too valuable to put it at risk. Lee wanted to extricate himself from the conversation and said, "Your Honor, I know you don't mean this, but cutting to the chase, you are asking me to represent you in this recusal hearing, and of course I have a conflict, so I can't discuss this with you."

The Cook County plaintiffs' lawyers never resisted these ex parte discussions, but Judge Higgins realized she was putting herself at risk and replied, "You are absolutely right. Thanks for the attorney-client advice, and consider this as if it never happened." She then hung up.

Judge Higgins had a dilemma. If she recused herself based on the papers on file, other defense lawyers would use the same papers to recuse her in future cases. If she did not recuse herself, Boxer would conduct a videotaped hearing in which Higgins could not attempt any intimidation and would have to allow Boxer to create a full and complete record of condemning evidence. Higgins *sua sponte* filed and served a simple notice recusing herself from the case and quashing the subpoenas and further sealing the record. Someone might try to use the record in the future, but the chance was remote. Higgins called the presiding judge and warned him about Boxer. She said, "Boxer is the type of lawyer who will complain about bias of the entire Cook County bench and seek a change of venue to one of the more conservative counties. He will impugn the integrity of the entire Cook County bench and try to damage our reputations nationwide."

The parties received the Higgins recusal, and before they could celebrate, the presiding judge (PJ), Jethro Pugh, assigned the Nobo extract cases to himself and reexamined Tate's *pro hac vice* petition with the thought of denying the petition and prohibiting Boxer from practicing law in Illinois. The presiding judge did not want Boxer seeking recusal of other Cook County judges including himself. The Cook County bench could not withstand a rigorous investigation, and the best way to avoid one at this time would be to deny Boxer even a temporary license to practice law in the State of Illinois.

Judge Pugh scheduled a CMC on two days' notice and included Boxer's *pro hac vice* on the agenda. Fortunately, Boxer had remained in Chicago and decided to appear in person rather than by phone. Lee decided to appear by telephone.

At the hearing, Judge Pugh announced he wanted Boxer to answer, under oath, some questions with regard to his *pro hac vice*. The presiding judge was focused on the large number of Jonas cases that Boxer would be handling in Illinois. He suggested that Boxer would probably be trying more cases in Illinois than a lawyer who passed the Illinois Bar Examination and practiced full-time in the state. Boxer pointed out that he would have experienced Illinois counsel appearing with him and that plaintiffs' attorney Dodge Lee was also national counsel for a number of Illinois individual parties. Ultimately, the PJ wandered off the *pro hac vice* issue and got into calendaring matters. He set dates for depositions, expert discovery, and production of documents. The end result was that Lee and Boxer both remained counsel of record.

Boxer reported that the PJ might be just as biased as Higgins but was much more surreptitious. It was as if the Cook County bench wanted a full and flourishing docket to manage. The legal profession has a saying to describe this phenomenon: "If we build it, they will come." The plaintiffs came and came and were rewarded by the judges and jurors of Cook County.

Victim from Cook County

Mamie McDermott always looked forward to her visits to the Cook County Bridge Center. She was a life master and was playing in the regional championships with her bridge partner of twenty-six years, Florence Duffy. They had come in second in the tournament last year and were the favorites to win this year. Like so many masters, when it came to bridge they had photographic memories. They could remember every card in a hand they played three weeks ago. They knew every rule and every exception to every rule. They knew all of the conventions. Younger players were in awe. They were eighty-three and eighty-one years old, respectively, and while they might stumble over the name of a grandchild, they did not stumble over a finesse or a takeout double. Mamie had played bridge through sore throats and colds and headaches. But on this particular afternoon, Mamie started to feel acute pain in her lower back. Usually, her powers of concentration overcame any aches and pains of aging, but Mamie could not ignore this ache. It slowly grew from dull to acute. Mamie missed a point count on an opening bid, and then she failed to respond to an overcall. By the end of the day, Mamie and Florence were out of the tournament. They adjourned to their hotel room for their evening glass of wine, but Mamie couldn't even take a sip. Florence ordered room service, but Mamie took a pass. Then when she was getting into her pajamas, Mamie briefly fainted. Mamie and

Florence were both getting panicky and decided that Florence should drive Mamie to the hospital, which was only half a mile away.

At the hospital Mamie was directed to an admissions officer who orally took her insurance and biographical and medical history.

Shortly thereafter Mamie was admitted to the hospital without a clear diagnosis. Her pain was exquisite and similar to kidney stones. The attending physician prescribed morphine. Florence called Mamie's son, Danny McDermott, who was a solo street lawyer in Chicago. He was married with three children. He dropped everything and drove to the hospital from his apartment in downtown Chicago.

By the time he arrived, Mamie was heavily sedated. Danny spent the night in Mamie's room asleep in a chair with blankets covering him. In the morning Mamie was slightly better because of the pain killers, but she still was somewhat out of it. Mamie signed the necessary powers of attorney and consent forms allowing Danny to approve the various procedures listed. Mamie would have an ultrasound, x-rays, MRIs, blood tests, and the total battery.

The head of the team was an oncologist, which severely frightened Danny. Of all possible diagnoses, Danny feared cancer most. His father, Mamie's deceased husband, had died after a long fight with prostate cancer. Danny realized his fears were somewhat unrealistic inasmuch as women don't get prostate cancer since they don't have prostates. But just the word *cancer* associated with an eighty-three-year-old woman who had only quit smoking at seventy was scary.

In the early afternoon, Danny was walking the hallway with other guests and nurses. The oncologist, Dr. Oso Lynch, and his intern caught him. They proceeded to a somewhat public consultation, which Danny found awkward. They informed him that it appeared that there was a small growth between his mother's pancreas and stomach. They suspected cancer but wanted to do a biopsy and other tests. They expected to have the results that evening. Danny had questions, but he did not want to ask them in public. The doctor said, "Let's have a more in-depth private conversation after we read the biopsy." Danny agreed and said he would have Florence and his two younger sisters in attendance.

That evening, the quiet, understated oncologist met with Danny and the family in Mamie's semiprivate room. It was awkward, because there was another patient in the room only separated by a sheet-like curtain. The oncologist, with no introduction, coolly announced that Mamie had pancreatic cancer. He explained that the pancreas was a large, compound gland situated near the stomach that secreted digestive enzymes into the intestine and insulin into the blood stream. He said, "The tests show that you have a malignant, invasive tumor on your pancreas." This pronouncement was met with silence. No one moved.

Danny had tears rolling down his face but did not want to dry them for fear his mother would see him. *This is not the time to show weakness*, he thought. He could see the sisters crying.

After what seemed liked five minutes, Mamie asked the dreaded question: "Is it fatal?"

Dr. Lynch: "Yes."

Florence and Mamie were the only ones not crying, and Mamie, in a businesslike manner, asked, "How long will I live?"

Dr. Lynch said, "It's hard to tell, but the average is about three months—sometimes less and sometimes more—and I have to tell you, the pain can be exquisite."

Danny, reasserting his role as the only son, asked, "Is there nothing that can be done?"

"There is a new drug, Nobo extract, which is extracted from the bark of a Nobo tree found only in Kenya," said the doctor. "It has stopped the tumor growth in some patients, and in a few patients the tumor has receded."

"Does it have side effects?" Danny asked.

Dr. Lynch responded, "There are some preliminary studies that suggest that if the Nobo stops the tumor growth in the pancreas, sometimes it causes tumor growth in the brain, which also can be fatal."

"It causes brain cancer?" asked Mamie. Without waiting for an answer, she asked, "If I get brain cancer, how long will I live, and will I be in pain?"

Danny was amazed at his mother's guts, but Florence saw her handling this like she was bidding a grand slam hand. She was looking for weaknesses in the opponent's cards.

The doctor decided this was someone who wanted and needed the details because she was still in charge of her own destiny. "The statistics are not large enough to give us any certain numbers, but if the pancreatic cancer recedes and brain cancer occurs, there is a possibility that you will have a twelve-month survival. Further, it is possible that the brain cancer could respond to treatment, in which event the survival rate can be several years. The pain from the brain cancer is generally much more controllable than the pain from the pancreatic cancer. You would probably be able to play bridge for a period of time if you suffer brain cancer. For the few people who are cured of pancreatic cancer and do not get brain cancer, they have a normal life expectancy."

Mamie said, "If I am not cured of pancreatic cancer, can I play bridge for the next three months?"

"Probably not," said Dr. Lynch. "You will be suffering disabling pain, and you will need more powerful drugs."

Danny couldn't take it anymore and said, "Thanks, doctors. The family will talk about this and will have some decision in the morning." Frankly, Danny had had trouble concentrating on the doctor's lecture.

Mamie quietly said, "I don't need to wait until morning. I know what I want to do now. I want the Nobo extract. I'm willing to take the risk of brain cancer."

Florence had expected as much.

Dr. Lynch said, "We can start you in the morning. Your first injection will be at 9:00 a.m. Afterward we will release you, and you'll have to return every morning for further injections. We will know if the pancreatic tumors have stopped growing in seven to ten days. We will know if there are brain tumors within ten days of the pancreatic tumor stopping."

Danny managed his practice in the afternoon and evening. He drove his mother to the hospital every morning. For the first week, there was no change in Mamie. She was bloated and bedridden and in pain. It was depressing. But on the eighth day she started to improve, and by the tenth day, Mamie was symptom-free. Florence said it was a miracle, and Mamie agreed. They returned to their duplicate bridge, and Mamie was sharp as ever.

They also resumed their postround glass of wine. Danny and his sisters celebrated Mamie's return to health with weekend family dinners, and life was good—for a while.

At the end of one of the bridge hands, Mamie started to notice a small headache. The pain was not terrible, but Mamie's anxiety level skyrocketed. She could not go on and asked Florence to take her to Cook County General Hospital. The cancer doctor shared Mamie's concern, and sure enough, she had a slow-growing form of brain cancer.

Danny and his sisters were devastated and angry. Danny wanted to strike out, and his most effective weapon was his law degree. He thought, *There must be a case here. The doctor said that Nobo caused the brain cancer. Therefore, we must have a case against the manufacturer of Nobo.* Danny knew he did not have the skill to bring such a case and set out to find a lawyer that did. Before long he heard about Dodge Lee in San Francisco.

Danny telephoned Lee, who said, "I have a hearing on my Nobo extract cases in Cook County in two days. Let's get together."

Dodge and Danny met. Dodge had a saying he used when making presentations to potential referring attorneys: "I don't care about good liability; I only care about good injury." A good injury, of course, meant a bad one in this case. Mamie's injury was good but not great. She was eighty-three years old and had a short life expectancy whether she suffered cancer or not. Further, the case would have been worth more if brought by her spouse—but he was dead. Dodge still liked the case. The McDermotts were a close, loving family, and a jury would like them. The medical evidence was clear. Nobo extract was killing Mamie. Dodge agreed to take the case. His plan was to file it with his other Nobo cases in Cook County. There was one problem, which he had with all those cases. The plaintiffs were residents of Illinois, and Jonas and the other defendants were residents of California. There was diversity, and the cases could all be removed to federal court, where the judges and jurors were more conservative. The only way to keep a case in plaintiff-friendly Cook County was to add a local defendant and destroy diversity. Each case would be looked at to see who could be added as a local defendant to destroy diversity. In *McDermott*, the obvious local defendant was the oncologist at Cook County General Hospital, Dr. Oso Lynch.

Danny had never liked Dr. Lynch, starting when Dr. Lynch conducted the first medical discussion in the busy corridor at the hospital, and Danny thus gave the go-ahead to file a complaint against the "usual suspects and Dr. Lynch." At Lee's request, the court appointed Danny McDermott as the first named plaintiff and guardian *ad litem* for the estate of Mamie McDermott.

Jethro Pugh

At the case management conference, Judge Jethro Pugh proved organized and decisive. Boxer had privately discussed the benefits of a federal venue, and Dr. Lynch's lawyer fully agreed to the strategy of trying to get Dr. Lynch dismissed, thus creating diversity and permitting removal to federal court.

The first item on his agenda was the motion of Dr. Oso Lynch to be dismissed from the case for fraudulent joinder. Boxer sat silently as Dr. Lynch's lawyer argued that the only reason Lynch had been named as a defendant was to destroy diversity and keep the remaining defendants from removing the case to federal court. Lee argued that Dr. Lynch was the learned intermediary and that he had failed to adequately warn of the risks of brain cancer. Lee further alleged that if Dr. Lynch had done his job, Mamie would never have taken Nobo extract. Judge Pugh nodded as Lee spoke. At the end he announced, "At this stage, I have to accept the allegations as true, so Dr. Lynch's motion to dismiss is denied."

The next item was Lee's motion to quickly set the case for trial. Lee argued that Mamie was fading and was in and out of consciousness and she had a right to go to trial before she died if at all possible. Boxer argued that the real reason Lee wanted to rush to judgment was that it would give the plaintiff an opportunity for double recovery. That is, the McDermotts could recover for the personal injury, and then her estate could sue again for wrongful death after she died.

Judge Pugh said, "The law of Illinois allows for recovery for her personal injury and the wrongful death. Thus, I am granting the plaintiff's motion and set trial for sixty days from today. I encourage both sides to cooperate with expedition of discovery and trial preparation." Boxer knew that if Mamie died before the sixty days, she would not be able to proceed with the personal-injury trial.

Judge Pugh further ordered that he would hear all motions to dismiss on the first day of trial. He said out loud what the lawyers were thinking: "This is going to be your 'show trial' and your 'bellwether trial.'"

Boxer further thought, *Judge Pugh is also assuring that Cook County Court will be the focus of future Nobo extract cases.* If there was one thing a plaintiff's attorney wants is to get to a jury. Judge Pugh was essentially announcing that if you filed a suit in Cook County, dispositive motions wouldn't be heard until the day of trial, at which time you might as well go ahead and complete the case, meaning you would get to a jury—and Cook County juries had proved themselves to be very generous.

The Demand

Dodge Lee was thrilled. The McDermott case was attracting publicity and lawsuits. Lee had billboards and TV ads all over Cook County. He was trying to precondition potential jurors to accept Jonas as a bad company and Patrick Jonas as a bad person who owned a bad company. Jonas made billions selling dangerous drugs. There were even word-of-mouth rumors that Jonas's forbearers had been Nazis who escaped from Germany after the war.

Within weeks Lee had filed 150 cases in Cook County. His official asking price to settle was $7 million per case for a total of more than $1 billion. Unofficially and confidentially, he told Boxer he would settle the McDermott case for $6 million, which would include both the personal-injury and wrongful-death cases. Lee said he liked McDermott as a bellwether case.

Boxer called his war counsel together. He gave his assessment of the situation. Of the 150 cases in Cook County, some of the plaintiffs would not have brain cancer, and some would not have been exposed to Nobo extract. Mamie McDermott had been treated with Nobo extract and did have brain cancer caused by Nobo extract. But in prescription drug cases, the law was slightly different from most product-liability cases. Pharmaceutical law accepted the fact that all drugs have side effects. The duty of the manufacturer was to timely and adequately warn the treating doctors of those side effects. Further, if the manufacturer did not advertise to the public, it did not have to warn the patient but only her treating physicians. It was thus up to the physician to adequately warn the patient. These types of cases were called failure-to-warn cases.

"So," Boxer said, "the first project is to find out how Oso Lynch will testify in this case. If he agrees that he was well warned, that would be important for us. Further, we will not have to point fingers at Oso Lynch. When the defendants point at each other, the plaintiff wins. Here, Mamie McDermott, prompted by Lee, will probably deny adequate warnings. If her denial is believed, it would put Oso Lynch at fault."

The next item Boxer raised was settlement. In evaluating cases, trial lawyers wore two hats—their advocate hat and their counselor hat. As an advocate, the McDermott case was triable on the failure-to-warn theory. Most of the cases that would get to trial would be failure-to-warn cases. Thus, the McDermott trial would have tremendous impact on the future of the litigation. Boxer said, "We're not going to get a bargain on this case. But if we win, this case we will get bargains on future cases; but if we lose, the price goes up. And we can lose, because we are in Cook County." After some discussion, it was agreed that if the McDermott case could be settled for five hundred thousand dollars, it should be settled. If the 150 cases could be settled in bulk, Box suggested that the defendants would pay twenty thousand dollars per case or a total of three million dollars, knowing that some of the cases would be worthless. Next Boxer discussed retention of a jury consultant. He wanted to see how a focus group would react to the facts of this case. He wanted to know how the failure-to-warn argument would work. He wanted to know how a jury would react to a cross-examination of Mamie. Should he waive cross, conduct a soft cross, or conduct an aggressive cross? He also wanted to show the focus group prior video testimony of Al Purcell. He wanted to see what the group liked and didn't like about Purcell. The testifying expectancy of a trial expert was limited. Each adverse cross-examination usually exposed a chip. After several cross-examinations, the chips tended to keep growing and turn into cracks that someday might crumble the witness. A home run for Boxer would be a defense verdict with no chips.

At Lee's request, Boxer and he met with a mediator to discuss settlement. Lee never made the Tommy Thompson mistake of underestimating Boxer. While Boxer was not as experienced as Lee, jurors readily forgave Boxer any mistakes in the courtroom. Lee didn't want to incite Boxer and thus treated him with respect. Each was wary of the other. Boxer thought the mediation would be a worthless exercise because Lee would want too much money, but Boxer did not mind making Lee think the case would settle and thus Lee did not have to spend too much time getting ready for trial. Lee's opening demand was six million, and Boxer's opening offer was two hundred thousand with an indication of more if Lee substantially reduced his demand. Lee would not, and that ended the conference.

On the way out, Boxer said he wanted to depose Lee's experts. Lee said, "If you admit causation, I won't be calling any experts."

Boxer said, "We do admit causation."

Lee replied, "That will reduce the time of the trial." Lee also announced that he would not have Mamie in the courtroom except for a very short direct examination. Lee's jury experts had counseled him that if a seriously injured plaintiff spent too much time in the courtroom, jurors became immune to their pain and suffering. However, if they did not appear at all, the juries became suspicious of the validity of their pain and suffering claims. Thus, experienced plaintiffs' lawyers only exposed their clients to juries for less than thirty minutes.

Victim Defeat

For even the most experienced lawyer, the first day of trial is the most exciting. The courtroom is filled with prospective jurors, most of whom are trying to get out of jury duty. They quickly identify the lawyers, because the lawyers are the only ones in ties and suits with shiny shoes. Some even approach the lawyers with questions. For their part, the lawyers are looking at the potential jurors, trying to see who might be with them, their clients, and their arguments. There are many generalized prejudices that don't hold true in individual cases. It was said that Melvin Belli, at a seminar of plaintiffs' attorneys, had announced that it was legal malpractice for a plaintiff's lawyer to accept an Asian juror on his San Francisco panel. The Italians were supposed to be warmhearted, and Netherlanders were supposed to be coldhearted. Accountants demanded great detail and exactitude. Teachers were liberal and nurses were conservative, and nurses did not believe in recovery for pain and suffering.

Boxer had come to believe that older jurors had seen it all and were less likely to reward a plaintiff. Retired jurors had greater respect for the dollar and were less likely to render large awards.

Judge Pugh's pretrial rulings had hurt the defense. He was going to allow punitive damages to go to the jury. Thus, Lee could introduce evidence of the defendant's wealth, which in the case of Patrick Jonas was now in the billions of dollars. He also had determined that several medical journal articles about Nobo extract were public pronouncements and sponsored by Jonas, thus vitiating the learned intermediary doctrine and requiring Jonas to warn patients directly of the dangers of Nobo. Thus, even if Dr. Lynch had been aware of the risks of Nobo extract, the plaintiff could still win if she had been unaware.

Rulings on jury selection were also plaintiff-oriented. The judge ruled that the fact that a prospective juror had seen billboards or TV ads for plaintiffs would not be grounds for disqualification; nor would the fact that a relative or friend was suing Jonas be grounds for disqualification; nor would the fact that the juror had read negative articles about Nobo. The best that could be said was that Boxer preserved the record on appeal by getting a number of those jurors to admit that Jonas was starting out behind in their minds.

Lee was successful in dismissing a nurse who thought Nobo risks were well known in the medical profession. Lee's theme in the opening statement was that Jonas Pharmaceuticals knew the dangers of Nobo extract and was slow in informing the FDA and in changing the labeling. Thus, the oncology community became attached to the benefits of the drug and failed to fully accept the reality of the dangers that were finally revealed. Lee no longer needed Dr. Oso Lynch as a defendant, since the time to remove to federal court had passed. Thus, Lee dismissed Lynch as a defendant. Without Dr. Lynch in the courtroom, Lee argued that even Dr. Lynch had been taken in by the initial labeling, which never mentioned the risk of brain cancer. When Lynch finally received the belated warnings, he subconsciously underestimated them when describing them to patients, such as Mamie, desperate for even the most remote possibility of relief. Brain cancer only prolonged the misery these victims were enduring.

Danny McDermott was Lee's first witness. His testimony played right into Lee's theme. Danny and his sisters were hesitant about using Nobo extract, but their desperate mother, Mamie, requested the drug and waived aside the obvious concerns. Mamie had not received from Jonas any warning letter or any public interest announcements. Jonas never used any of the billions of dollars he received to publicly warn of the hidden dangers. The McDermotts were forced to rely on the oral presentation of an overly optimistic oncologist, Dr. Oso Lynch.

Boxer's cross-examination of Danny was designed to be short, and it was. He had Danny authenticate his guardian *ad litem* documents and handed him the informed consent. Boxer asked Danny to identify the document. Danny said, "It's a piece of paper drug companies use to try to avoid liability."

Boxer said, "Danny, you are a lawyer, correct?"

Danny paused and said, "What do you mean?"

Boxer said, "An informed consent is designed to tell a consumer the dangers of a product, right?"

Danny evasively responded, "I don't know what Jonas designed this for."

Boxer persisted, "Well, Mr. McDermott, please read Paragraph 4.2."

Danny finally said, "'Nobo extract has been shown to cause brain cancer in some individuals.'"

Boxer said, "Please identify the signature at the bottom of the document."

"Well, it's mine."

"And Mr. McDermott, what does it say right above your signature?"

Mr. McDermott shouted, "It says, 'I have read and fully understand the risks set forth above,' but I didn't read it and I didn't understand my mother was going to die from your client's product."

Boxer said, "No more questions for the witness, Your Honor."

The McDermott sisters echoed the testimony of Danny, and Mamie's oncologist's nurse was called to the stand and narrated a sixty-minute day-in-the-life video of Mamie's painful confining illness and her fears of death. The film showed the nurse bathing and feeding Mamie. It showed Mamie and Danny holding hands and praying. It showed Mamie moaning with pain. It showed her caressing her daughters. Florence Duffy was the last witness of the day, and she testified to Mamie's love of bridge and how she now missed that discipline and camaraderie. She showed the jury Mamie's life master plaque and testified about how proud Mamie was when she received it. Several jurors were in tears, but Boxer asked one question: "Isn't it true that Mamie got to play more bridge than if she had not taken Nobo extract?"

Florence answered, "Yes."

Silence.

The next morning immediately after the jurors were seated, the back doors to the courtroom were thrown open, and two orderlies walked Mamie into the courtroom. She was lying in a hospital bed. Mamie must have weighed less than ninety pounds. She was bald, and her skin was light yellow. She had plastic bags dripping liquid through plastic lines into her emaciated wrists. Lee fixed a microphone in front of her mouth, but the jury still could barely hear her hollow voice. Lee, however, did not have her there to illicit testimony but rather to illicit sympathy, and she did. It was a disturbing sight.

Lee had Mamie identify herself and then asked her how she spent her days. She said, "I spend them in bed waiting to die. I wish I had never taken Nobo." Lee looked at Boxer and said, "Your witness."

Boxer slowly rose. He had been hurt by this display. He really thought that Mamie had fully consented to the risks of brain cancer caused by Nobo, but bringing that out and not inflaming the jury called for great delicacy. Boxer respectfully said, "First, thank you for coming. I just have a few questions. Do you remember when Dr. Oso Lynch talked to you about Nobo?"

"Yes."

"Did he tell you that Nobo in a very few cases could cure pancreatic cancer?"

Before Lee could object, Mamie said, "Yes."

"And did it cure your pancreatic cancer?"

"Yes."

"Did Dr. Lynch tell you that even if it cured your pancreatic cancer, it might cause brain cancer?"

"Yes."

"Was Danny there?"

"Yes."

"Did Danny say, 'We will think it over and give Dr. Lynch a decision later'?"

"Yes."

"And did you say that you did not need time—you knew you wanted to receive the Nobo extract?"

"Yes."

"Is there any danger associated with Nobo that you did not know about?"

"No."

"Were you aware that the brain cancer could destroy your life?"

"Yes."

"And were you aware that the final stages of brain cancer could be just as you are now suffering?"

"Yes."

Boxer glanced at the jury and they were rapt. Boxer was aware that he might be asking one question too many, but he thought, *This is an honest woman, and the jury wants the answer to this question.*

"So why did you testify that you wish you never took Nobo?"

Lee jumped to his feet. "Objection. Mr. Tate is harassing the witness."

Before Judge Jethro Pugh could speak, Mamie said directly and clearly into the microphone, "Mr. Tate, I apologize. I'm near death, and I don't want to go out with a lie on my soul. I'm glad I took Nobo, but Mr. Lee said I would have to say this to get money for my children."

Lee tried to cut her off, but she looked at him and said, "See? I told you this wouldn't work."

Lee moved to strike his client's testimony as nonresponsive and rendered under the duress of a browbeating of counsel. Boxer chose not to speak, because it was clear that Judge Pugh was thinking.

Judge Pugh paused, looked Lee in the eye, and announced, "Denied." It was the only ruling he had given in favor of the defense, and the jury knew it.

Lee offered no further witnesses; nor did Boxer, and after a brief closing argument, the jury returned with a defense verdict in twenty-two minutes.

Boxer Victory

Before Boxer could get out of the courtroom, he was surrounded by the media. Boxer reveled in the attention. Next day, the legal press headlines read, "Boxer KO's Nobo Case." The stories told of Boxer's successes in California and West Virginia leading to the defense verdict in Cook County. They also described Tate's courage in confronting hometown judges and the speed with which he managed a case from start to finish. His bills were low and his profile high. Jurors were quoted as saying they liked him because he talked directly to them and described law and medicine in plain English. He did not overstate his case. He carried his own briefcase and was not surrounded by minions.

Fortune was quoted as stating, "Boxer is the best trial attorney in Atlas's large stable of trial lawyers. He loves trial and is always super prepared." Surprisingly, Tommy Thompson gave a quote: "Boxer is good, but he gets close to the edge."

Fortune made her comments without benefit of counsel. When Boxer asked her why she had done this without talking to him first, she said, "Because I knew you would have advised against it. Furthermore, I think it will help our national strategy. I'm already getting phone calls from general counsel of companies we insure and general counsels of companies we don't insure. I think we are going to get more business, and so will you—it will be good for both of us. My boss is thrilled, as is our board of directors," Fortune continued. "I heard that after your last victory you conducted the celebration and postmortems in Carmel."

Boxer chuckled and replied, "Yes, but I wasn't employed by that confidante. And besides, how do you know that?"

Fortune said, "You forgot who pays your expenses. The dinner at Mission Ranch and suite at La Playa were on the expense reports and then crossed out. Why, I don't know."

Boxer said, "I crossed them out because Audi Johns was giving me personal professional advice, not advice on Nobo litigation."

Fortune said, "I will be glad to pay. Just remember there is no such thing as a free dinner. And besides, I don't think we will need Audi this time, as I will be happy to give you all the personal advice you need. Let's say I make the reservations and we meet at the La Playa at 7:00 p.m. this coming Friday?"

Boxer made no wisecracks and asked for no details. He just said yes.

There were five days until Friday. Boxer thought they would go slowly, but not so. His time was packed.

He convened a war council of his Nobo team. After back slaps and handshakes and high fives all around, they had to get to work. There were still more than three hundred Nobo cases pending in Cook County. Dodge had been keeping a low profile on the McDermott case. There were no public statements or attempts at backdoor communications. Boxer solicited ideas. Bill Dawes said, "I've been thinking about this. The McDermott case shows that we can win a failure-to-warn case in which the exposure to Nobo occurred after the change in warning. What are we going to do with a brain cancer case in which ingestion is pre–brain cancer warnings? Obviously, there must be some of these, because that's why Jonas changed the warnings."

Karen Klein said, "I've been researching this. It will likely come down to a question of fact to be decided by the jury. Was the warning added in a timely fashion? In other words, when Jonas became aware of the risk of brain cancer, did it timely change its warning? Thus, if a plaintiff was the first one in the world to suffer brain cancer from Nobo, she cannot recover, because there was no evidence that would cause a reasonable drug company to change its warnings at that point. Further, Jonas cannot change its warnings without FDA approval, and it took the FDA almost ten months from the first adverse event until it permitted the labeling change. We obtained the preemption dismissal in California because of the FDA delay. In Cook County there is no preemption defense, and the plaintiff can try to show exigencies that would require Jonas to make the changes without FDA approval. Of course, Jonas would run the risk of severe sanctions from the FDA for making changes without its approval."

Boxer said, "We would have paid five hundred thousand dollars to settle McDermott before trial, but Lee held firm on his six-million-dollar demand. Now we wouldn't pay costs of defense to settle McDermott, because we have already spent this money, and of course we got a defense verdict." Boxer continued, "I would be happy to reapproach Lee, but I suggest we pay nothing on a case unless plaintiff presents proof she had pancreatic cancer, she took Nobo extract, and she developed brain cancer within two months of taking Nobo extract. If plaintiff took the Nobo extract right before the change in warnings, we offer her two hundred thousand dollars. We reduce the offer the longer she took Nobo before the change in the warnings. In other words, if she took Nobo eighteen months before the change, we offer nothing, because we had no scientific reason to change the warnings at that time. If she took it after the change in warnings, we offer a hundred thousand. If she took it after the change in warnings and we can show that her doctor and/ or she actually knew of the danger before she took the Nobo, we offer fifty thousand dollars."

There was general discussion. Fortune Jones for Atlas and Kenny Clark, general counsel of Jonas, both expressed approval. Fortune said, "I like it, because it won't encourage new suits. In other words, the warning was added three years ago. Those people who did not get cancer won't sue. Those people who got cancer will probably be barred by the statute of limitations and by their knowledge and assumption of the risk."

Clark said, "Based on past statistics, probably 60 percent of the claimants won't be able to show Nobo exposure and real brain cancer. We will have a McDermott-type warning defense in 30 percent of the cases, and only 10 percent or less will have prewarning exposure. Worst case, this amounts to twenty-five plaintiffs. If we paid each twenty thousand dollars, that would add up to three million. We would be delighted to put these behind us for that money. Just the business interruption value is many times higher."

Boxer said, "I agree it would be a good result for us. How do we sell it?"

Dawes said, "We push discovery hard. Lee is not going to invest more money after three big losses. If we notice two depositions in each case, that will be almost six hundred depositions, and that's just for starters. We will subpoena at least five sets of medical records in each case and five sets of employment records in each case, and the list goes on. Lee does not have the bench strength to handle this, and he won't want to associate in other lawyers with whom he may have to split fees."

Boxer looked at the clients, and they nodded. Boxer said to Dawes, "Let's do it."

Running the Firm

Boxer met with the two other owners of the firm—Bill Dawes and Audi Johns. Boxer had been out of the loop for the last sixty days because of the McDermott trial. All agreed it was time well spent. Boxer gave a brief summary of the trial, spending most of his time talking about his telephone conference with Fortune Jones and his upcoming business trip to Carmel with her. This caused some winking and smiles. Audi was stone-faced.

Nevertheless, Bill was delighted with the prospect, particularly since Audi had been spending money rapidly. She had successfully subleased the various San Francisco offices to others and signed a new lease that would put the firm in new space for a hundred lawyers starting in two months. She had already hired seventy lawyers from the Thompson firm. Thus, she had about twenty vacant offices. One of the keys to the financial success of a law firm is accurately estimating future space needs. If twenty spaces remained empty, they could become a drain on profits. Audi said, "I am bullish."

Boxer and Bill agreed. In fact, Boxer said, "I am concerned we will run out of space in six months."

Audi said, "I have paid for options that will give us fifteen new offices per year for the next five years. If we fill all these offices, it will put us at a hundred seventy-five lawyers in San Francisco in five years."

Boxer said, "I am comfortable with that. How are we going to manage the national growth?"

Audi said, "I have been in contact with the Atlas real estate people. They have about a hundred offices nationwide. In each office they will dedicate a Tate, Johns, Dawes suite."

Audi continued, "Atlas will use the suite on a regular basis, but the office directory will have the name of the Tate firm, and when offices in the suite are needed by Tate lawyers, the Tate name and particular lawyers' names will be slipped into a holder next to the suite office door. Atlas will bill us for the use of the offices at the lowest rate they charge.

"We won't list the offices on our letterhead unless we have one of our lawyers working at the office and admitted to that state bar. We already have lawyers in the firm who would like to relocate to DC and Chicago. The Chicago lawyer is already admitted to the Illinois bar. I have told the DC lawyer we would pay for his taking the bar exam. They both love the idea of being the senior Tate person in their own offices."

Boxer asked, "How are we paying for this?"

Audi said, "Out of the Thompson accounts receivable, but they are coming in slowly. We have been able to pay salaries but we have had to obtain a line of credit to pay the overhead. The three of us have not had a distribution yet. When our bill for the McDonald case is paid, we should be able to pay off our line of credit."

Boxer said, "What do you suggest?"

Audi said, "We are going to need a bookkeeper at some time. I think we should hire one now and do an audit of the Thompson accounts receivable and work in progress."

Boxer said, "Do it. And if Thompson gives you trouble on the audit, let me know. Right now associate salaries are well below the going rate, which makes us vulnerable to poaching."

Next Boxer asked about the status of Bryan Malloy. Audi reported that he had finished his rehabilitation and was back at work. "He appears tired and bored. Miller Johnson is monitoring his work."

Boxer said, "I'll stop by and see him. Governance?"

Audi passed a draft partnership agreement to Bill and Boxer. She said, "You and Bill are the first people I have shown this to. It is fairly rich on distribution of points, because I worry that we won't be able to pay as much as needed at the front end, and we will then have to make it up by giving more lawyers a greater equity stake.

"I have also written it to discourage turnover. One of the sections promises raises and bonuses payable in the future but only if the lawyer is still at the firm. This strategy has been successful in the investment-banking community. It works best if income is going up. We might have to alter it to promise raising percentages of future income as opposed to precise amounts. This is counter to the present trend of making fewer equity partners and more nonequity partners and of-counsel members and senior counsel and senior associates.

"I also propose that departing partners forfeit their interest in WIP and accounts receivable. This too makes it hard to leave."

Boxer said, "Try to get a sense of the firm on these matters. I would rather go slow and get it right."

Finally, Audi said, "We are all moving to the new space in two months, and there is the issue of who gets what offices."

Boxer said, "I will give up a corner office and even give up a big office if my office adjoins my very own war room. I have lusted for such a space, and I think it would make me more efficient. Otherwise, I delegate who gets what office to the two of you. I think you two should have first choice and then be the arbiters of the others. After we get in, I would like to have a reception for all personnel and clients."

62

Thompson's Decline

Thompson expected his firm to flourish after the departure of Dawes and his group. Thompson was more interested in SEC, price-fixing, antitrust, intellectual-property, and white-collar crime work than mass torts and class actions. He called this glorified tort work. He could get higher hourly rates handling his business cases. Also, when a mass-tort matter came in the door, it required a number of bodies that had to be devoted to the matter. The problem was when the case was over there were always a number of bodies out of work. Thompson had no trouble just laying these people off, but it was an irritant and hurt morale.

Thompson believed he was getting rid of the weakest parts of his business. But the loss of all these lawyers and their clients and cases was a prestige buster. It was tarnishing his image. Tate's success in the courtroom further embittered Tommy.

For some reason, the Thompson firm income had been going down even before the Dawes departure. The losses were starting to accelerate. Thompson had lost a few more partners, and he grew very tired of answering questions from judges and media about the firm's financial status. Also, recruiting was becoming harder.

Thompson needed another Dawes. He liked lawyers out of the US attorney's office. A number of them were ready to leave after five or six years to make more money in the private sector. As a former assistant US attorney, Thompson had an excellent reputation with the office. He usually used Audi Johns to set up these interviews. Without her, he decided to use one of his senior associates. He reported back. There was no one available in the US attorney's office. Tommy knew that was unlikely. For a price, there was always someone available. But he decided to call the placement office at Boalt. They always had alumni who wanted to change firms.

After a week, Tommy got a call to set up an interview with a ten-year graduate. The young man arrived. He was a partner in an LA firm who had married a San Francisco lawyer and wanted to move to San Francisco. He had an SEC background, and Tommy thought there could be a fit. But the candidate was not enthusiastic. Thompson asked why.

"The word on the street is that the firm is going downhill. You are losing clients, and you are losing business, and even more scary, you have a lot of empty offices."

After the recruit left, Tommy picked up the phone and threw it against the wall. His secretary called in. "Is everything okay?"

He said, "Leave me alone."

She tried to calm the situation by bringing in mail. The top item was the *SF Legal Journal* with a headline about Boxer Tate's victory in Cook County. Thompson held his temper until she left. Then he ripped the front page in half.

Thompson was becoming more and more bitter. He grew to hate Tate, Dawes, and Johns. He had assumed the Tate firm would not survive, and when it did, he believed it was at the expense of the Thompson firm. His conversation with the Boalt graduate solidified his decision to slow pay the accounts receivable to the Tate firm and increase his own draw so that the amount of the receivables would look even less. He justified this by reexamining the departure of Dawes. While all had agreed that the Tate firm and the Thompson firm would split the Thompson accounts receivable, this was not in writing. He figured he would not tell Dawes that he considered the accounts receivable deal unenforceable because it was not in writing.

Tate's new bookkeeper called Thompson several times, but Tommy did not respond other than to leave a voicemail explaining that because of the Dawes departure the Dawes clients weren't paying their bills and thus the receivables were down.

Tommy was also of the view that it was Boxer's victories that were hurting the Thompson firm and that those victories had been obtained through Boxer's dishonest unethical conduct. In particular, Thompson considered Boxer's strategy of undermining the reputation of his adversaries unethical. Thompson justified his underpayments based on Tate's unclean hands. Of course, Thompson did not reveal his secret self-justification.

One of Thompson's antitrust lawyers was passing his office when Thompson was yelling at his secretary and decided to check on him. Another partner followed, and they asked what the matter was. Tommy said he was busy and did not have time to talk.

Privately, Tommy was of the view that he had to retaliate against Boxer, but he wasn't going to tell anyone. He wanted to ruin Boxer's reputation and any chance Boxer might have to become successful. So far the judges in West Virginia and Illinois didn't like Boxer at all.

Tommy thought one of his best chances of retaliation would be with the help of Dodge Lee. He set up another lunch. The lunch was in Tommy's private dining room. Lee was still smarting from the McDermott defeat, and he knew that Tommy was smarting from the Dawes departure.

Lee thought he did some of his best work in Tommy's dining room. At the outset, Lee asked, "Tommy, don't you have a conflict talking to me?"

Tommy said, "I am no longer involved in the Nobo cases and no longer represent Jonas or any of the defendants, and thus there is no conflict." Then Tommy asked, "What are you going to do about the McDermott verdict?"

Lee said, "I can ask for a new trial or appeal, but I doubt either would be successful."

Tommy asked, "What are you going to do about the other Cook County cases?"

Lee said, "Boxer has served me with carloads of discovery requests. They are all relevant. To respond, I will need at least twenty paralegals and five junior lawyers. I worry that the discovery will show that a large percentage of my cases are worthless."

Tommy was surprised at Lee's candor. He asked, "Won't Boxer need many people to analyze your responses?"

"Yes," said Lee, "but he has got the clients to pay for it and seventy of your lawyers to work on the cases."

Tommy remarked, in an effort to disclose Boxer's weaknesses, "I heard Boxer is having some cash-flow problems." Tommy went on to say, "The Cook County local rules have many traps for the unwary. You should hire a local lawyer who will look for the technical flaws in the Boxer papers. For instance, has Boxer been admitted *pro hac vice* in all of the cases in Cook County? Has he paid the correct statutory filing fees? Are his pleadings properly authenticated?

"Lee, I know you named the treating physicians as defendants in Cook County to destroy diversity. Perhaps one of their lawyers will offer you favorable testimony by his physician to get him out of this case. It would help your case immensely if a physician would testify that Jonas's representatives told the treaters not to believe the brain cancer warning and it was just put there to satisfy the FDA."

Lee was not thrilled with these ideas, particularly the last one. He said, "This sounds like suborning perjury."

Tommy said, "It is not suborning perjury if the doctor says it is true. Further, I would be willing to approach the doctors if I get a cut of any attorneys' fees obtained on cases in which I could turn the doctor against Jonas."

Lee said, "I'll think about it." Lee was also thinking about the additional percentage he would have to give up if he hired local counsel, which looked like what he would have to do.

On his way out, Lee checked the recorder on his iPhone to make sure it was working.

Fortune, Superstar

Before coming to Atlas, Fortune was in the New York insurance bond business. She loved trading bonds. She had the magic touch. It was easy. She bought low and sold high. An early client was a billion-dollar pension fund. Fortune and her team persuaded the firm to move $100 million from a high-risk, high-yield book to a lower risk but lower return portfolio. A manager for the fund insisted that he sit by Fortune's side and watch how she did it.

Fortune explained, "I can't just dump the whole portfolio on the market at once, because it would cause the bonds to go down in price. I will start today by buying a few of these bonds. I want the financial community to think I am a buyer. If the price goes up, I will sell in the afternoon." The pension fund representative sat at Fortune's side for a month and watched his funds go from high risk to low risk and actually go up in value by $20 million. Fortune did the same thing for four other accounts during the same month and continued at this pace for several years. She was a superstar. Her salary was relatively low, like most financial people, but her bonuses were high—in the millions of dollars. Some of the payments of the bonuses were deferred for a year or more. This was her firm's way of keeping the superstars. If you were not still at the firm when the bonus was payable, you did not receive it. It was called golden handcuffs.

Her firm was making so much money that they were bought by an even richer New York investment firm. This sale triggered a clause in Fortune's contract accelerating the payments of these bonuses and causing Fortune to receive all of her bonuses and exercise all of her options at once. Fortune was also offered a new job by the new purchaser in their New York office, but since she now had $20 million in the bank, she decided to move to San Francisco as a free agent.

With her work history and résumé, Fortune was in demand. Stanford MBAs ran the San Francisco financial market, and they tended to hire other Stanford MBAs. Fortune just happened to have one of these treasured degrees. The only problem was that she had gone to Berkeley as an undergraduate and didn't know who to root for at Big Game.

Fortune had several offers and more overtures. She sought advice from her high-profile father, Jackie Jones, who was CEO and principal shareholder of Atlas Insurance Company. Coincidentally, Atlas was having financial issues. Jackie said, "I am thinking of hiring a consulting firm to analyze the situation, and I see they all have résumés similar to yours."

Fortune said, "I did buy and sell insurance bonds and had an opportunity to investigate winning and losing strategies." She said, "I am willing to spend four months analyzing your business, but I don't want a salary; I want bonds and bond options."

"Agreed," he said.

Fortune started by filing a Freedom of Information Act request to the California Insurance Department seeking reserve filings of California insurance companies. She found that there were several large insurance companies that had enormous reserves set aside to pay potential asbestos claims. The San Francisco Bay Area had in excess of a hundred thousand potential asbestos claimants who had been exposed to asbestos as far back as World War II as a result of work they did on naval ships stationed in Alameda, Oakland, San Francisco, Martinez, and Port Chicago. Bay Area Insurance Company insured most of the asbestos suppliers in the Bay Area.

Bay Area Insurance had $8 billion in reserves, but most of the claimants exposed to asbestos were not suing Bay Area Insurance, because discovery against their insureds did not reveal that they had Bay Area Insurance policies.

Bay Area Insurance's large reserves had a negative impact on the price of its bonds. Fortune pointed this situation out to her father. She said, "If you can buy Bay Area Insurance for one billion dollars, you stand to make a seven-billion-dollar profit on the eight billion dollars in reserves after they are liquidated. This potential will also drive up the interim sales price of the bonds."

Jackie said, "I'll buy Bay Area Insurance if you will stay in the business and not quit after four months and we can work together at Atlas. I will make sure the board of directors awards you significant stock and bond options. Your earnings will surpass your investment bank income." Fortune agreed.

Atlas then bought Bay Area Insurance, and while the California insurance regulators would not let Bay Area Insurance immediately liquidate the bond reserves, the business community assumed liquidation would ultimately occur, and thus the Atlas bonds and equities went up in price.

Unfortunately, as time went by, the number of asbestos claimants did not go down. It went up. Originally, oncologists thought the latency period between exposure to asbestos and the incidence of cancer was about fifteen years. Atlas bought Bay Area Insurance almost forty years after most asbestos was removed from ships and shipyards. Unfortunately, it turned out that some of the most virulent cancers, such as mesothelioma, had latency periods of fifty or more years. In other words, the first signs and symptoms of cancer did not occur for fifty years after the original exposure. Insurance carriers in the Bay Area had to worry that time would reveal more injured victims and more sources of exposure.

After most of the asbestos manufacturers were forced into bankruptcy because of their asbestos litigation, plaintiffs' attorneys searched for more sources of money. They scoured the records of the suppliers and ultimately found that Bay Area Insurance was an upper-layer carrier for several of the largest suppliers. The largest of these suppliers had obtained excess coverage from Bay Area Insurance Company almost thirty-five years after the claimants were exposed to asbestos. Bay Area Insurance never expected to be at risk for these asbestos claims. It was not until well after Atlas bought Bay Area Insurance that such claims started to be filed in large numbers.

At the beginning, the suppliers did not give Bay Area Insurance or Atlas notice of the claims. The suppliers' records retention policies did not call for their insurance policies and certificates to be retained for that long of a period. It was not until hundreds of plaintiffs' personal-injury attorneys had scoured through suppliers' warehouses for documents that copies of the destroyed insurance policies started to appear.

The plaintiffs' attorneys were clever. They did not want the suppliers to declare bankruptcy; that would stay the litigation. They really wanted the suppliers to ignore the complaints and allow the plaintiffs' attorneys to take default judgments against the suppliers. Thus, even if a case was unmeritorious, plaintiffs' attorneys could take defaults if no responsive pleadings were filed by the suppliers. Default judgments were quickly taken against the suppliers by the thousands. Each default was for a minimum of $10 million, and some were for as much as $25 million.

The plaintiffs' attorneys agreed not to execute against the suppliers, in return for which the suppliers assigned their insurance coverage claims back to the plaintiffs' attorneys. The plaintiffs' attorneys filed bad-faith coverage claims on behalf of the suppliers against insurance companies like Bay Area Insurance, which now tendered the defense of these cases to Atlas.

Atlas and Jones hired the most sophisticated coverage lawyer they could find. He was J. J. Strauss of New York, and he had been the coverage lawyer for the insurance industry in the multibillion-dollar Twin Towers coverage litigation in New York.

Strauss was abrasive, abusive, and arrogant. He was mean to his adversaries but worse to his clients. Insurance CEOs hired him to cover their asses. He was usually retained when a company might have to pay billions or more to resolve ticklish situations. Boards of directors would approve such payments when recommended by a J. J. Strauss. Jackie and Fortune did not want to pay big money on these coverage suits. They wanted to get out, and that's when Fortune thought of Boxer.

Fortune and Boxer
at Carmel

Fortune loved Carmel and the Monterey Peninsula. Because of her work life, Fortune had drifted away from her PhD boyfriend so she loved planning her weekend with Boxer. She studied where they would eat, where they would hike, and where they would brainstorm. But most of all, she loved planning their round of golf. This was going to be a surprise. They had never discussed the sport, but she knew Boxer at one time had been a scratch golfer. Boxer did not know that she had a six handicap and had played golf at Berkeley undergraduate. Fortune made reservations at Pebble Beach, and she also made room reservations at the lodge, which overlooked the eighteenth fairway and the Pacific Ocean. The waves would crash against the retaining wall and splash onto the fairway. She couldn't wait to surprise him.

In glowing terms, Fortune told Jackie about Boxer. She told her father that she and Boxer were going to play Pebble Beach and she planned to get Boxer's insights into the Bay Area Insurance matter.

Since Fortune's business responsibilities caused her to share many amicable social situations with men, Jackie assumed that Fortune's trip to the Monterey Peninsula was one of these platonic events.

Thus, as the competent businessman he was, he unilaterally made some small changes in this Atlas business meeting and documented them by e-mail to Fortune. He was sure she would be pleased. He said,

"It sounds like Mr. Tate could be a great resource for us going forward, and your Carmel meeting seems like a good opportunity to get to know him."

Fortune thought, *I thought it would be a good opportunity for me to get to know him.*

Jackie proceeded to advise that he had added his name to what was now the Jackie Jones foursome. Fortune thought this was an excellent idea, but she thought it would be even better if Jackie just came to Pebble for the day. But there was more: "I have made reservations for dinner at Monterey Peninsula Beach House. And I have changed the room reservations to three adjoining suites."

The beach house was literally right on the water. It was usually reserved for twenty or more people. But Jackie had set up an intimate dinner for them—at a price for twenty.

Fortune loved her father, but it was moments like this that made her regret agreeing to work with him. They were a great business partnership, but he had no conception that she might have a love life. The problem was she didn't. Her business commitments made it impossible. She was probably crazy to think she could possibly enjoy anything but an amicable relationship with another business partner like Boxer Tate. Fortune wanted to scream at her father, but while she could be candid and frank and aggressive with him in business, she was overwhelmed by him socially.

Fortune had no idea how to tell Boxer that their private victory celebration was turning into a business weekend. She just forwarded her father's e-mail to Boxer and hoped for the best.

Boxer read the e-mail, and it was as if a bell went off in his head. He knew Fortune would be conflicted about including Jackie but Boxer was delighted. He further forwarded the e-mail along to Audi Johns and Bill Dawes. Both were thrilled. Getting to play golf and have dinner with *the* Jackie Jones was a huge business breakthrough for the firm.

Boxer e-mailed back to Fortune, "Does this mean we can't hold hands at dinner?"

She was delighted that he could still flirt his way through this situation.

It turned out to be a great weekend. Jackie loved the special attention Boxer lavished on Fortune. When Boxer draped one arm over Fortune, Jackie would also drop his other arm over her. When Boxer raised his glass to Fortune, Jackie would touch his glass to both of their glasses. At the end of the evening, Jackie announced a group hug.

Boxer thoroughly enjoyed the golf. He gave Jackie a stroke a hole and gave Fortune a stroke every other hole and appropriately lost money to both. The golf pro gave them tips and helped them read the tricky greens.

They talked business but only briefly about Bay Area Insurance. Boxer spoke as a friend and trusted adviser not as a salesman. Fortune found herself relaxed and happy. She did not have to prove herself with Boxer. They would be best friends forever and maybe more. Boxer and Jackie made a date to play golf at the San Francisco Golf Club in a month.

The next week, Jackie said to Fortune, "I think we should take advantage of not only Boxer's legal talents but also his leadership abilities. Why don't you have him look at the Bay Area Insurance files?"

Fortune said, "Boxer is not a coverage lawyer."

Jackie agreed but said, "We have the best coverage lawyers in the country on the case, and we're getting nowhere. I'm not saying we should get rid of J. J. Strauss, but he certainly is not going to be our trial lawyer when these cases get filed in San Francisco."

Fortune said, "I'll call him," and she did.

Boxer told her he had loved the weekend. He asked, "Does this qualify as a date?"

Fortune answered, "Yes, but not to worry, I'm only chaperoned on overnights." Then she said, "Jackie wants you to open a case file on the Bay Area Insurance matter. I will have the papers copied and sent over. Try to read J. J. Strauss's coverage analysis first. You should have a young lawyer assigned to the file with you, because the papers take up five filing cabinets. Ultimately, you may need a much larger team.

"Also, I'm inviting you to discuss the case Friday night at Sam's. If you don't bill for the discussion, I'll pay for dinner, and yes, this is our second date."

Boxer said, "Get that table where you have to slide up against me."

"I will," said Fortune. "That helps me to think better."

"Well, you may have to think better, because a reporter from the San Francisco legal press called this morning asking for a quote about the Bay Area Insurance cases. I was slightly evasive. I said I was unaware of the filing of such cases. The reporter said there would be an article tomorrow."

Fortune said, "Can you get me a copy of any complaints?"

"Yes. I can get them electronically after they are filed."

Boxer obtained a complaint that afternoon. He quickly skimmed the document. The complaint had been filed in San Francisco Superior Court, and to Boxer's great surprise, the plaintiffs' attorney was Tommy Thompson. Boxer's first thought was *Doesn't Tommy have a conflict since at one time he represented Atlas, which is a defendant in these new cases?* Boxer then forwarded the complaint to Fortune and his team. He called a team meeting in the war room for early evening.

Defense of the Bay Area Insurance Complaint

Boxer called the team meeting to order. He first asked Bill Dawes to present his preliminary analysis of the complaint. Dawes explained, "The plaintiffs were four asbestos suppliers called in the complaint 'asbestos suppliers.' The suit is brought against Atlas as the parent of Bay Area Insurance for bad-faith refusal to defend the asbestos suppliers when they were sued by injured asbestos victims. The complaint, which is 120 pages long, lists the names of nine hundred victims who had sued asbestos suppliers and obtained default verdicts averaging ten million dollars per case for a total of nine billion."

Dawes went on, "The complaint alleges that Bay Area Insurance issued policies that covered asbestos suppliers but failed to honor these policies and wrongfully failed to defend the suppliers in the cases brought by the victims. Further, Bay Area Insurance failed to pay judgments against these suppliers.

"The complaint goes on to allege that Atlas bought Bay Area Insurance and all of its assets and liabilities. Atlas intended to strip Bay Area Insurance of all of its assets in order to avoid paying its liabilities." Dawes commented, "Tommy has employed his typical tactic of naming not only Bay Area Insurance and Atlas but also Fortune Jones and Jackie Jones as defendants."

"Thompson alleges that the Joneses conspired to avoid paying any of their insurance obligations."

Fortune was outraged. She said, "I can't believe this! I discussed the Bay Area Insurance with Tommy before Atlas even purchased it. What a snake! I told Tommy there were some documents that concerned me. Tommy recommended himself as trial attorney and J. J. Strauss as coverage counsel."

Boxer pointed out that Tommy had technically not been hired by Atlas, but Tommy still had a duty of loyalty under these circumstances.

Dawes said, "Let's talk about possible actions we should take. I think we all agree that we should consider moving to disqualify Thompson. The one problem is that Thompson will point out that disqualification is our typical ploy. And he is right. But it isn't our fault that there are so many shady characters out there."

Boxer said, "I think we should talk to Tommy. He knows that a motion to disqualify him will be our first response, and he probably has some ideas up his sleeve."

At that, Boxer's secretary stuck her head in the room and said, "Tommy Thompson is on the line and says it's important." All agreed that Boxer should take the call, but they all quietly listened in.

Tommy said, "Have you read the complaint?"

"Yes," said Boxer, "but I can't see how you can represent the plaintiff against your old client Atlas."

"Why am I not surprised that this would be your first response? But don't react too quickly. It might not be a bad idea to have a friend on the other side. I have an idea."

"What, pray tell?" asked Boxer.

Tommy answered, "I am aware that Atlas bought Bay Area Insurance for a billion dollars hoping to get the eight-billion-dollar reserves. If I remain as the plaintiffs' attorney, I could work out a settlement in which Atlas paid a hundred million dollars for release of all possible claims against Bay Area Insurance or Atlas and get it approved by the

California Department of Insurance, thus allowing Bay Area Insurance to release all of its reserves to Atlas."

"How would we do this?" Boxer asked.

"We would have all of the asbestos suppliers declare bankruptcy. I would become the trustee in bankruptcy, and I would agree to settle and to release Atlas and Bay Area Insurance from all future claims. We would have to give public notice of the settlement, and assuming there were no objectors to the settlement, the bankruptcy court would approve all past, present, and future dismissals. Atlas would get the remaining seven billion free and clear."

"What if there is an objector?"

"I think a hundred million dollars paid in settlement would be enough to persuade the court to reject and dismiss the objectors," said Tommy. "Remember under this settlement each claimant would receive an average of one million dollars."

"Won't the objectors argue that your past representation of Atlas precludes this from being an arm's length transaction?"

"I never represented Atlas in any Bay Area Insurance matters," Tommy reminded him.

"Let me talk about this to my people, and I will get back to you."

After Tommy hung up, everyone started talking at once. Boxer said, "I hate to get in bed with this scoundrel."

Audi asked, "Will this idea work?"

Fortune said, "Good question. Let's get an opinion from J. J. Strauss."

The next morning after the legal news article about the complaint against Bay Area Insurance and Atlas was published, Boxer received a phone call from Dodge Lee.

"Did you see the new complaint against your client Atlas?" Dodge asked.

"Yes. I am surprised you aren't the plaintiffs' attorney."

"So was I, but I knew nothing about the case until twenty minutes ago when I first saw it in the press."

Boxer said, "First I or my clients heard about it was yesterday when I got a call from a reporter."

"I suppose you will be making your usual disqualification motion," Dodge said.

"Too early to tell," Boxer said.

"Well, I have some information which might help you."

"What is that?" asked Boxer.

"Too early to tell," Dodge said.

"Give me a hint. I need as many facts as possible to make a decision."

"Tommy gave me confidential Atlas information."

Boxer said, "I need more."

"Also, he volunteered to turn the testimony of the treating physicians in the Cook County cases."

"How?"

"He proposed that he would go to each of the doctors' attorneys in Cook County and say that he could get them out of the case if they would testify against Jonas. They would have to testify that the Jonas sales representative said that the brain cancer warning was not true and was only put on the labels as a sop to the FDA."

"Why are you telling me this?" Boxer asked.

"Two reasons," said Dodge. "One, I think Tommy should be disbarred. Two, I want the Bay Area Insurance cases."

"Why would I want you to have both the Cook County cases and the SF Insurance cases?"

"Because right now I will discuss settlement of all the Cook County cases in bulk on terms you will like."

Boxer paused to refresh his recollection. He recalled that Dodge had three hundred Cook County cases counting the McDermott case, and Boxer's analysis was that a total payment of six million dollars for all the cases would be a good deal. That would be an average settlement of twenty thousand per case. It would cost much more to complete discovery and try all of these cases. And if they were all tried, there would always be several runaway plaintiffs' verdicts.

Boxer said, "I have already evaluated the Cook County cases as they are now. Let me get back to you with the numbers after I talk to my people. But any number I give you will be a first and best offer." Boxer went on, "With respect to the Bay Area Insurance, I can try to get Tommy disqualified, but I doubt the asbestos suppliers will solicit my advice if they have to select new counsel."

"Just give me the names of the people running the show at the asbestos suppliers, and I will take it from there," said Dodge.

Boxer quickly arranged a conference call with Fortune Jones, Patrick Jonas, Kenny Clark, Bill Dawes, and Audi Johns. Boxer said, "Since your interests are overlapping, I want all to agree on the strategies, since they impact each other. We may now have an opportunity to settle the Cook County cases. Remember, I had recommended to you a total settlement payment of three million dollars. I'm not sure that this amount would settle all of the cases, but I thought this was a good time to get a bargain, so I am seeking authority to offer the full three million."

Kenny Clark said he would be happy to pay even more, and Fortune agreed.

But Boxer said, "I do not want more authority now. I like being able to tell adversaries that I am offering all the money I have."

The Bay Area Insurance matter was more difficult. Dawes had talked to J. J. Strauss. "Not an easy conversation," he said. "The price Tommy wants to settle, a hundred million dollars, is in the ballpark, but it is likely there will be objectors who will say the price is too low and the court should not approve it. Further, the objectors, probably led by Dodge Lee, will want to disqualify Tommy if for no other reason than there would be an appearance of self-dealing between Atlas and Thompson, who represented Atlas in the past."

Boxer said, "If we don't move to disqualify, it may look like the fix is in and we have conspired with Tommy to give us a good deal, which is, of course, true." Boxer went on, "But in most mass torts, bulk settlements are negotiated in detail before seeking court approval. First, let's approach Dodge Lee. We will propose that if we can settle the Cook County cases we will also agree to try to disqualify Tommy, and we will not oppose Dodge Lee's appointment as attorney for the suppliers. Our deal must be that if we fail in our attempt to disqualify Tommy, the Cook County deal is still in place. But if we cannot settle the Cook

County cases, we won't try to disqualify Tommy. This will give Lee more incentive to settle the Cook County cases with us."

Boxer called Dodge Lee and presented the $3 million offer in the Cook County cases. He explained to Dodge: "I usually do not offer all my authority, but I know you have to get approval from each of your clients to the settlement and this will take time. I don't want you to have to go through this process again and again; that's why I'm offering the entire three million now. I know that some cases are worth more than the average and some are worth nothing. I don't care how you allocate the money; I just want releases from all at the end of the day. Also, remember if we settle these cases, part of our deal is that we will move to disqualify Tommy from the Bay Area Insurance cases. While I am not happy about Tommy taking those cases, moving to disqualify him will likely create more publicity and discovery than I want."

Lee replied, "Let me talk to my people, and I'll get back to you. Note—I did not say no."

Several days later, to the delight of all, Dodge Lee confirmed the Cook County settlements. He said, "I even gave some of the money to Mrs. McDermott, who was thrilled." Boxer still had a soft spot for Mamie, who had been the key to his victory. He would have agreed to any amount she got, even though the jury had given her nothing.

The conversation did not go as well with Tommy Torts. Tommy said, "This is the typical Boxer Tate strategy. I thought we had a deal. If this case has to be litigated, I will get into the Atlas business records to show how the Joneses were trying to make a quick seven-billion-dollar profit at the expense of asbestos victims."

Boxer said, "Look, Tommy. If we do not move to disqualify, there will be objectors who will do this."

Tommy answered, "I will do what is always done in these mass tort cases—if the objectors are competent, qualified trial counsel, I will make them cocounsel with me and give them a percentage of my legal fees. If they are not competent, the court will overrule their objections."

"If we do not move to disqualify it will set a terrible precedent," Boxer argued. "Corporate America cannot have former counsel suing them and blackmailing them into a settlement with the threat that the many confidential internal documents they learned about will become public records available to all. For years Atlas has turned to you for advice. Now you are turning against them. Finally, we think what you're doing is unethical. We cannot condone it."

Tommy hung up midsentence.

Thompson DQ

When plaintiffs' attorneys file mass torts complaints, they usually list the plaintiffs in alphabetical order. Thus, the first case would be *Aaron v. Jonas*. But here, the court clerk named the case *In Re Bay Area Insurance*, knowing the case would garner more publicity, and it did. The financial section of every newspaper in the country called it by that name—*In Re Bay Area Insurance*. Thompson loved the name and the publicity it brought him. He was interviewed by reporters and talk-show hosts. This was more effective than billboard and TV publicity. Plaintiffs and their lawyers were desperately looking for deep pockets to sue in the asbestos cases, and Tommy had found Bay Area Insurance.

Tommy was the perfect advocate for asbestos victims. He characterized the *In Re Bay Area Insurance* cases as his "effort to obtain financial recovery for two thousand asbestos cripples." The *In Re Bay Area Insurance* cases required significant seed money and thus further slowed the flow of money from Thompson's accounts receivable to Tate. Thompson saw himself getting richer and richer and started acting like one of the superrich. He had a Town Car and chauffer waiting for him all hours of the day. It took him and his associates to three-thousand-dollar dinners at the French Laundry in Napa Valley. He rented private jets to take him to suites he reserved at Bellagio in Las Vegas. It was as if he was trying to squander all of his cash before going into bankruptcy.

Boxer filed his motion to recuse Tommy Thompson before the presiding judge in San Francisco Superior Court. The PJ set the matter for hearing before herself in thirty days. Each side was invited by the PJ to submit briefs, declarations, documents, and evidence. The hearing and papers would be available to the public and not filed under seal. Witnesses would testify live. The PJ had read the criticism leveled at Judge Higgins in Cook County and did not want it repeated in San Francisco.

Tommy and Boxer cross-noticed each other as live witnesses at the hearing. The legal community could hardly wait. For thirty days, the legal press played the hearing up like a Super Bowl. Commentators speculated on whether each lawyer would testify and also act as the lawyer at the hearing. Boxer would go first, as he had the burden of proving Tommy should be recused.

The courtroom was packed on the day of the hearing. The PJ had allowed cameras in the courtroom. This was not a trial, and there were no jurors. The PJ would be the decision-maker. She invited Boxer to proceed. The cameras were rolling. The news reporters were taking notes. The air was electric but chilled somewhat when Boxer did not give an opening statement. He decided to tell the Atlas story through Tommy, whom he called as his first witness. Tommy objected and said since Boxer had the burden of proving any testimony from him, he should come last. Tommy Torts well knew that lawyers were quarrelsome and generally made bad witnesses—himself not being an exception.

The PJ overruled the objection and directed Tommy to take the oath and be seated.

Boxer started his cross-examination in a subdued, serious fashion. The audience could hear the court reporter's keyboard as she typed out the transcript. He had Tommy briefly explain the attorney-client privilege. Tommy quibbled. He said there were many exceptions to the privilege. "A criminal lawyer cannot have his client testify differently than what the client told the attorney. A lawyer has to advise appropriate authorities if he thinks his client is going to commit fraud or perjury."

Boxer led Tommy by asking, "Isn't it true that the attorney-client privilege is sacrosanct?"

Tommy said, "No. I believe the attorney-client privilege is superseded by my obligation as an officer of the court."

"Doesn't a lawyer have a duty of fidelity to his client?"

"Not if it enables the client to profit from wrongdoing."

Boxer had to become more aggressive: "Mr. Thompson, were you attorney for Jonas Pharmaceutical Corporation and Patrick Jonas, the owner?"

"True," said Tommy.

"You also defended Jonas's Medical Director, Al Purcell, at his deposition, correct?"

"Yes."

"And you spent many hours preparing him for his deposition, right?"

"Yes."

"And those discussions were confidential, right?"

"Yes."

"And Dr. Purcell is the Medical Director of Jonas Pharmaceutical?"

"I already answered that—yes."

"And you considered Al Purcell your client?"

"Yes."

"It is also true, is it not," Boxer went on, "that you had conversations with plaintiffs' attorney Dodge Lee about the Nobo extract cases, correct?"

"Yes."

"And you suggested to him that he should sue Purcell as a method of destroying diversity, right?"

"Well—I think that was after I stopped representing him."

"But you *did* suggest to Mr. Lee that he should sue Purcell, right?"

"Well, I said that it would help the parties come together for settlement," Tommy said.

"Did you tell Jonas or Purcell or Atlas or anyone that suing Purcell was a good way to bring the sides together?" Boxer asked.

"I don't remember."

"You have had several in-person meetings with plaintiffs' attorney Dodge Lee, haven't you?"

"Yes, that's not unusual for adverse lawyers."

"Is it usual for one lawyer to give his adversary advice on how to win the case?"

"No, but—but again, you use a lot of hypotheticals to move settlement discussions along."

"You admit that you and Dodge Lee were adversaries, right?"

"Well, sometimes."

"Were you adversaries when you proposed to him that you were willing to suborn perjury from the treating doctors who were codefendants in Jonas Nobo cases?" Boxer asked.

"No."

"No, you weren't adverse or no, you didn't propose suborning perjury?"

"No to both."

Boxer said, "Well, you did propose that for every treating doctor you turned that you would get a percentage of any money paid on or behalf of your clients Jonas and Atlas."

"No. That's not true."

Tate then turned to the PJ and said, "May we approach the bench?"

"Yes, you may," the judge answered. And Mr. Thompson, you should probably be here also."

Boxer, in a low voice, said to the judge, "Your Honor, at this time, I would like to interrupt the testimony of Mr. Thompson to put on a witness who will directly impeach him. I think the testimony will shorten this hearing."

The PJ asked, "Who is the witness?"

"Mr. Dodge Lee."

Thompson said loudly, "This is preposterous. Any of our conversations were work-product and thus privileged."

"Not if conducted for fraudulent purposes," Boxer replied.

"Well, put him on and let's see where this goes," the judge said. "Mr. Tate, you will conduct direct examination of Dodge Lee, and Mr. Thompson, you will conduct cross-examination."

Lee took the oath and, for the first time in his career, sat in the witness chair. Lee was not happy to be on the stand, but he was not surprised. This really was the only way he could take over from Tommy as counsel for the suppliers. He was ready.

Boxer had Lee identify himself and his relationship to the party and the fact that Boxer had subpoenaed Lee to testify here. Boxer then got right to the point: "You had a conversation with Mr. Thompson about the Cook County litigation—true?"

"Yes," said Lee.

"And did he talk about strategies you could use against Atlas and Jonas?"

"Yes."

"And were any of these conversations about settlement?"

"No."

"And did you tell Mr. Thompson that you thought he had a conflict of interest in these conversations?"

"Yes."

"And did Mr. Thompson propose that he would talk to the plaintiffs' treating physicians and try to turn them against the defendants, your former clients, and Atlas, and did he then say that if he was successful, he should get from you a percentage of your attorneys' fees?"

"Yes."

Boxer knew that Lee had recorded this conversation with Tommy but decided to leave it as a bombshell on Tommy's cross-examination. He tendered Lee for cross-examination by Thompson.

Tommy asked for a five-minute bathroom break, which was granted. After he returned, he said he was surprised by Lee's testimony and asked if he could talk privately to Lee. The PJ looked at Lee, who shook his head no, and the judge denied the request. Tommy had never thought Lee would turn against him. In fact, he was so surprised that he took more chances on cross-examination than he should have, thus giving Lee a chance to reinforce his testimony.

Thompson began, "Mr. Lee, just as you have talked to me about the Cook County cases, you've also talked to Boxer Tate about those cases, correct?

"Yes."

"Did you also talk to me about the *In Re Bay Area Insurance* cases?"

"Yes."

"And you were upset that I was the plaintiffs' attorney in those *In Re Bay Area Insurance cases*, right?"

"Yes. I thought I could do a much better job for the plaintiffs," said Lee.

"And you suggested that Tate attempt to disqualify me from them, true?"

"Yes."

"Why?"

At this point, it seemed to dawn on Tommy that he was putting his career in jeopardy. He had made a first-year law student mistake. He had asked an open question on cross-examination.

Lee said, "I told Tate that I thought you should be disbarred. You are unethical. You can't be trusted by your own clients to keep a confidence, and you cannot be trusted by anyone."

Now Thompson lost his cool. "You are making these things up, aren't you?" Before Lee could respond, Thompson added, "There was no one in the room when these claimed statements were made, right? You have no corroborating notes, do you? You have no proof, do you?"

Here Lee interrupted. "Yes, I do—I have you on voice memo on my iPhone, which is right here."

The PJ intervened. "Can you play it?"

"Yes," said Lee. "I can play it into the court's microphone."

And he did. Lee turned up the volume when Tommy said, "It is not suborning perjury if the doctor says it's true. Further, I would be willing to approach the doctor if I get a cut of any attorneys' fees on cases in which I could turn the doctor against Jonas." The PJ placed the iPhone itself into evidence.

The courtroom was in silence. The tape did not make Lee look good, but Thompson looked despicable. It was clear that Tommy wanted to turn the doctors' testimony but was trying to persuade Dodge Lee this wasn't suborning perjury.

Finally, the PJ said, "I am directing the court clerk to send a copy of this tape to the state bar and the district attorney. I am disqualifying you, Mr. Thompson, from being the plaintiffs' lawyer in these cases."

Boxer was ambivalent with this result. He liked to win, but he was watching the downfall of one of his heroes and it bothered him. He was also concerned that the deal that he had with Lee to settle the Cook County cases in return for Boxer moving to disqualify Thompson would come out. It didn't.

Date Night at Sam's

Fortune didn't even have to tell Boxer this time. Jackie just showed up for the Sam's dinner. He wanted to be part of the celebration of the Thompson disqualification and the settlement of the Cook County cases. True, Boxer's reputation was growing, but what really thrilled Jackie was that drug and device companies and insurance companies and, indeed, corporate America were all looking at Atlas as the insurance company of choice for bet-the-company litigation. The business plan whereby Atlas had Tate's firm running their major cases supported by less expensive local counsel was drawing praise from business periodicals around the country.

Jackie's first business item was marketing. He wanted the Atlas marketing group to tout the Atlas-Tate lawyer-client relationship. He also wanted Atlas marketing to get one of the major news outlets to run a profile on Boxer himself. Boxer, never a shy man, loved the idea, but he also suggested that the story should be about both him and Fortune and how they had pushed down insurance rates for corporate America while at the same time providing better, cheaper legal services. Boxer liked the Atlas marketing approach better than billboards and TV ads.

Sam himself served the dinner. They all had Dover sole washed down with DuMol chardonnay, but they were so embroiled in business they hardly noticed the delicious fare.

Jackie's next issue was the Bay Area Insurance case. He was pleased that Tommy was recused, but he needed the insurance case resolved quickly. Its pendency was a severe drag on Atlas stock. Jackie had paid $1 billion for bonds worth $8 billion, but the bonds were being held in reserve because of the roughly $200 billion in default judgments taken against Bay Area Insurance insureds. Boxer said that these defaults had been taken with no opposition from the asbestos suppliers who were the insureds. These defaults were astronomically overvalued. Boxer roughly calculated that asbestos victim claims were actually worth about $100 million total. Jackie said that he would still pay $1 billion to settle these claims, because the California Department of Insurance would then release the remaining $7 billion worth of bonds.

Boxer said, "Since Tommy is now disqualified, there's no one to negotiate with. There is temporarily no lawyer representing the plaintiffs. Tommy could appeal his disqualification, but that would take time. That would take months, if not years, and would probably be unsuccessful for Tommy. Further, I think Tommy is going to have trouble keeping his license. We will have to decide if we should file charges with the state bar against Tommy. The judge's referral of the iPhone tape may be enough to trigger an investigation, but the Bar Association is understaffed and would welcome our help in the prosecution of Tommy."

Jackie said, "Let's solve the issue of the Bay Area Insurance cases first."

Fortune, touching Boxer's arm, said, "What about helping Dodge Lee become the lawyer for the plaintiffs in these Bay Insurance cases? He wants the job, and he will give you credit for helping him get it."

Boxer mused, "You're right. Lee certainly was responsible for getting Tommy tossed. But the problem is our judge doesn't think much of Lee's ethics. When I told Lee that I didn't think I could get him the job, he said, 'Do not worry. Just let me get close to the plaintiffs themselves.'

"Lee is not totally trustworthy, but there are many worse. I suspect he could agree on a reasonable settlement number if I agree to tell the judge I thought Lee would well and honorably represent the plaintiffs. I could further remind the judge he would be approving not only the settlements but also Lee's fee."

Jackie asked, "How much would it take to settle the Bay Area Insurance cases?"

"Maybe as much as a billion, but I'd try to get it for less," said Boxer.

Jackie said, "Fortune tells me that—going back to Lumpy Griffin days—you like a piece of the action."

Boxer laughed out loud and thought back to the deal with Fortune when she had allowed him to keep whatever he saved on the $75,000 settlement authority she gave him to resolve the *Lumpy* case. Boxer had walked off with $25,000.

Boxer said, "I have been undercharging Fortune ever since."

"I'll give you a chance to get it all back," said Jackie. "Your fee will be anything you save on the billion-dollar settlement authority we will give you. And you have to get the settlement deal done within one month. Also, out of your fee, you will have to assist the state bar in its prosecution of Tommy Torts."

Boxer said, "Well, I better get out of here right now and get to work, and no more date nights for the three of us during the next several months."

Jackie said, "I'll give you two months if we can still have date nights."

"Deal," said Boxer, mentally calculating his potential legal fee in this case. He was also considering how to split the fee with his partners.

Dividing the Money

At the weekly meeting of named parties, Audi cryptically said, "I love these post–date night reports."

Dawes said, "Maybe we should make Fortune an equity partner. She and her father are bringing in more business than anyone else."

Audi went on to say, "It comes at a good time, because the Thompson firm is continuing to default on its payments to us. Nevertheless, I hate to rely on oral statements of the likes of Fortune and Jackie."

"Even if we are successful in settling the Bay Area Insurance cases, it will be several months, at best, before we get paid," said Boxer.

Dawes said, "I have an idea. Most of Tommy's time is going to be spent defending himself against the bar investigation. Plus, he will have to hire lawyers to help. The remaining partners at his firm will start to lose confidence in the stability of the firm. As Audi knows, the Thompson firm will become a target for headhunters. We should beat the headhunters to their doors."

Audi said, "If we could engineer a takeover merger, it would be preferable to our picking off lawyers one at a time."

"Explain," said Boxer.

Audi answered, "Right now we are entitled to roughly half of Thompson's work in progress and receivables, and we are not getting them. If we merged, the remaining lawyers could bring the rest of the WIP and receivables and the money Tommy is supposed to be paying but is not. And Tommy would be at a firm with no money coming in and no distributions to make to himself."

Boxer said, "It would have to be a merger in which we remain in control. In other words, I want the Tate, Dawes, and Johns name to remain the same, and the three of us must have at least a plurality of the points and the new lawyers will not share in the Bay Area Insurance fees. Bill, can this be accomplished?"

"After Tommy, the most powerful partner is Sam Hawthorne," said Dawes. "He was tempted to come to Tate with the rest of us but stayed at Thompson because he thought he would make more money. I doubt that he has. I think that we should approach him first. If he and most of his team comes to us, it could start a panic. The younger, less secure lawyers would start to worry about the survival of the firm. No one wants to be the last soldier standing. Furthermore, the good name of Thompson will start eroding, and the lawyers will worry that their clients won't want to come there."

"Bill, should you be the one to make the first approach?" asked Boxer.

"Yes. I will set up a meeting with Hawthorne soonest."

"Now, let's talk about the disbarment of Tommy," said Boxer. "Do we have any in-house experts on suspension and disbarment procedures?"

"Yes," said Audi. "Karen Klein worked for the attorney sanctions section of the bar before she came to Thompson."

Boxer said, "Audi, work with her. I assume that we should first talk to the bar association and see what they advise? I suspect that there is much more than his suborning perjury on the iPhone tape. For one thing, I bet that he was stealing from his firm."

"I'll get on it," said Audi.

Boxer continued, "I will contact Dodge Lee and start work on the Bay Area Insurance settlement. I am going to need more bodies. Look around and give me some suggestions.

"Finally, how are we going to divide between the three of us the legal fees we are going to get in the Bay Area Insurance settlement?"

"Some firms set up a points committee to distribute percentage interest in the profits of the firm," Audi suggested. "The committee interviews all of the equity partners and then makes a recommendation to the equities, which is usually rubber stamped."

Boxer said, "I'm not sure I like that."

Audi said, "Usually the points committee system is used by second-generation firms—firms in which the founders have retired or are near retirement. We are a first-generation firm. Our founders are building the firm and run the firm, and they really should be the ones dividing the money."

Boxer said, "I would really like to have a profit-sharing plan in place before merger talks with ex-Thompson partners. We will have to give some of their lawyers points, but I like the concept that we are giving them points from our ownership shares."

Dawes and Johns agreed, but Dawes said, "Boxer, how are the three of us going to reach an agreement on our shares?"

"Let's each take an identical slip of paper and write each of our names in with a percentage next to the name. The total must add up to 100 percent. Print carefully so no one else will know whose writing it is. We will put the slips in a hat, and we will withdraw all the slips and vote on which slip comes closest to the way we want the points divided."

All agreed, and Boxer handed out the identical slips and identical blue pens. They thought for close to five minutes before secretly writing out their proposals and placed them in Boxer's Giants baseball hat.

Boxer then turned over the slips. The first slip read:

Tate	60 percent
Dawes	20 percent
Johns	20 percent

The second slip was identical to the first. The third slip read:

Tate	33 1/3 percent
Dawes	33 1/3 percent
Johns	33 1/3 percent

Dawes and Johns looked at each other and knew it was Tate who had proposed the even three-way split, and both said to Boxer simultaneously, "No way."

Johns said, "You are our face man, our rainmaker; if you get rich, we get rich."

Dawes said, "At this stage, we rise or fall on you. We need you working twenty-four seven. We need you taking Fortune's dad on your dates. I propose we use the 60-20-20 split for three years, and if things change, we can revisit."

All three hugged in agreement.

Privately, both Johns and Dawes were thrilled. They wanted Boxer locked in for at least three years to get their vision off the ground. Both of them worried that no matter how much Boxer made here, he would make more building Atlas into a financial juggernaut. Johns could see Fortune trying to switch Boxer from a legal superstar to an insurance superstar. He invoked her name in conversation all the time. The firm calendar showed more and more telephone conferences scheduled for the two of them. Audi was inadvertently displaying a sour expression at the sound of her name.

69

Dealing with the Devil

Dodge was expecting Boxer's phone call. He believed that Boxer owed him. It had been his tape and testimony that caused Tommy Thompson to be recused as the plaintiffs' attorney in the Bay Area Insurance cases. Dodge played it close to the line sometimes, but he considered Tommy Thompson's conduct outrageous. Tommy was going to use confidential information that he received from a client against that very same client. Lee also didn't like the idea of Tommy walking on his side of the street. Finally, Dodge thought he was the most qualified lawyer in California to represent the plaintiffs in the Bay Area Insurance case.

"Hello, Boxer. How can I help you?"

Boxer did not want to sound anxious. He certainly did not want to announce, "I'll help to get you appointed and approved as plaintiffs' counsel if you settle with me for less than one billion dollars."

Instead Boxer said, "I am worried about getting you approved as plaintiffs' counsel in the Bay Area Insurance case. While the PJ was furious at Tommy, he wasn't too pleased with you. If you had applied for the job at the hearing, he would have disqualified you also."

Dodge said, "The judge will realize based on my past successes that I have the best chance of getting the victims the most money possible."

"Yes, and my client, Bay Area Insurance, knows you are a barracuda and that you will try to bully it into paying more than the case is worth. We looked at one of the underlying cases in which a default of ten million dollars was taken for a man who had a chronic cough.

Tommy's settlement demand in that case was for one million when the case was really worth about fifty thousand.

"Also, there were several wrongful-death cases in which the decedents were over eighty-five years old at death, and the default judgments were entered for fifteen million dollars in each case. Tommy wanted a million each case."

"I am not foolish enough to ask for those amounts," said Dodge.

Boxer asked, "How do I know?"

"I have a thought," said Dodge. "You give me a copy of the medical records. I will have my nurse paralegals review them, and you can have yours do the same. Based on their summaries, we will each propose a settlement figure in each case. I know you will quote low, and you think I will quote high. But there is a way to avoid that. We will then jointly hire an arbitrator who will look at the summaries and look at each settlement number and pick one number or the other—nothing in between. By way of example, if the arbitrator thinks my number is too high, the only other number he can pick is yours."

Boxer said, "What if the total of all of the numbers is more than my client is willing to spend?"

"I thought about this. If the arbitration total is higher than the number we agree on, all of the numbers will be reduced pro rata to get to the preagreed total."

Boxer thought about this and realized the only number he cared about was the agreed high number. Boxer had authority to offer one billion dollars. The difference between that and what he paid went to Boxer's own attorneys' fees. Boxer said, "I can see why you like the idea. It reduces the conflict you have in representing different plaintiffs all looking for money from the same pot."

Dodge said, "True, but if you want a quick resolution, this is the way. The objectors will have a difficult time showing the settlement number in each case isn't the result of an arm's length transaction. To make it even easier for the court to approve the settlement, we could let the judge preapprove our choice of arbitrator."

"What do you have in mind for the high number?"

"It depends on the attorneys' fees. The higher my contingency fee, the lower the recovery I need to get to that number, so you shouldn't mind what I ask for in attorneys' fees."

"The court will have to approve the choice of counsel," said Boxer. "One of the things she will look at is how much you are going to charge. I think you should ask for 20 percent of the total recovery. We will use that as an argument why you should be approved by the PJ. But from your perspective, we should get some credit for setting you up as counsel of record for the plaintiffs. I think you should give me your best number right now, and I will take it to my clients."

Dodge said, "Okay, my total demand is one billion dollars, but you have to pay the amount within thirty days of court approval."

"I can't take that number to Bay Area Insurance," Boxer said. "They will not even give you a counter. Hell, at 20 percent, your attorneys' fees would be a hundred sixty million, and you haven't done a day's worth of work. Cut the number in half, and I will bring them to the client and I think they will be willing to talk."

"Okay, but you personally have to argue in favor of my appointment at the hearing before the PJ," said Dodge.

Boxer said, "I will orally take the five-hundred-million-dollar offer to my people and get you a response in the next several days. I frankly don't think they will accept this number." Dodge did not object.

Boxer called Jackie and Fortune immediately. They loved the high low and wanted to accept it on the spot. Boxer said, "We cannot do that, or Dodge will worry that his opening number was too low. I suggest that we respond at three hundred fifty million."

Jackie said, "Okay, but I don't want our nickel and diming to cost us a settlement."

Boxer said, "Also we have to address the J. J. Strauss fees. Fortune, could you call him before news of a settlement gets out and tell him you have hired me to do the settlement negotiations because Dodge and I have such a great relationship and tell him to send his bill overnight? His bill today will be much lower than it will be after news of the terrific settlement becomes public."

The next day Fortune put in a call to J. J. Strauss about the same time that Boxer put in a call to Dodge Lee. Boxer and Lee connected, and Boxer offered the $350 million. Lee was disappointed but said he would think about it. Boxer said, "I can only keep the offer open for twenty-four hours."

Strauss called Fortune back. "I am glad you called. I need to make some changes to my coverage opinion."

"What changes?" asked Fortune.

"There is about half the coverage I thought there was due to certain personal-injury exclusions."

"Actually, we have made a three-hundred-fifty-million-dollar offer."

"Given the personal-injury exclusion, I think that is about two times what you should be offering."

Fortune said, "I had better get off the phone and talk to Boxer immediately."

"Okay," said Strauss, "and I will rerun the numbers with the Bay Area Insurance personal-injury exclusions."

Fortune got Boxer off another conference call to tell him about the exclusions. Boxer said, "I told Dodge he could have twenty-four hours to think about my offer. I could call him now and withdraw the offer. There would be a fight as to whether he could accept, and we would probably win. Or we could wait, and we would probably get a counter trying to get us to pay more than the three hundred fifty million that we have on the table. I could say no and announce that our three-hundred-fifty-million-dollar offer is withdrawn. This would give us time for J. J. to more carefully consider his coverage opinions.

"The worst result would be if Dodge e-mails and accepts the offer on the table. This has the best chance of a binding settlement."

Fortune asked, "What do you recommend?"

Boxer said, "Let me call and withdraw the offer before he can say another word. I want to be sure about the coverages we are responsible for. There is too much money to guess at the right analysis."

Fortune said, "Okay, but we want these cases resolved!"

Boxer called Dodge Lee, and before Lee could say anything, Boxer said, "The offer to settle is withdrawn."

"Why?" asked Lee.

"Because our coverage counsel says the insurance policies have a number of personal-injury exclusions that significantly reduce our exposure."

Dodge answered, "You lost these exclusions when you failed to defend your insured at all and set them up for default on both covered and uncovered portions of the policy."

Boxer worried that Lee had a point. He wished Atlas had gotten his firm in on an analysis of the coverage issues sooner. In retrospect, he felt he should have pushed harder and sooner to get personally involved in the coverage. In the future, he would not give so much deference to New York lawyers and their fancy résumés.

"And further," said Dodge, "I am withdrawing any offers I made."

Boxer, trying to maintain his dignity and class, said, "I will see you in court."

Boxer reported his conversation to Fortune and Dawes. Boxer recommended that they not relieve Strauss at this time but ask him for his updated analysis in writing. Boxer then said to Bill Dawes, "Let's go over all of the policies until we are satisfied we have all of the coverages properly analyzed."

Bill said, "The team and I will have to pull all-nighters, but we will do it."

"Do it, and keep me in the loop," said Boxer.

70

|||| |||| |||| |||| |||| |||| |||| ||||

J. J. Blows Policy Analysis

Analyzing insurance policies is tedious work. The policy language is sometimes referred to by the courts as "seas of ink." The lawyers like J. J. Strauss who do this kind of work are called coverage lawyers. Some key words or phrases in insurance policies have been the subject of litigation in which these single words or phrases were the topic of judicial opinions that ran on for pages. Coverage lawyers have these opinions in mind as they read the exclusions and inclusions and limitations and endorsements in the policies, and these boilerplate phrases become terms of art in the insurance world.

Furthermore, different courts in different states interpret the same language differently.

Dawes reported the next morning. The policy in question had a personal-injury exclusion for on-the-job injuries to an employee—something called a workers' compensation exclusion.

Dawes said, "It is true the Bay Area Insurance Policies did not cover workers compensation claims, but they do cover products liability claims to the injured shipyard employees. Employees of the suppliers cannot sue the suppliers. Their exclusive remedy against the suppliers is workers' compensation. But the asbestos workers who were injured on the job, while they cannot sue their own employers, can sue the asbestos suppliers who provided allegedly defective asbestos and are insured by Bay Area Insurance. Thus, the exclusions Strauss thought reduced coverage do not, and Bay Area has coverage." That meant Bay Area should have settled!

Dawes and Boxer called the arrogant Strauss, who had to concede that his latest analysis was wrong and the Dawes analysis was accurate. Strauss sheepishly agreed to put his new opinion in writing and said he would submit a discounted bill.

Boxer said, "Okay, but by paying the discounted bill, Atlas is not waiving any claim for malpractice."

J. J. Strauss icily accepted the condition.

With the approval of Fortune, Boxer called Dodge and said, "Our offer is reinstated."

Dodge, ignoring his prior arrogance, said, "I will accept the high of three hundred fifty million if there is a low of two hundred fifty million."

Boxer said, "I'll put it in writing and present it in person myself."

"I'll see you," said Dodge.

Boxer and Dawes were ecstatic. Basically they had just settled the case for a maximum of $350 million, thus generating a legal fee of close to $650,000 million. Not only would they be very wealthy, but in the short run, the Tate, Johns, and Dawes firm would survive even without the Tommy Thompson payments.

Jackie and Fortune were thrilled, because they had essentially obtained $8 billion at a cost of $2 billion: one billion for the initial purchase price of the company and one billion to resolve the supplier litigation. They could not wait for date night at Sam's, where they could plan the future of the Atlas and Tate relationship.

Rules for Lawyers

The state bar investigators were overworked and underpaid. The adversary system created enemies. The call to zealous advocacy promoted more hate than happiness. One of the bullets in the trial lawyer's arsenal was a complaint to the state bar. The state bar was aware that its offices were sometimes misused and thus took some complaints lightly; but a complaint from a sitting presiding judge was a call to action.

The bar investigator handling the Thompson matter interviewed the PJ, Dodge Lee, and Boxer Tate. He also listened to the Lee recording of the Thompson Lee meeting and read the transcript proving the Thompson perjury.

Tommy had retained a former state bar lawyer who said there was a chance that the bar association would recommend to the California Supreme Court that they revoke Tommy's license for good. "The best that we can do," said Tommy's lawyer, "is negotiate a suspension." Tommy asked what this meant practically. His lawyer said, "You can't go to court, you can't represent litigants, you can't give legal advice, and you can't draw up contracts."

Tommy asked, "Can I represent myself? I may want to sue someone. Can I act pro se or in pro per?"

His lawyer said, "Yes, but if you are thinking of suing Baxter Tate or Dodge Lee, it is not a good idea. These grudge matches spawn very nasty litigation in which one side or both step over legal lines."

Tommy said, "Well, I will make that decision. What's the best deal you can get me?"

"Probably a one-year suspension."

"Okay, do the best you can," said Tommy.

Tommy next had to report the anticipated suspension to his law firm, which would have to remove his name from the letterhead and all pleadings and would have to advise the legal malpractice carrier, which would then take Tommy's name off the policy, meaning Tommy would not have malpractice coverage during his suspension.

Most of this made Bill Dawes's telephone call to Sam Hawthorne a fairly obvious move. Sam said he expected most of the Thompson lawyers would be willing to move to Tate.

The Thompson lawyers had heard good things from their former partners and associates at Tate. The new merger structure was in place and had worked out.

Privately, Boxer was thrilled. He had bragged about running the Thompson firm someday but never really had thought it would happen—certainly not in four-and-a-half years.

Tommy Still Doesn't Listen

Tommy's lawyer worked out a deal with the state bar that Tommy would receive a one-year suspension. Tommy had to personally appear before the bar to orally agree to the deal. It was almost like a perp walk. Thompson was greeted with cameras and TV film.

Questions were shouted: "Tommy, what will you do for a year?" "Tommy, should Boxer Tate and Dodge Lee have been suspended?" Involuntarily, Tommy put his hands up to avoid the flashing lights. This only made him look guiltier. Inside, the presiding bar examiner lectured him on the importance of integrity in the practice of law and how Tommy's actions undermined the justice system. Tommy was humiliated but not sorry. The fury continued.

All of the California monthly legal publications listed the lawyers who had been disciplined by the state bar, and Tommy was listed with about fifteen others. Most of the others were unknown, small-time practitioners. Most of the violations involved comingling trust funds, stealing from clients, mishandling files, failing to communicate with the clients, and other mishaps frequently associated with drugs and alcohol. Tommy's was the only recognizable name on the list. The practice of law was his life. He was good at it. He had built a great firm, a great reputation, a great lifestyle, and a lucrative income. All of this had changed after he became involved with a young, undereducated Boxer

Tate. In Tommy's mind, this kid had stolen his practice, his firm, and his reputation. He had accomplished this by cheating and lying.

Tommy had little to do for the next year. His one way back to the courtroom was to sue on his own behalf, and the one person he thought needed suing most was Boxer Tate.

A lawsuit against Tate would be vicious. Tate was the one person in the world who could provoke his anger. He had been warned that one way to put his return to the bar at risk was to provoke a malicious confrontation with Tate. Tommy had thought it through. The suit would be for libel, slander, and intentional interference with contractual relations. He wanted to allege intentional misconduct, because insurance companies did not cover intentional actions and Tommy wanted the cost of defending the lawsuit and any plaintiff's verdict to come directly out of the pockets of Boxer Tate.

Tommy would depose all of the former Thompson partners and associates who were now at Tate and get them to admit they had left Thompson because of Tate's interference and initiatives. Tommy would depose the officers and directors of Atlas and Jonas. He would demand production of documents regarding cases that Tate had handled, and he would show how Tate had stolen Bryan Malloy's firm from him.

Even if Tommy did not win, and he knew his odds were poor, he would keep Boxer and his firm tied up for the next several years. The trial itself would take weeks. Defense costs would be in the millions.

Against the advice of his own lawyer, Tommy filed the lawsuit against Tate, Johns, and Dawes individually and the entire firm jointly. The case was reported in the front pages of all the legal periodicals around the country.

The vast majority of the Jonas cases had been resolved with Dodge Lee deals. But Boxer was working on some of the remainder when he was served with the Thompson complaint.

Audi Johns immediately referred the summons and complaint to the firm's malpractice carrier, which predictably denied coverage.

Date night at Sam's started out glum. Boxer recited the details of what he called the Thompson malicious prosecution suit. Jackie said, "It seems to me that a large part of the damage claims rest on his being wrongfully recused from the Bay Area Insurance cases. He argues that the contingency fees that Dodge will get should have gone to Tommy, right?"

Boxer agreed.

Jackie went on, "It also seems that you were working for me and that you were proceeding at my direction."

"True," said Boxer.

"And Atlas made six billion dollars from you efforts," said Jackie. "Therefore, legally and morally, I think Atlas should defend and indemnify you and your firm. You are becoming a very important asset to Atlas, and it is in our best interest to have the Tate firm thrive and flourish. Further, I don't want your time consumed defending a malicious, unmeritorious lawsuit. We need you building a world-class firm, which would be at our disposal."

Boxer said, "I can't say no to that."

"We use a great outside firm to represent lawyer insureds who get sued," said Jackie. "And while I shouldn't discuss it right now, this boutique legal malpractice firm might be a good merger candidate." Jackie also said, "The lead lawyer's name is Drew Richmond. I will set up a meeting for you next week."

The next week, Tate, Johns, and Dawes met with Drew at his office. Richmond was slightly nerdy but well-spoken and obviously knowledgeable. Johns had done some background work. Drew had successfully tried a number of cases for some big-name lawyers in town. It soon became apparent he could stand up to the likes of Tommy Thompson.

Drew's zest for information was insatiable, and he drilled the named partners for hours. One of the things they told him about was the defense and indemnity offered by Atlas together with the PR assistance Atlas proposed. At the end, Drew said, "I want to digest all of this and do some research, and then I will give you my analysis and recommendations."

Dawes said, "We want a lawyer who will represent the entire firm. We would like to present a united front. If you agree, we would like you to make your presentation before all the lawyers in the firm who are potentially your clients."

Drew agreed. He said, "I think the united front is the way to go, but we have to make sure all of the lawyers agree. Representing a large number of lawyers creates some conflicts. To start with, I seriously doubt that the nonequity partner can be vicariously linked for the acts of the named partners. Nevertheless, I will ask them to waive any conflicts in their individual retention letters."

Boxer the Bully

One hundred fifty Tate lawyers gathered in the conference room thirty minutes before their attorney, Drew Richmond, was to arrive. Boxer wanted to brief them himself first. He assured them that Atlas would defend and indemnify each of them and that Atlas had proposed Drew Richmond as their lawyer. Drew agreed that a united front was important to the successful defense of the case. Drew wanted to draft individual retainer agreements for all in which he would ask them to waive any conflicts. "If you decide not to retain Drew, you can retain your own lawyer but at your own expense."

One of the quick-witted, aggressive associates raised his hand. "I thought the labor code required employers to defend and indemnify employees who were sued for on-the-job actions."

Boxer said, "Yes, and we are doing that through Atlas, but since we are defending and indemnifying you, we control the strategy. If you don't like the strategy, you can go your own way, but then we won't pay for your defense. Sorry to be so dictatorial, but we feel tied to a united front. We want to win. We think victory is key to the growth and prestige of the firm. We want you to be proud of yourselves and the firm."

Boxer proceeded, "As we go forward, please ask questions and make comments. The goal is for all of us to be intellectually and emotionally committed."

At this point, Boxer saw Drew in the back of the room and asked him to come forward. Boxer gave a brief introduction including a short description of some of Drew's trial victories on behalf of some stalwarts of the California Bar Association.

Drew took the floor, but before he could speak, another one of the Tate law reviewers said, "Can't we sue Thompson for malicious prosecution?"

Drew replied, "A plaintiff can sue with malice and still win. In other words, a person injured by a car that ran into his rear end can maliciously sue and still win if his case has merit." Drew continued, "I believe Tommy's case has no merit and is maliciously brought. While it is tempting to sue Tommy for malicious prosecution right now, such a suit would be dismissed by the court as premature. If we settle Tommy's case, we can't sue for malicious prosecution. The only way we can sue for malicious prosecution is to win the case. Frankly, most people who ultimately win are so sick of the judicial process that they just rejoice in their success. Thus, I suggest we wait till another day before we consider a malicious prosecution suit."

The associate said, "But we have other possible claims against Tommy."

Another chimed in, "When some of the Thompson lawyers broke away from that firm, a deal was made in which in return for the Boxer firm becoming responsible for the rent on their space, Thompson would pay to Boxer his share of the WIP and accounts receivable."

Yet another said, "My understanding is that rather than paying these sums, Tommy diverted the money to himself in the form of partnership distributions. In other words, he stole the money."

Boxer said, "I don't disagree. We have sought to have the Thompson books reviewed to verify our concern about the distributions, and Tommy did not permit the review by our bookkeeper. Thus we have a good claim for an accounting. We also want to see if Tommy took money by submitting false expense reports or making firm payments to fictitious suppliers controlled by him. If we find out he was stealing, we will turn the information over to the San Francisco District Attorney's Office."

A different associate spoke up. "Doesn't Boxer have a claim for libel and slander?"

Drew answered, "What is said in court pleadings and statements in the courtroom is privileged and cannot be the subject of a libel or slander action, but Thompson repeated those things to reporters outside the courtroom. Thus you are correct—we can now sue him for libel and slander."

"What is your recommendation, Drew?" Boxer asked.

"I think we should draft lawsuits against Thompson including all of the things mentioned and adding other things that each of you may come up with in interviews with me," said Drew. "I think I should present these to Tommy in person and urge him to drop his suit against partners and associates alike in return for our not filing cases against him and agreeing not to sue him for malicious prosecution in the future. But he has to permit our bookkeeper to do an accounting, and he will have to repay sums that he owes. I will point out that he is not only putting himself at risk of being prosecuted for felony theft of money but also risks losing his bar card permanently. If he doesn't drop the suit, we can discuss attacking the complaint for allegation of vicarious liability, among other things."

"Good," said Boxer. "Any further comments before we take a vote?"

Drew said he would make himself available for personal questions and also ideas on additional causes of action against Tommy.

Drew later reported to Boxer, "Everyone has signed the retainer agreements. Everyone hates Thompson. His firm was not a partnership. It was a monarchy. There was no communication. There were no meetings." Drew said, "There are no additional ideas for causes of action except one of the female associates said Thompson had an affair with her. It was consensual, and it is now over. I assured the associate that I would not reveal her name to you but thought it would be helpful if you were aware of the situation without her name. The associate agreed."

Boxer said, "I am not surprised and will merely file the information in my brain. What's next?"

Drew said, "I will meet with Tommy and try to talk him out of this craziness."

Boxer said, "Let's talk first."

Preparation for the Thompson Meeting

Boxer had sandwiches and coffee brought into his war room. He did not like to waste time at lunch. Neither did Drew. Boxer began, "Over the last several years, I have had talks with Tommy about the two of us practicing law together in one form or other. This has caused me to ask around."

Tommy's reputation as a U.S. attorney was stellar. Not only was he a superb trial lawyer, but he was greatly admired for his honesty and integrity. Lawyers said his word was his bond.

Drew said, "Well, I have had some off-the-record conversations with lawyers who have faced him recently. They say things changed about three years ago. His marriage broke up, and he went through an acrimonious divorce. Even former Thompson partners say he was less-than-prepared in court and in client meetings. He downstreamed much of his work but took credit for the good results. Associates did not want to work for him, and his profits went lower and lower. His mishandling of the Al Purcell deposition was one of a number of breaches of the standard of care. I also found out about several more affairs—one with a law school applicant to his firm. While the applicant also considered her affair with Tommy consensual, I found a pattern of Thompson's dating and romancing women over whom he had control."

Boxer knew about the Purcell matter, but he was floored by the other revelations.

Drew said, "That's not all. The word on the street is that Tommy can no longer be trusted. Every deal has to be documented in writing. He 'misremembers' oral agreements, and the super prompt, quality service he gave clients generally has slowed down."

Boxer said, "It sounds like an attorney who is abusing drugs or alcohol." But Drew had found no evidence of that. There were no DUIs or missed court appearances or missed meetings. Boxer said, "I haven't seen anything like that either."

Boxer said when he first observed Tommy, he was a towering figure. "To my surprise, he has changed. He is now manipulative, untrustworthy, and self-indulgent." Boxer wondered if Thompson had just masked his true self or whether he had changed over the years. Boxer was well aware of the stresses on a trial lawyer. People's careers and fortunes rode on the outcome of trials. When lawyers lost cases, they blamed themselves—not the facts. Sometimes it took months to shake off losses. The life of a trial lawyer was hard, and many dropped out or turned to an office practice. Boxer said, "Did I misread Tommy, or have the years taken a toll?"

Drew said, "Frankly, I had forgotten about all of his past successes. My review shows that his problems started at the time of his divorce."

Boxer said, "I'd like to learn more. I think I should be at the meeting."

Drew was dubious about Boxer's attending the meeting with Tommy. He said, "I can be more aggressive and threatening without you." Drew thought Tommy would be more candid if it was just the two of them in the room. Boxer insisted as the client and promised to let Drew take the lead in the conversation.

Drew telephoned Thompson, who answered his own phone. Drew's excuse was compliance with the local rules in San Francisco Superior Court, which required adversaries to meet and confer at key stages of the case. Drew proposed an in-person meeting at Tommy's conference room. Tommy said he would like it to take place at Drew's office.

Drew replied, "Okay, and my client insists on attending. Also, I have a proposed draft cross-complaint I will have delivered to you in advance."

Tommy said, "Temporarily, I am working out of my apartment. Could you drop them off there?"

Drew replied, "Of course."

Boxer the Magnanimous

Thompson arrived at the meeting with the Drew draft pleadings in hand. Thompson appeared to be a beaten man. His usual bravado and self-confidence were no longer in evidence. He did not stand tall. He did not talk over others in the room. He was not angry. He was just defeated.

It was clear that he understood Boxer would never back down and would fight the Thompson suit to the bitter end. It was also clear that Tommy understood that the Boxer suit would put Tommy at risk for follow-up criminal proceedings. But Tommy was still a clever man.

He said to Boxer, "I consider your proposed cross-complaint against me extortion. I know the main reason you have drafted it is to get me to drop my case against you. I also assume Jackie Jones is bankrolling your defense."

Tommy said in a determined voice, "Well, you win. I will drop my suit if you agree not to file yours."

Drew said, "We might be able to make a deal, but the one cross-complaint we cannot drop is for accounting and restitution of the money we believe you have taken."

Tommy said, "I figured you would try this, and my response is that if you do, I will have to declare bankruptcy."

Boxer intervened. "Why? You have made tons of money over the years. Even if you gave half of it to your ex-wife, you should still have enough to pay back the illegal distributions you took for yourself."

Boxer could see the last vestige of self-respect drain from Tommy's whole body. He dropped his head, paused, and said, no longer in a determined voice, "Gambling. I got involved with some rich plaintiffs' attorneys who took me to the cleaners. I lost my home and my wife and now my job."

Boxer said, "Have you gone to rehab?"

"No—why?" asked Tommy.

Boxer said, "We have one of our attorneys in alcohol rehabilitation, and I am hopeful that he can recover."

"Oh, let me guess," said Tommy. "Bryan Malloy. That doesn't give me much hope. He has fallen off the wagon repeatedly. And besides, I don't have the money."

"I don't know why, but I think there is something to be salvaged," said Boxer. "My partners will kill me, but I have an idea. We will pay for your rehabilitation. You will work for us as a paralegal and management consultant for the year you are suspended from the practice of law. Out of your salary, we will deduct the rehab and the money taken for what we consider were illegal distributions. You will dismiss your libel and slander suits, and for now, we won't file our suits against you. If you go back to gambling, all bets are off."

Drew said, "Boxer, I think you need authority from the firm to make this deal."

"Yes, I will need their authority."

"Oh, now we have Saint Boxer," said Tommy. "I don't love this, but I will even accept this humiliation if I can return to the practice of law."

"I can't promise you a job as a lawyer at the end of your year, but if you can clean up your act, you can start over," Boxer said. "And with your talent, I can see you in court again."

Tate, Dawes, and Johns the Magnanimous

"Are you crazy?" said Audi Johns. "When you get a guy like Tommy Torts on the ground, never let him up."

The rest of the partners were stone silent. Boxer nodded to Drew Richmond, who said, "Well, there are some good things about this deal. One, it gets you out of a hugely time-consuming litigation. Even though Atlas is going to pay for your defense, it will not reimburse you for the business interruption. You will lose thousands of billable hours.

"You will also get back the diverted distribution, since Tommy has agreed not to declare bankruptcy and allow the sums to be taken out of his salary.

"Finally, it gives you the option of having Tommy back as a lawyer if you want to."

Dawes then stood. "It also gives us the possibility of rehabilitating a great lawyer. As a clerk, I saw Tommy in court. He was one of the most effective advocates I observed that year. As his associate and later partner, I can say he is one of the most brilliant lawyers I have ever seen. There are a number of keys to the success of a law firm. But the most important key is having spectacular trial lawyers. They're hard to find, and many of them are difficult people. But I would like to be known as the house of great trial lawyers. I think we should create an environment that supports the idiosyncrasies of these rare people. I think if Tommy spends time rehabilitating and the rest of the time working with us at the end of his suspension, we will know if this should be his house."

Audi Johns said, "On the one hand I think this is crazy, but as an ex-headhunter, I was always looking for a Tommy Thompson. They are one in a thousand. If we can make this work, it will help us build the type of firm we want to be. If we want him to return to being a lawyer here, we may have to impose some monitoring procedures—particularly in his expense reports. We also may need to monitor his timesheets to make sure he is working the hours he reports. He may not accept these conditions, but he may welcome them as a safety net to keep him from falling off the wagon."

It was agreed that Tommy could return as a legal assistant.

On the way out of the meeting, one of the junior partners could be heard saying to the other, "Did you notice how Tate never said a word, except nodding a few times, yet he still got exactly what he wanted?"

The other replied, "Speaking of gamblers ... but then Tate never loses."

Date Night Again

Jackie and Fortune were delighted. Fortune said, "Atlas had reserved one-point-five million dollars to defend and resolve the Thompson suit, and now it's gone for no pay. Drew Richmond told us you were a great client and a great firm leader. While there are some risks having Tommy work for you, there is a big upside."

Boxer said, "Drew himself is an excellent lawyer. Presenting the proposed cross-complaints to Tommy was extremely persuasive. We are having lunch with Drew next week."

Jackie said, "How can we most effectively take advantage of our most recent successes?"

"I have been thinking about that," said Boxer, "and I have several proposals. We have been so busy we haven't had time to do some team building. I would like to have a two-day firm miniretreat at our SF offices. Associates would be included. The theme would be 'path to greatness.' I think a highly successful father and daughter should be the keynote speakers. This would be a fabulous kickoff. I would put Audi in charge."

Jackie said, "I know the mayor. I'll bet I can get her to come by and say a few words. And while we are planning, I think parts of the event should be open to non-Tate lawyers. If you approve, I would like our PR department to work with Audi."

Fortune was excited. She said, "Yes, I would love to be a keynote speaker. Jackie, are you in?"

Jackie said, "Of course."

Fortune continued, "I think your miniretreat could be a prelude to a bigger retreat. I think Atlas should sponsor a retreat for all its regular outside lawyers nationwide. I am not sure what to call it, but my purpose is to introduce the Tate, Johns, and Dawes firm as our national counsel and to discuss how this model will improve legal services to our insureds. I want our present lawyers to remain loyal. I want to teach them that good lawyering will help make Atlas a great insurance company and will be a win-win for both of us. And Boxer, I want you to be the keynote speaker."

They ordered a second bottle of Heitz cabernet. The ideas kept coming, and Jackie made no move to go.

Boxer called the next day and said, "Fortune, I think date night is misnamed, but it is too late to change. But how about TV night Saturday?"

Fortune said, "Great. Come to my place, and I will make dinner."

Boxer said, "No Chaperones?"

"None."

The Audi Affair

When all three names were in the office, they met informally in Boxer's war room. There was no set agenda. Boxer described date night. At this point, he didn't yet want to mention Saturday-night dinner at Fortune's. He did want to tell Audi about the retreats and how Fortune wanted Audi to work with Atlas's PR department. Audi commented sarcastically, "It sounds like you and Fortune are becoming our firm's management committee."

In the same spirit, Boxer replied, "You forgot Jackie."

Audi did not laugh or even smile. "Do you and Fortune hold hands during these meetings?"

"No, she sits on my lap."

Audi asked, "How do you separate business from pleasure?"

Trying to change the awkward mood, Dawes said, "Audi, you had many business dinners that had both a social purpose and a business purpose when you were a headhunter."

Audi said, "Yes, and as Boxer well knows, I never let romance into the equation, and I don't think Boxer should either."

"Even if the firm benefits?" said Boxer.

Audi asked, "Is that why you are doing this—to benefit the firm? Are you going to go after all pretty women who are potential clients?"

"Not unless I fall in love with them," said Boxer.

Audi said, "Oh please, you hardly know her."

"Do I detect some jealousy?"

"You wish! Besides, I don't have one-point-five million to spend on defending you when you get sued." Audi firmly slammed the door as she left the room.

Boxer looked at Dawes, shrugged his shoulders, and said, "She has known for some time about date night. I am surprised she reacted so hostilely to it this time." He added, "I am going over to Fortune's for dinner Saturday night, but I don't think Audi knows about that, and furthermore Audi is the one who rebuffed my advances. She made it clear that she would not date me. She said that even before we were partners."

Dawes said, "Well, I think we should let it sit for a while."

"Okay," said Boxer, "but I want Audi to get closer to Atlas and Fortune and Jackie and their PR department. Bill, for your benefit and the future, it is just as easy to fall in love with a rich woman as a poor one."

Dawes said, "That is how well you know me outside the office. I am married."

"Well, as you can tell, I am not, and can you see why? I am going after Audi and try to straighten this out."

"Don't ..." said Dawes, but Boxer was already on his way out the door.

Boxer returned to his office torn. Outside of Fortune, he really had no social life, and despite calling it date night and a little flirting, from early on, it was all business. Boxer totally enjoyed Jackie, but he robbed the evening of romance. He was still lonely and frankly frustrated about the lack of progress in his personal relationship with Fortune.

Boxer knocked on Audi's office door and entered simultaneously. Audi was standing by the window looking out. Boxer came to her, and she turned to him in tears. They hugged, and she sobbed. "I love you."

Boxer said, "Well, you have a funny way of showing it. You were quite clear that there would be no romance between us—no dating at all."

Audi said, "Well, I made a mistake. I want you so much that it hurts."

Boxer thought to himself, *I should have listened to Dawes. What am I doing here?* He was highly attracted to Audi but thoroughly enjoyed Fortune. He knew fishing off the company pier was a dangerous sport. He was concerned that if he stopped coming on to Fortune it could hurt their business relationship, which would cost the firm millions. Besides, he liked her company.

By now Audi was pulling off his shirt, and there was no going back.

At the end, Audi looked into his eyes and asked, "Do you love me?"

Boxer said, "I could, but I don't know at this point. If we go forward, it could have an impact on the firm. Our having a relationship could be very complicated. Our partners would think we were a power block, that we always voted the same way because of love and not merit. Fortune might not like it. She could become jealous. Jackie might think, *I paid a lot of money for this philanderer and I am not paying any more.*"

Audi said, "Okay, but we don't have to decide now. I want to see you tonight. We have a lot of time to make up for."

Boxer hated his weakness but said, "Okay." And so they met again that night. She said as he was leaving, "If you come over Saturday, I will cook dinner for you."

Boxer looked at her. "How did you know?"

Audi said, "I asked your secretary to e-mail your calendar to me so that I could schedule some meetings for you and I saw your dinner with Fortune there. Please don't go."

Boxer said, "I have to go. It would be very rude to break the date."

Audi's business judgment took over. She realized if she forced him to do things that interfered with business she risked losing him. She chose to consider Saturday night business, and she replied, "You are right. You have to go."

The Fortune Affair

Boxer arrived with a bottle of Silver Oak cabernet sauvignon, which Fortune opened and decanted. She offered him a cocktail starter. She had premixed some manhattans. Boxer had never had one but drained his first and asked for a second. Not only did he love the taste, but to his surprise he was nervous. He realized he had never been alone with Fortune. She then showed Boxer the apartment. He was stunned. He knew Fortune and her father were both rich, but he never had pictured Fortune in these surroundings. He only saw her as a smart, powerful working woman.

The apartment was the height of royalty. It was two stories high at the top of her building, which was at the top of Nob Hill. It had a 360-degree view of Alcatraz, the Golden Gate Bridge, and Marin County to the north; Treasure Island, the Bay Bridge, Berkeley, and Berkeley Hills to the east; the Peninsula and San Jose to the south; and the Pacific Ocean to the west.

They stood together and watched the sun dropping quickly. Boxer pointed out that the scene changed by the minute. Fortune said, "I know. I live here." Sailboats were racing between the Golden Gate Bridge and Alcatraz. A large cruise liner was going under the Golden Gate Bridge. Fishing boats were coming into Pier 39.

Boxer said, "You should share this more often."

Boxer swore he saw a flash of green at the point the sun fell below the horizon right below the Golden Gate Bridge. Fortune said that it was his imagination. The sailboats turned east toward home, the San Francisco Yacht Club. Their white sails contrasted with the red halo from the sun.

Looking down to the street, Boxer pointed out limousines dropping the anointed at the front door of the Pacific Union Club.

Fortune said, "Jackie is a member there. We'll have to go."

Boxer joked, "He's not coming tonight, is he?" They both laughed. They selected the Coit Tower view and sat on a large white sofa. Indeed, the main theme was white. The rugs, the walls, and the furniture all had a white motif. On the walls hung impressionist and contemporary oil paintings set off with subtle lighting. Fortune was a vision. Boxer had never seen her so beautifully presented.

She asked about Tommy. Boxer said, "I really want to see Tommy return to the superstar he was. Not only would it be good for Tommy, but I think it would be good for the firm."

Quietly, Fortune swelled with pride. She said it was her fantasy that Tommy would again lead the law firm and that she and Boxer would run Atlas-Tate together. She said, "By the way, you look good in here. I can see you and me living here."

"We could play golf at the San Francisco Golf Club followed by dinner at the PU Club. No more impossible airport security procedures. We'd just have our driver drop us on the runway and walk onto our private jet. Insurance and law are natural partners, and we could capitalize on those synergies."

Two manhattans and a Silver Oak were having their effect. A certain euphoria was floating over Boxer, and he liked it. In the back of his mind, he thought about Audi but less so after the next Silver Oak. The mood was interrupted when an older, heavyset woman in chef's wear entered and invited them to the dining room. It overlooked the Golden Gate Bridge, and they both sat on the same side of the table so they could both see the view.

He suggested they walk to the top of Coit Tower after dinner. She said, "I have some other ideas."

And he said, "Is Jackie coming for dessert?"

She nuzzled his neck and bit his ear. Neither of them finished their after-dinner cordials. In fact, the next thing Boxer remembered was a small cup of coffee being brought to his bedside by Fortune in her silk pajamas. She still looked perfect. The sun was rising, and she wanted to make plans for the day. There was a special exhibit at the De Young showing one of the rooms she had donated to the museum.

Boxer had to pack for a trip to Chicago that night and had to pass on the De Young exhibit. On the cab ride to his apartment, he considered his position. He was in big trouble. Even though Boxer was good looking and charming, he really had little experience with women. He wasn't into casual sex and had no idea how to manage two girlfriends at one time. He wasn't very good handling one girlfriend at a time.

Audi already knew about Fortune, and invariably Fortune would learn about Audi. Boxer thought Audi was the type who might just tell Fortune herself.

Liaisons are not unusual in law firms. Already as chairman, Boxer had had to counsel one of his young married partners who had been hitting on a female secretary. Basically, Boxer's counseling was "knock off the affair or we will fire you." The firm already had a broad antinepotism clause that held if two lawyers were married, one had to leave the firm. Thus, if Boxer and Audi got married—big problem. One would have to leave the firm, or they would have to change the partnership agreement, which would take a two-thirds vote of the partnership. If they lived together—no problem.

If Boxer and Fortune married—no problem. Partnership issues aside, Boxer tried to analyze the situation.

Boxer's immediate concern was Audi. He had left his iPhone home because he knew Audi would be trying to reach him and when she did she was going to ask questions he could not answer. Actually, he was worried that Audi would be waiting for him at his front door.

Audi was not at the front door, but he had e-mails, text messages, and iPhone messages from her:

"How was the dinner?"

"How was her apartment?"

"Where are you?"

"Why aren't you home?"

"Are you spending the night?"

"I need to talk to you—now!"

Boxer thought of waiting until he got to Chicago and calling her from there saying he had left on a plane last night and had not spent the night with Fortune and basically trying to lie his way out of the situation. But he knew that the lie strategy might possibly work in the short run but certainly not in the long run.

He decided to call Fortune first and tell her the Audi story. Fortune was cool.

Fortune said, "I am not a virgin, and I never thought you were. The fact you have another girlfriend, while disappointing, is not a shock. I seduced you, and I will try it again and again. I think that we are a great couple, and I will fight for our success."

She never used Audi's name and never commented on the fact that Audi and he were law partners. He was relieved, embarrassed and ashamed. He then returned Audi's calls and e-mails. She was sobbing before he could say a word. She yelled a succession of questions. The same ones she had asked in her e-mail, basically. "You slept with Fortune, didn't you?"

Boxer said, "Yes. It was the first time." This response helped nothing at all. He said, "I guess I was more attracted than I realized."

She said, "You lied to me. You led me to believe it was all business, all platonic, all jokes and flirting. We need to talk at my place when you get back. After our making love, I know we should be together. Please let's try. I forgive you for Fortune. I blame it on her. Come to my place, and if it doesn't work, I won't bother you again."

Boxer wanted to tell her a night with Fortune would never happen again. He wanted to do anything to get her off the phone. The truth was he was not in love with Audi and never would be. He could not allow her to think otherwise.

He told her, "Audi, I have always been sexually attracted to you. You caught me off guard in your office, and I knew I should not have made love to you but could not stop myself. I am sorry, and I won't let it happen again."

It was almost as if Audi came out of an anger scene. She seemed to wake up and calmly said, "Apology accepted, and I won't let it happen again either."

After Boxer got to his hotel room in Chicago, he called Fortune again. He couldn't help flirting.

"I know you think that I can satisfy two women at once, but I now realize that I am into monogamy."

Fortune said, "How do you know I am?"

"Because who else but me would take your father on so many date nights?"

Fortune said, "True, but if we are going to be monogamous, we will have to see each other a lot more. Once a month just won't cut it."

Boxer said, "I suppose you are going to want more variety—i.e., we have to find more restaurants."

"Yes, I was thinking of dinner at your place next weekend."

"Done," said Boxer, "but you will either have to help me cook or bring your chef."

"I'll bring the wine and have the meal delivered to your place. The coffee I brought you for breakfast this morning is the most I can do."

After the phone call, Boxer was happy. He loved being around her—and her father. He loved her brains, her beauty, and working with her—and yes, he even loved her lifestyle. In fact, he knew people would talk behind his back and say he was dating her for her money. Boxer could not bring himself to concede that he loved her, but he sure looked forward to seeing her. He enjoyed her wealth but recalled he wanted to be with her before he realized the true size of her fortune.

Fortune was not surprised at Boxer's apartment. The best view was a very large, high-definition flat-screen TV. Boxer could be persuaded to watch *Downton Abbey* when there wasn't a Niners game on. Friday-night date nights were soon followed by Saturday nights. The couple couldn't have been happier.

The only fly in the ointment was Audi. Her ability to grow the firm was a key. Audi had a sharp tongue, and if she turned it directly on Fortune, Fortune could hold her own. But if she used it to stab Fortune in the back, it could be a different story. Boxer would warn Dawes of this concern.

The Resurrection of Thompson and Malloy

Most of Tommy's rehab was on an outpatient basis so he could make use of his small interior office at Tate. A great deal of what he did was work with documents. He produced them; he reviewed them; he indexed them; he summarized them. But what he did best was analyze them. He could capture the gist of a file cabinet full of documents in a few paragraphs. For instance, "These research files show that the company performed the necessary clinical trials but never calculated the true risk of injury." Tommy could easily see failures of data and weaknesses in data.

He was also valuable in drafting lists of questions he expected the adverse attorneys would ask at depositions or cross-examinations at trial. He also suggested responses.

Some lawyers even asked him to draft proposed opening statements or closing arguments at trial.

Tommy was becoming a modest man. When he ran the Thompson firm he was too busy to teach continuing legal education (CLE) to the associates. Now not only did he teach CLE, he acted as a tutor and a mentor to many of his favorites. He would go to their depositions and court appearances and critique them afterward.

He would sit as a moot court judge for lawyers who wanted to practice their presentations and legal arguments in advance.

He brought his homemade sandwiches to work and ate in the cafeteria, and not only associates but other paralegals and secretaries would eat with him and relish his war stories. Most of them involved victories, but Tommy threw in a few defeats.

Bryan Malloy was still going through his alcohol rehabilitation. Tommy was aware that Malloy had suffered some relapses, but he did not tell anyone; instead he invited Malloy to lunch. The first day Malloy did not understand the cafeteria concept and had to share part of Tommy's lunch. Malloy was flattered that Tommy would spend time with him but figured out Tommy's motives when Tommy drafted Malloy to help with the CLE and the tutoring. Tommy also drafted senior associates to help. The program became a showcase, and junior lawyers and in-house lawyers came from their corporate departments to obtain their CLE credits at the Tate firm. It was great marketing.

Bryan and Tommy also taught leadership and marketing skills. Tate associate-training innovations helped in the recruiting of new associates. Most good law schools taught using the Socratic method. They taught you to think like a lawyer but not to behave like a lawyer. Thompson and Malloy taught the associates to act like lawyers. It was a rare firm that had two lawyers who had tried as many cases as Thompson and Malloy.

Malloy had thought that his career was over. Alcoholism is a stigma, but Thompson gave him pride. The two of them gave in-house seminars and then started receiving requests to preside over outside speaking events. The Tate firm started leading the polls as the best place to work. The barriers between partner, associate, paralegal, staff, and assistants started to vanish. People came to Tate to stay.

Tate gave them a career and a sense of pride. Boxer himself publicly got a lot of the credit but couldn't see why. Fortune said, "Yes, Thompson and Malloy are doing a lot of the work, but who salvaged their careers?"

At the end of Tommy's one-year suspension, the partnership met to consider the future status of both Bryan Malloy and Tommy Thompson. Unanimously, the partners wanted both to stay at the firm as lawyers.

The question was what their status should be. Partner or associate? Or of counsel? Or senior counsel? Or some other euphemism?

Some of the partners thought senior counsel was appropriate. They argued that both should work their way back into the partnership. Others thought there was a risk of recidivism and that the firm should wait another year to see if both could remain on the wagon.

Eyes kept turning to Boxer, and finally he rose. He said, "We took a chance on both Thompson and Malloy, and they didn't let us down. Either one of them could screw up again, but that is true of any one of us. If they relapse, we deal with it. We can vote them out of the firm, or we can suspend them, or we can fine them, or we can seek restitution for anything they take just like any other partner. There are downsides, but I think the upsides are greater. Both of them bring a sense of history and institutionalism to the firm. Malloy can be one of the best insurance-defense lawyers in California; Tommy can be one of the great trial lawyers in the country. We have invested in these two, and I think they know it. I think in a year or two their excellent reputations will be even greater, and the headhunters will be out for them. I want them here.

"Finally, I think they're better men and we are a better firm for having suffered this penance. I see them returning to leadership at the firm. I move their partnership at the firm."

There was a chorus of ayes, and it was deemed unanimous.

In anticipation of the vote, Boxer had asked Thompson and Malloy to remain available for a possible emergency. He called them in and announced the firm's two newest but oldest partners—Bryan Malloy and Tommy Thompson. They received a standing ovation, and each of the partners paraded by them, giving high fives, forearm shivers, and tears.

Boxer thought, *This is one of those moments that justifies the sacrifices of practicing law.*

Press releases prepared by Audi with the help of Atlas were distributed to both the legal and lay media and the employment offices of the top law schools in California. Boxer was quoted extensively in the press. Malloy and Thompson received media training from Atlas and were encouraged to give in-depth interviews.

The theme of most of the stories was "Tate seeks greatness on the outside by taking care of its own on the inside."

Audi Reacts

Audi was sure that Boxer hadn't told anyone about their fling. Nevertheless, Audi felt like everyone knew and everyone was staring at her. Audi avoided Fortune and Boxer and Jackie and had trouble dealing with the Atlas PR group.

The truth was Audi did not feel like a lawyer at Tate. She felt more like an in-house headhunter. That was the role given to her by Boxer, and she filled it well. Tate and Dawes were pleased with her success in bringing the Thompson lawyers over. But they generally did not include her in discussions of legal strategy. She did not feel like a true lawyer partner.

Boxer asked Audi to give a presentation on firm growth. Boxer stated that he wanted "a review of where we came from and where we are going." Boxer said, "I want Fortune to be there for the presentation, since so much of our growth is linked to Atlas's business."

Audi did not say no, but she didn't exhibit any enthusiasm.

Several days later, Dawes dropped by Boxer's war room, where Boxer was hiding and preparing for a big court appearance. Dawes said, "I have been getting feedback from some of the partners. Audi does not like Fortune coming to her presentation. She said she thinks the firm is being run by your girlfriend."

Boxer said, "The last time I said I was going to talk to Audi privately, you said not to. You were right. Maybe you should talk to her. I think that our growth strategy is good. It will allow us to attract and successfully manage mass torts, class actions, and complex litigation. Atlas is our anchor client. It will help drive our growth. Audi is a key to that growth."

Dawes agreed to talk to Audi and keep Boxer in the loop. When Boxer was in the war room, interruptions were to be kept to a minimum. But Boxer's cell phone rang, and he answered. Fortune was on the line and said, "We have to talk."

"What's up?"

"Your friend Audi is causing problems," said Fortune.

"How?" Boxer asked.

"She called me and said our romance is interfering with operations of the firm. She said you had directed that I should attend the meeting when she is to give a presentation on firm growth."

"Well, I really think you should be at the growth meeting since part of our growth strategy is sharing your offices and lawyers, but politically I think it best you not attend. I now realize I should have a meeting solely to discuss our relationship with Atlas. I think Audi is out of touch with the rest of the firm on that issue."

"I agree," said Fortune, "but I worry that you will not get the support you want, because some partners might think this is an outgrowth of our relationship. I also worry that she is using Atlas-Tate as a way of breaking us up."

"For now I think you should call Audi and decline attendance at her presentation. Then I will add Atlas-Tate to the agenda. I expect everyone but Audi will be in favor of partnering with Atlas. Then it will be hard for Audi to say the strategy is driven by our friendship."

"Is friendship the way you describe it?" she asked.

"Yes, when it suits my purposes," said Boxer. "In fact, I am glad you brought this up. The one thing that does worry me is that if you and I should drift apart, will it break up our business relationship? I don't think it will, but I do think we should talk about it."

"I think my father and I can separate business issues from domestic issues. So I am confident that any breakup we suffer, while it may change our personal interactions, won't change our corporate interactions."

Boxer said, "If I need to, can I quote you in order to gain support for our growth strategy?"

"Is this why they say not to fish off the company pier?" said Fortune.

"Probably, but I think if there is one relationship that can survive, it is ours."

"Okay. You can quote me confidentially but only if you have to."

"I have commandeered Bill Dawes to talk to Audi. I will try to intercept him," said Boxer.

He walked down to Dawes's office, and Dawes's secretary told him that Audi Johns was in the office. Boxer hesitated and then knocked and went in.

Audi said, "Bill and I are having a private conversation."

Boxer said, "Yes, but I just got off the phone with Fortune, and I want to bring you up to date on my present thinking."

"I feel like I am working for Fortune, and I did not sign up for that," Audi said. "Further, I think Fortune has too much impact on partnership decisions even when she is not there."

Boxer said, "Well, she will not be in attendance at your growth presentation, and I think we should also have a meeting to frankly discuss our relationship with Atlas."

Audi said, "Boxer, I think that your relationship with Fortune taints your business judgment. I think that if we have a relationship with Atlas, you should not be the one running it."

Boxer was tempted to repeat his conversation with Fortune, but he decided that this was not the right time. Instead he said, "Audi, I think a number of our partners are aware of your concerns, and I think that you can voice them at our meeting. But if we are going to be completely candid, do you think I should reveal your relevant romantic interests?"

Audi said, "I think my situation is totally different, and if you bring it up I will quit on the spot."

"I apologize," said Boxer. "I shouldn't have brought it up, and I won't again."

Bill Dawes was befuddled but said not a word.

Audi Presents

Audi's growth presentation was valuable. In just four years, Tate had grown from five lawyers—Boxer Tate, Bill Dawes, Audi Johns, Bryan Malloy, and Miller Johnson—to 300 full-time lawyers and 150 available local counsel employed by Atlas but available to Tate.

Johns went on to report that she was negotiating mergers with a thirty-lawyer firm in Texas and a fifty-lawyer firm in Florida. She predicted annual growth of about 20 percent interspersed with potential mergers and acquisitions depending on partnership ambition and approval.

Boxer asked about the correlation between size and income. Audi stated that statistically there was a direct correlation: "Partners in large firms make millions. Partners in small firms make thousands. Big firms get hired by big clients to handle big cases. Big firms also get the best associates."

Boxer then announced the meeting to discuss the Fortune Jones–Boxer Tate issue. Boxer could tell the word was out. He decided to be blunt. "One major issue to be discussed is the firm's growing relationship with Atlas and my relationship with that client. We will discuss this in-depth."

Pay to Delay

Jonas's general counsel, Kenny Clark, telephoned Boxer, who was thrilled to hear from him. Clark did not engage in any pleasantries but got right to the point and asked if Boxer could attend a corporate board meeting at Jonas. Boxer said, "Sure, but why?"

Clark said, "The Jonas patent on Nobo extract is expiring, and competition from generics is going to have a disastrous effect on the company."

Boxer said, "I know it is a dirty word, but Tommy Thompson is the expert in this area. Can I bring him?"

Clark said, "This meeting is highly confidential, and in the Nobo cases he violated the most important confidences and privileges we have."

Boxer said, "Let me bring him. He is a changed man. I think you will be impressed. If he makes you nervous, we can send him on his way."

Kenny said, "I want an oath from him in front of my board."
Boxer said, "Okay."

Boxer arrived at Jonas with fond memories. He looked forward to spending time with his old friends Al Purcell, the medical director; Patrick Jonas, the CEO; and Kenny Clark, general counsel.

Kenny Clark started the meeting. He said that experience with Nobo in the marketplace had been very successful. The incidence of curing pancreatic cancer had gone up, and the incidence of causing brain cancer had gone down. Since Jonas held both the patent and the new drug approval from the FDA, Jonas had a monopoly.

At this point, Clark stopped and looked at Thompson. "I hate to ask this, but do you agree everything we say here is attorney-client privileged and you will not violate that privilege?"

Thompson said, "I agree—I apologize. It took me a year's suspension to get it right."

Kenny Clark said, "As a monopoly, Jonas can charge what it wants. Profits have gone up from fifty million dollars per month to a hundred million dollars per month.

Clark explained that Congress wanted to create incentives for drug companies to invest in research and development for new therapies. Statistics showed that the average cost of bringing a new drug to market was $1.2 billion dollars. For Nobo extract it was considerably less, about $200 million total.

The Nobo extract patent was scheduled to expire within the year. Basically, generics could merely manufacture another Nobo pill that had the bio-equivalency of Nobo extract without replicating any of the research and development done by Jonas. Traditionally, brand manufacturers lost about 90 percent of their profits in the first year of competition from a generic.

Kenny said that several generics had given Jonas notice that they planned to enter the Nobo extract market.

Boxer said, "Most of these patent-type cases are filed in the Federal District Court for the Northern District of California and are assigned to a judge who is an expert in intellectual property. Tommy went to Boalt with this judge and has appeared before him a number of times. I think that you will find Tommy a changed man and you will be favorably impressed. Tommy, could you give us a few words on this type of litigation?"

Tommy said, "Something called the Hatch Waxman Act controls this. This act extends the patent protection in drug cases for the amount of time the manufacturer took to get FDA approval. I think it took Jonas about three years to get approval, so that has to be added to the exclusivity, and that adds about three-point-six billion dollars to the income generated by Nobo."

Tommy went on, "There are additional ways to delay the expiration of the patents. Just before expiration, we can start a lawsuit seeking an injunction, keeping the generics from manufacturing and selling Nobo extract until after a ruling on our injunction. While our ruling is pending, none of the generics can compete with us—even if the injunction is unmeritorious and ultimately unsuccessful.

"Finally, during the pendency of the injunction, we can settle with the generics based upon their stipulation to a permanent injunction giving up only a small percentage of Jonas profits. These settlements have been attacked by the Federal Trade Commission as a violation of the antitrust laws and as an illegal monopoly. The FTC calls this strategy 'pay to delay' and says these deals cost US consumers billions each year.

"The brand names have won two of these cases and lost one. The Supreme Court has granted a hearing in the case, which was lost by the brand manufacturer.

"This is a risky area, but the rewards are so high you must exhaust all options. Every day of exclusivity is worth millions of dollars."

Kenny said to Tommy, "I am sorry I am skeptical, but I have to ask: Hypothetically, if a generic approaches you tomorrow, how do we know you won't take its case?"

Tommy recognized the question as a direct but warranted attack on his integrity. He thought back to what his response would have been before his suspension from the bar. He had been as arrogant as they come. He was pleased to recognize the humility and strength of character he had built through his own rehabilitation but even more so through his struggle to help Bryan Malloy stay sober. All of these thoughts went through his head as he struggled to find an answer to Kenny Clark's question.

Tommy said, "That isn't so hypothetical. In the next decade, thousands of patents are scheduled to expire, and generics and brand names will engage in acrimonious, bitter struggles that will put billions at stake. I have published the lead bar review article on the topic.

I expect many inquiries. I will, however, make you a deal. If you hire me and Tate for your case, I will accept no cases from generics. In other words, I won't take the side arguing in favor of restricting the length of patents. I will represent other brand-name manufacturers arguing to lengthen patents, thus helping your status." Tommy went on to add, "I will sign a retainer that says if I violate your confidence you will get my license for life."

Kenny said, "Hypothetically, what if a generic approaches you before you sign such a retainer? Frankly, your word is not much good here, Tommy."

Boxer interjected, "If anyone was injured by Tommy's misconduct, it was me and my firm. We took a chance with him, and he delivered. We are aware that potential clients may avoid us and Tommy. We have paid an extra legal malpractice premium for a Tommy Thompson rider with a huge excess umbrella. That's how much confidence we have that Tommy is a changed man."

Tommy said, "First, thank you Boxer. It took a lot of guts for you to bring me to visit with the firm's top drug and device client, particularly after all of the malfeasance and malpractice and the money I have cost Jonas. I realize this is my last chance. If I am successful, I can help you earn billions on a drug that you took a chance on and that has been a boon to mankind. I would be proud to be a part of that success."

Tommy was struggling, and Kenny intervened, saying, "I will retain you and the Tate firm. Not because of anything you have said here but because of our respect for Boxer. We owe him, and we know his word is his bond. Someday I hope that we can have that same relationship with you."

Tommy answered, "You and Boxer are an inspiration. I hope I can be half the men you are. I will not let you down."

After Tommy and Boxer got out of the Jonas building, Boxer turned to Tommy and shook hands and said, "You did it. Great job."

Tommy said, "Boxer, you have a disciple for life, and by the way, I am behind you on the Atlas strategy. Not because I necessarily believe in the strategy but because I believe in you."

Boxer realized that the job of chairman was bigger than he was and that the only way he was succeeding was by talking people into helping him succeed. He thought of Audi. He had helped her rise from a mediocre headhunter to a highly successful big-time law partner. In turn, she had been highly instrumental in the growth of the firm. But right now, she probably was not trying to help Boxer. In reality, she wanted to hurt him.

Atlas Meeting

Of Tate's three hundred lawyers, thirty were equity partners and forty were nonequity partners. Equity partners did not get a salary; they received a percentage of the profits, called points. If the firm made no profit, they received no income. This was purely hypothetical, because the equity partners would fire associates and reduce wages and overhead enough to ensure a profit. The chair and the management committee could manipulate the timing and amount of expenses in order to come close to making budget and getting the partnership share close to the amount predicted.

The nonequity partners basically received a salary and sometimes a bonus.

At Tate, all partners received a full vote except that the nonequity partners had no vote when it came to income distribution to lawyers. Thus, at the goal-setting meeting, which did not set income distribution, all partners were invited. Boxer wanted all to be invested in the future of the firm.

Boxer started the meeting. Even though nonequities had no say in income, Boxer revealed the firm's gross income, expenses, and profits per partner. In reality these amounts were estimated and published in *The American Lawyer*, so lawyers could see averages of not only what lawyers at Tate made but also lawyers at other firms. Knowledge of this data contributed to the free agency of lawyers. Most lawyers could estimate what they would make if they left and went to another firm or opened their own firm. Before this openness, senior partners could pay the underlings less than they were worth because the market information was unknown and younger lawyers could get financially screwed. Boxer recited this situation to an already sophisticated partnership audience. But he emphasized their role as owners. He explained the obvious importance of money not only in the partners' lifestyle but also as a means of measuring their success. Finally and most importantly, Boxer emphasized how critical money was to building the firm—hiring associates and staff and paying the rent.

Boxer said, "The other side of the equation is culture. Intellectually, lawyers live in very close quarters. The asshole factor is critical. Selfish, dishonest braggarts are hard to live with. In a perfect world, lawyers would handle challenging, interesting, lucrative cases in which important issues are decided. Partners would share clients, research, and ideas. They would be people of integrity and would be hard workers, smart, and creative, and all would become good friends—and most importantly, they would not fight over money. This is in a perfect world.

"Stability also contributes to a healthy culture. Some turnover is healthy. It allows the best to rise. Frankly, not every associate is suited for partnership. Nor are they necessarily fit to practice in a three-hundred-lawyer trial firm. But too much turnover is unhealthy and expensive. If we spend three years training an associate and the associate leaves, we lose the amount we paid the associate together with overhead.

"Finally," Boxer said, "good clients are critical. Some weeks you will spend more time with clients than with your partners and your family.

"Surveys show that the most satisfied lawyers are the rainmakers, and these same studies show that the rainmakers who generate the most business are the trusted advisers who help their clients look good. We want lawyers who treat the client's work as if it were their own. We want lawyers who become experts in their clients' business.

"Today I want to identify not just the areas of law we want to practice in but the companies we would like to represent and how closely we can get to these companies. Specifically, I want to talk about Atlas.

"For Atlas we have done insurance-defense work, coverage and bad-faith work, mass torts and class actions. We have gone from the mundane to the sophisticated. We get slightly more than the going rate for insurance-defense work and slightly less than the going rate for complex litigation. We have gotten close to management and ownership at Atlas, meaning that they have become not only business partners but social friends. When we were sued, they paid for our defense. They have suggested lawyers we should recruit. They are aware of and have endorsed our rehabilitation of Tommy Thompson and Bryan Malloy. With that, I will open it up for questions and comments."

Audi thought, *This isn't a brainstorming session. Boxer is using this as a campaign platform. How can I follow that speech?* But she raised her hand anyway and said, "Can I ask some questions?"

Boxer said, "Of course."

Audi asked, "Is Atlas a client of the firm or your client?"

"Well, it is a client of the firm," said Boxer. "The firm sends bills to Atlas, and Atlas makes payment directly to the firm."

"Do you discuss firm issues with Atlas?" asked Audi.

"Yes, I have discussed firm marketing issues with Atlas, and as you know, we have been given access to their marketing department. I've also discussed our future relationship with them, and indeed they know we are having this meeting."

Audi said, "Has Atlas ever given you gifts or taken you on vacations?"

"I have gone to dinner, played golf, and been to Carmel with Fortune and Jackie Jones. We talked business on all of these occasions, and I assumed they expensed these trips. Sometimes I have paid and turned in chits to the firm. Incidentally, we did have some nice wine on these occasions," said Boxer.

Audi asked, "Have you talked to them about your becoming CEO of Atlas?"

He wanted to say it was none of her business, but in fact it was something his partners should be aware of, so Boxer replied, "In fact after a glass or two of wine it has come up, but not seriously; no offer was made or accepted. It was a wouldn't-it-be-fun type of comment."

Audi said, "As I recall, it would be unethical for a law firm to be owned by or run by a nonlawyer. Are we putting ourselves in a position where someone can make that argument?" Boxer paused, and Audi went on, "What if Atlas offered you a job as CEO—would you take it? Could you be CEO at the same time you were the chair here?"

"All these things are purely hypothetical," said Boxer, "and as we say in court, they are incomplete hypotheticals."

Tommy said, "Further, we as a firm would be thrilled if these hypotheticals came true. What an endorsement of our firm if our chair was recruited to become a captain of finance, and I am sure any offer from Atlas would be conditioned on Boxer resigning from our firm. Further, Boxer should be a role model for all of us. We should all be promoting the firm as well as he does. No client is going to give us as much work as Atlas gives to Boxer without getting as close to us as Atlas is getting to Boxer."

Bill Dawes added, "I think that our challenge is to help Boxer. We need more people to get close to Atlas. I don't see Boxer Tate as a thirty-two-year-old lawyer with his career in front of him leaving the firm. I hope that we are all so successful that we make him rich and in turn make ourselves rich. Nevertheless, I do think we should have a succession plan in place for all of the senior partners."

The meeting dragged on, but it became clear that a consensus had developed supporting the continued growth of the Tate firm and its continued relationship with Atlas.

Boxer knew that he couldn't win Audi over, but he hoped that when confronted by arguments in favor of the Atlas approach Audi could be persuaded. He now realized that Audi would not be here for the long run. Boxer knew this was all okay as far as Fortune was concerned.

Boxer gave Fortune a blow-by-blow description of the meeting at his sparse, underdecorated apartment. Boxer brought hot seafood pasta and cold white wine from the local deli, and they watched the Warrior game on his wide-screen, high-definition TV.

Boxer said, "Life is good."

Fortune said, "I didn't know you were thirty-two."

Malloy in Rehab

After Boxer essentially told Malloy either go to rehab or look for another job, Malloy took the cab directly to the rehab center. He entered with mixed emotion. In one sense, he was a failure—again; in another, he was being given another chance.

As he waited for admission, he mentally reviewed his story.

He usually started at noon with a vodka over ice and club soda. He liked it because it wasn't so obvious that he was having alcohol. It looked like ice water. In his younger days he would have martinis at a bar for lunch. Now he wouldn't go to a bar; rather, he would have the drink in his office using a water glass. If he proceeded slowly, he could make two large drinks—four shots—last until 2:00 p.m. At the beginning of his career, most lawyers openly had cocktails with lunch. His drinking buddies were now gone—either retired or deceased. There was no longer anyone to drink with. Drinking at lunch was now frowned upon. The issue was further complicated by the fact that he had become tolerant to alcohol. So to get a high, he had to drink quite a bit. He would reach the legal limit with few obvious side effects. Thus he had been convicted of DUI several times before he figured out he was legally drunk without realizing it.

Malloy could make it through the afternoon with just a few more shots. His serious drinking started after he entered his empty house. His wife had divorced him after several unsuccessful rehabilitation attempts. He watched TV and drank. At home, his favorite was Grey

Goose martinis on the rocks. He went through almost a fifth a night, frequently passing out in his favorite chair and waking for his shower in the morning.

After the admission interview, Malloy was told he would probably have to stay for one month. He was disappointed but not surprised. A month seemed like an eternity. Actually, just staying sober for a day seemed like an eternity. Malloy completed the program, but with no wife and really no friends, Malloy's only reason to stay sober was his job. Even that wasn't critical, because he had plenty of money. Further, Boxer and Audi and Miller were too busy to spend time with him.

Miller Johnson had given Malloy rides home on several occasions in the last year and could not understand how he continued to practice law. Miller was thrilled and surprised when Boxer got Malloy to agree to try rehabilitation again.

Then Boxer got a phone call from Malloy in a holding cell. Malloy had fallen again and, this time, had gotten a DUI citation.

Boxer was furious. He felt betrayed by Malloy. He had persuaded his partners to elect Malloy back to the partnership, and Malloy had proven unworthy.

He told Malloy at the jail that he was suspended from the firm pending a formal partner meeting he had called for the next day.

Tate Picks Him Up

Boxer invited Malloy to tell his side of the story at the partnership meeting. Malloy said, "The firm gave me the company car. The firm knew I was driving it. They paid for the gas. I even told them I had driven intoxicated. I really did not intend to drive that night. I did not feel intoxicated."

Boxer had planned to let others talk first, but he could not resist. He said, "Frankly, I don't trust you anymore. Yes, we didn't watch you closely enough. Yes, we gave you a car, but we did not think you would drive after drinking. We can't babysit our partners. They are supposed to be the leaders, the teachers, and even the disciplinarians. Bryan, you did not just put yourself at risk, but you also put the firm at risk. And finally, the biggest risk is to others on the road. If we don't do something about this, it will put us at more risk the next time."

Before anyone else could speak, Bryan said, "I have a proposal. I will remain suspended from the firm. I will not be listed on the letterhead or anywhere else. I will enter the Betty Ford clinic and stay as long as they think I should. If I am able to say that I have gone three hundred sixty-five without a drink, I will reapply to the firm. You do not need to promise me a job. It will be my burden to prove I am worthy. I desperately need this small possibility. Without it, I worry that I will never have the will to recover."

Boxer asked Bryan to leave the room for the roll-call vote. After Bryan left, Boxer asked for comments. Audi stood. She was a figure of iron strength and said, "I think we should fire him, and I don't think suspending him fits the crime. We have already given him chances. I have seen too many firms brought down by failure to address alcoholism."

Bill Dawes said, "After his first apology, I would have agreed with you, Audi. It sounded like he had already granted himself forgiveness. He didn't seem to get it. He blamed us for his sins, but I think that his second statement saved him. I think to survive he does need to see a light at the end of the tunnel. When we made him partner we were aware there might be a relapse. I think he will be paying a much bigger penalty than we will. But I think our penalty is suspending him for a year but agreeing to consider him again after a year's sobriety. He should be warned that we might not take him back."

Boxer rose in a contained manner and said, "This was partly my fault. I agreed that he should be given another chance, and he let us down again. I agree he should be suspended for a year. He may never be a productive lawyer at the firm again, but he gave me my first chance as a lawyer and I feel like I owe him. My plan is to check up on him regularly. I will see to it that he goes to rehab, that he goes to AA, that he work outs, and that he doesn't drink. I will drop meals at his house and check to see that he is taking good care of himself. I doubt he will ever practice law again, but at this point my goals are modest. I just want to save his life. No vote is needed. This is not intended as a firm project. It is only my chance to give back to him."

Several partners said quietly, "Let me help," and Boxer nodded and wrote down their names.

After a few more comments, the so-called Bryan Malloy proposal was accepted.

IIII IIII IIII IIII IIII IIII IIII IIII

Audi Leaves Tate

Boxer was spending almost every day in court. His business was booming, and the clients wanted him on the front line all the time.

Atlas and Fortune were referring new cases daily. Boxer assigned the cases around the firm but did not assign any to Audi. He was worried that Audi might try to sabotage the Atlas business.

After court one evening, Audi showed up in Boxer's office. She said, "We have to talk."

Boxer replied, "What can I do for you?"

Audi asked, "Why am I not getting any Atlas cases?"

Boxer said, "Well, you said you weren't interested in trying cases."

"I don't think you're being honest," said Audi. "I think you don't trust me."

Boxer said, "I trust you; it is just I think you have grown to dislike Fortune and my being with her."

Audi said, "No, it is just I think you are allowing Fortune to have too much say in the management of our firm."

"We had this discussion at the partners meeting, and your partners disagreed with you," said Boxer.

"Well, I think that I should practice somewhere else."

"Do you have some place in mind?" Boxer asked.

Audi said, "As a matter of fact, I do."

"Who would that be?"

"Rand Ryan."

"Are you kidding?" Boxer asked.

"No. In fact, I am giving you notice. Here is my resignation letter."

"Audi, we have had our disagreements, but we are a good team. You are great at growing the firm. I am great at bringing in business."

Audi said, "Boxer, you treat me like an in-house headhunter, not a lawyer, and Fortune treats me like part of her marketing department. Now she doesn't trust me around you. In fact, I don't trust me around you either. I really have to leave, but don't worry. Remember those thirty lawyers from Texas and fifty lawyers from Florida I brought in a couple of months ago? They are going with me."

Boxer was taken aback. He was on such a roll he was beginning to think he was invincible. He was aware that most courts were allowing lawyers to leave their law firm under the premise that clients had the right to pick counsel of their choice, but Boxer thought he would try to talk Audi out of this.

Boxer said, "You really don't want to leave on bad terms, do you? I will get an injunction to keep them from leaving, and I will sue both you and Rand Ryan for damages. Besides, the clients won't like getting bounced around like that."

"Well, we will see who wins," said Audi. "The clients get to choose who will represent them, and they have chosen Rand Ryan."

Boxer said, "It sounds like I also have a cause of action for intentional interference with contractual relations, to say nothing of the eighty lawyer offices that will become vacant. The damages will get big—fast."

Boxer then called security and ordered new locks to be put on Audi's office.

Audi said, "Don't worry—I cleaned out my office last weekend. If you had been paying attention, you would have noticed how unhappy I have been. I am not about to let Fortune build her empire on my misery."

Boxer said, "I guess I was right not to assign any Atlas cases to you."

"Maybe so."

Boxer talked Audi Johns's departure over with Bill Dawes. Both agreed this was a setback for the firm. Dawes said, "I think we should try to make the best of a bad thing. We can tie her up in litigation, and it will hurt her financials—but it will also hurt us not only financially but publicity-wise. It will make people think we're falling apart.

"I think we should turn it into an amicable win-win for both sides. I think we should tell Audi we will not pursue litigation against her but we should get the accounts receivables. There also should be a nondisparagement agreement."

Boxer said coldly, "Okay. I agree, but I'm not going to handle it. You should."

Dawes said, "Will do, Boss."

Boxer was not mollified. He said, "I have an idea. Why don't we encourage Audi to be our outside headhunter? If she gets the eighty lawyers she was taking to Rand Ryan to come back to Tate and Dawes, we will give her 10 percent of their first-year income. If the average salary is a hundred thousand per year, that will be eight million dollars. Tell her we will pay it over eight years if she gives us first choice on all future opportunities. Then we won't need to replace her as a partner."

Love at Pebble

Fortune, Boxer, and Jackie decided they needed another retreat. They talked about Palm Springs, Yosemite, and Mexico. But they decided to return to Pebble. They loved the golf, they loved the food, and they loved the company. The three of them had had so much fun on the last trip that they decided to try it again. Only this time they took two suites.

Friday night before dinner at Cypress, Jackie and Boxer decided to walk the sixth hole into the Pacific sunset each with a Grey Goose on the rocks while Fortune got dressed in the room. Boxer said, "I guess you've figured out I love your daughter."

"Yes, and I'm thrilled. You treat her like a queen, and I love to see the two of you together."

Boxer said, "Well, I love being together also. I have been thinking about this for a long time. I would like to be together with Fortune forever, and I would like your permission to marry her."

Jackie stopped. He said, "It would make me the happiest man in the world. I've always wanted a son, and now I'll have one. But one question: Does Fortune know?

Boxer said, "No. I intend to ask her tonight."

Jackie said, "Isn't that a bit risky? What if she says no? What if she is offended that you are not doing this in private?"

Boxer said, "I don't think it is that risky. In fact, I think she will love it. I think she might worry that our marriage will make you feel you are no longer in the triumvirate. I think that this will show her how much I love the two of you."

Jackie was in tears, but he said, "Okay, but don't blame me if she says no."

Boxer said, "I am so confident I already bought the engagement ring without her knowledge."

The dinner at Cypress was fabulous. Jackie had reserved a small room so they could talk business privately. Fortune had no inkling that the occasion would demand even more elegance and privacy.

After the Stag's Leap Cask Twenty-Three cabernet sauvignon came, Boxer said, "There is something I want to say." He rose. "Fortune, I love you and I love your father. This evening on my walk with Jackie, I asked him for your hand in marriage, and he said yes. You would make me the happiest man in the world if you would say yes also."

Fortune got up from her chair, walked around the table to Jackie, raised him, hugged him and kissed him, and said, "I love you, Dad." Then she went to Boxer's chair, raised him, and said, "I love you too, and yes, I will be your wife."

The three of them laughed and cried and hugged, and Boxer then pulled out the box with the ring. "We can take it back, but I like this one and I know it will fit."

Needless to say, Fortune loved it.

Epilogue

While Boxer and Fortune had date night once a month in Carmel, Boxer had a trial that delayed the honeymoon more than a year. The honeymoon was a unique experience—no Carmel and no Jackie Jones. The Tates rented a condo in Le Sirenuse on the Amalfi coast in Italy. The condo looked like it was attached to the cliffs. When you looked straight down, you saw the Mediterranean crashing into the cliffs below. The sun set over the Isle of Capri due west, and the coast could be seen as far as six miles in each direction north and south.

One day they had a car to drive them to Revello. They had a late lunch at Caruso, where they looked over a vanishing-edge pool with the mountain below and the ocean in the distance.

On their second bottle of wine, they were again toasting their great good luck. Fortune said, "You know, the Tate firm is built on second chances."

Boxer asked, "What you do mean?"

Fortune said, "Well, take Tommy, for example. Tommy lost his firm, lost his license for a while, and like a phoenix came back from the ashes to become a named partner again when you and Dawes named the firm Tate, Dawes, and Thompson."

Boxer said, "Tommy proved my maxim again that the best route to fame as a lawyer is winning big-time trials. *The American Lawyer* included him in their list of the ten best trial lawyers in the country.

They called him 'attorney for the damned' in honor of his hero, Clarence Darrow."

Fortune said, "As I recall, you were also on the list." Fortune went on, "We were happy when he won that victory on behalf of our tobacco insureds."

Boxer thought back. Blue Cross had sued seeking return of all the money it had spent on medical expenses to treat tobacco-related injuries. Blue Cross had sought $2.7 billion in the first of fifty trials around the country. The jury had decided that Blue Cross had not lost money but actually made money through the increased premiums it charged and thus Blue Cross was not damaged. While the firm received media criticism for defending big tobacco, corporate America was of the view that if Tate could win on behalf of tobacco, it could win for anyone. Thompson justified his representation of corporate America by stating, "When unpopular defendants are sued is when due process is at greatest risk." Big pharma, big chemical, big insurance, and big industry lined up to hire the Tate firm.

Tommy's suspension from the bar for suborning perjury was an obstacle, to be sure, but in the long run it only made his success sweeter. Tommy's return to the role of Boxer Tate's mentor made both of their careers even richer.

Boxer said, "Bryan Malloy certainly made good on his second chance. He returned to the firm in an of-counsel role after three hundred sixty-five days of sobriety and now is working on day nine hundred thirteen. While he is no longer trying cases or running the insurance-defense group, he is religiously attending and assisting at the Alcoholics Anonymous. He is also dating a lovely woman and enjoying life without alcohol. His income is modest, but his pleasures are great." Boxer quoted Malloy: "'My downfall was the firm and my resurrection was the firm.'" Boxer said, "His sobriety is one of my proudest achievements. Not only is he a good person, he is one my best friends."

Boxer asked, "Who else do you think cashed in on a second chance?"

Fortune said, "Audi Johns's second chance was the rekindling of her old headhunting firm. Her biggest and best client is Tate, Dawes, and Thompson."

Boxer agreed. "Johns helped us to grow to over a thousand lawyers. She helped us open offices in most major cities. I think one of the keys to this growth is your friendship with her. Not only can the two of you claim credit for the success of Tate, Dawes, and Thompson, but both of your own firms flourished as a result.

"Of the thousand lawyers who came to Tate, almost seven hundred came through the new Audi Johns firm. She knows exactly what lawyers to recruit. They have to be as smart as the Yale-educated Bill Dawes, as glib as the Boalt-educated Tommy Thompson, and as savvy as the Stephen A. Douglas-educated Boxer Tate."

Fortune said, "Next to you, she's my best friend."

Audi had originally criticized the Tate firm's close ties to Fortune and to Atlas. Audi had changed her mind and was enjoying the benefits of working with Fortune. In fact, she had started insisting on participating in date night in Pebble. Who was her date? Well, Jackie Jones, of course. All of them enjoyed their loudest laughs when they rehashed the Boxer Tate marriage proposal to Fortune and Jackie.

As Tate's portfolio of clients had grown, many corporations had found that insuring with Atlas gave them greater access to the Tate firm. Also, the efficiencies of this relationship meant lower premiums and coverage better geared to their corporate needs. At Atlas, corporations could procure products-liability coverage, directors' and officers' errors and omissions coverage, excess coverage, self-insured retentions, environmental coverage, and so on, all at one company that was well aware of the specific underwriting risks of each client and each industry.

Atlas solidified its relationship with Tate by making Boxer a member of its board of directors and making his wife president of the company. Jackie remained chairman of the board. Inside betting was that the next chair would have the last name of Tate.

While some criticized the insider atmosphere, Atlas stock prices flourished. Most analysts thought the stability of management and strong relationships with outside counsel tailored to corporate insured needs was a benefit.

The date night regulars were let in on Fortune and Boxer's second-chance club and decreed that the one who had capitalized most from his second chance was Baxter "Boxer" Tate. He had been turned down by all medical schools to which he applied and, likewise, to all law schools except the unaccredited Stephen A. Douglas School of Law. He had to be the most successful graduate of Douglas in the history of the school. He was the largest wage earner at one of the largest law firms in the world. His story was written up in *Forbes* magazine, *The National Law Journal*, and *The Wall Street Journal*. He had received honorary degrees from Georgetown, NYU, and Columbia, but on the negative side, he didn't own a car or a home. He lived in his wife's apartment and used her driver. He could no longer break eighty on the golf course. Nevertheless, he would tell you he was the luckiest man in the world. He loved his wife, and she loved him.

Edwards Brothers Malloy
Oxnard, CA USA
September 29, 2014